Echoes of the Past

An American Rose Abroad Novel

Riona Kelly

Echoes of the Past

When an American schoolteacher sets out for a summer in Wales, she plans to work on her thesis, explore the stunning and historic countryside, and maybe enjoy a summer fling. The charming ticket collector on the coastal train might fit the bill if she can draw him out of his shyness.

Then she discovers a dead woman on the beach, and everything changes as she's drawn into the intrigue surrounding the victim's death. Although the newly arrived guest at her hotel is sultry and sexy, he sets her trouble radar spinning. A man to avoid. Then she learns he has a connection to the victim and an undue interest in her.

Finding herself entangled in the mystery, can she maintain her distance and not end up a victim?

Echoes of the Past

An American Rose romantic suspense novel set on the current-day Welsh coast.

Echoes of the Past

This book edition is published by:
Pynhavyn Press

Ebook First Edition: June 2018
Revised: May 2025
http://www.pynhavynpress.com

Cover Art: Designed by Rene Averett and executed by Art Space.

Echoes of the Past

Table of Contents

Echoes of the Past

Chapter One

"... on waves of the summer sea..."

I loved this coastline.

Felt it in my very bones, as if I'd known it all my life—even lifetimes before. It stirred something ancient in me, something I couldn't explain. Maybe that was why I'd come here in the first place—to remember something I hadn't yet lived.

The beach stretched out in a wide horseshoe, the northern end barely visible in the morning fog while the southern tip disappeared completely from view. At my feet, the chill waters of the Irish Sea lapped gently up to anoint my bare toes, a quiet welcome home.

Behind me, sand dunes rose tall, crowned in long grasses, and in the distance, the stark silhouette of Harlech Castle perched like a stone sentinel on the cliff, watching the sea.

I turned my gaze northward and noticed something bulky on the beach—out of place, awkward. The tide often delivered debris, sometimes something dead. I squinted.

This looked like more than driftwood.

Unease unfurled in my stomach. I began walking, feet slapping softly on the wet sand, then I broke into a run.

The shape resolved into a woman—curled inward like a shell, hair splayed across her face and shoulders, as if trying to shield her from the world. I dropped to my knees beside her, pushing the wet hair aside with trembling fingers. Her skin had turned a pale bluish gray; her lips were purplish and still.

I leaned in, willing to hear breath—any sign of life—but there was nothing. Her body was swollen from the sea. Her limbs folded toward her center as if the water had drawn her inward.

No movement. No breath. No heartbeat.

Dead.

A sharp gasp escaped me as I recoiled, scrambling backward through the sand. My heart pounded in my ears. She was beyond help—beyond anything. With shaking hands, I fumbled for my phone and called emergency services. As I relayed what I'd found, the horror crystallized. The words made it real.

Holy crap. I'd just found a body.

The operator remained calm and professional—probably the only reason I didn't fall apart completely. She instructed me not to touch anything and to wait for the authorities. I nodded automatically before remembering she couldn't see me. "Yes," I croaked aloud. "I'll wait."

I dropped into a crouch on a nearby dune, hugging my knees. Only a few yards from the body, I had a clear view—and no one else had yet appeared on the beach. It was too early. Just me, the sea, and... her.

It hadn't stormed last night. So how had she ended up here? She looked about my age—late twenties, maybe thirty. Fit. I couldn't help wondering who she was. What had happened. Whether someone would miss her.

Needing something to do—anything—I retrieved my camera. It felt morbid, but I told myself it might help. If someone came by and interfered, I'd have proof.

As I crouched to photograph her face, I noticed a chain clenched in her right hand. A locket. A Claddagh design, etched in silver: hands cradling a heart beneath a crown.

Like the one my father had given my mother. A gift of love, loyalty, and friendship. Sadness surged unexpectedly. My throat tightened.

I straightened, wiping my eyes and turning toward the road. At last, I saw a car parked near the public path—and two men in yellow vests approaching.

The police.

One of them waved as they neared shouting distance. "Kathleen Donaghue?" the taller one called.

I nodded. "Yes, that's me!"

As they quickened their pace, a movement in the distance caught my eye—another man, farther down the beach, just barely visible in the thinning fog. "Until now, no one else has been around," I said, gesturing.

The younger officer peeled off to intercept the figure. The man turned and retreated before breaking into a jog. The constable gave chase, calling out.

The taller officer stopped beside me, offering a clipped nod. "PC Hughes." I acknowledged him, trying to keep my voice steady.

"You say you found the body?"

"Yes. She's just ahead."

We walked together, his tone calm, all business. I fell into step beside him.

"Tell me what happened," he said.

"I'm staying at the Thornhill Hotel," I said, gesturing up the bluff. "I came down early to photograph the sunrise over Snowdonia. I was walking the shore when I spotted what looked like a bundle—or maybe a seal—until I got close."

He nodded as we approached the scene. "Did you see anyone else? Someone who might've brought the body in?"

"No," I said, startled by the implication. "She was already soaked. There's seaweed. I think... she washed up." Still, the idea lodged in my mind like a pebble in a shoe. Could someone have dumped her?

His gaze flicked to me. "You're American, yes?"

"Yes. I'm here on summer break. I'm a teacher—doing research on coastal communities."

He raised an eyebrow but said nothing as we reached the body. The younger officer was already roping off the area.

"I'll call for the team," he said and jogged back to the car. Hughes studied the sand around the woman. "Your footprints?"

"Yes. And those are my knee marks—I tried to check if she was breathing."

He gave a faint grunt of disappointment—probably wishing the scene had been untouched. "Anything else you noticed?"

I shook my head. "Only the locket. She had it in her hand."

He made a note. "You're staying across the road. We'll be in touch." "For how long?" he added, almost as an afterthought.

"A month. Maybe longer."

He gave me a short nod and turned his attention back to the victim.

I stood there for a beat longer, looking down at the girl. She could have been me. That thought wouldn't go away.

Finally, I turned and walked back to the dune, slipping into my sandals with shaking hands. I glanced back once—at the dark shape curled on the sand, now surrounded by yellow tape.

A lone gull cried overhead. The morning fog was already thinning. The sea was calm again. But I couldn't shake the feeling that something had been left undone—some dark current still pulling beneath the surface.

Something had happened here. And I had a strange sense it wasn't finished with me yet.

My hotel, a charming bed and breakfast, stood partway up the side of a bluff just across the coastal highway. Like Harlech Castle in the distance, it faced the sea with a similar grandeur—though my little room looked inland, towards the ancient stones and the winding town.

I climbed the steep steps slowly, past dewberry vines whose thorny tangles explained the Thornhill name carved into the old wooden sign. At the garden landing, I paused, catching sight of the beach road below. Another police car and an ambulance-style vehicle had joined the first. Tiny figures moved briskly across the sand—investigators, I guessed—each one a reminder of the woman who would never leave that shore alive.

With a sigh, I took the remaining stairs into the inn. The memory of her lay heavy on my shoulders, dimming the usual lilt in my step.

Though it was early June and the start of tourist season, the inn remained mostly quiet. Poor weather and fewer American travelers this year had slowed the hospitality trade, or so Mrs. Linton had told me. Aside from myself, only two couples were currently registered.

In the four days I'd been here, I'd claimed a favored table in the small dining room—by the window, with a clear view of Snowdonia and Harlech Castle. I slipped into my usual chair without waiting to be acknowledged.

Mrs. Linton bustled over moments later, tea in hand. She'd discovered my breakfast tea habit on day one and now delivered it without asking.

"Did you have a nice walk, love?" she asked in her ever-cheerful English lilt. Neither she nor Mr. Linton were Welsh; they'd bought the Thornhill to escape city life.

"Yes, thank you," I said, hedging. It had been a nice walk—until it hadn't.

Her brow furrowed as she glanced out the window. "Looks like quite the to-do on the beach. Police cars and a mortuary van. Someone must've drowned, poor soul. You didn't see anything, did you, Miss Donaghue?"

I kept my tone light. "Something washed up, I think. Possibly a body. The police were already there when I left."

She clucked sympathetically. "A shame, but it happens from time to time. You'll hear more on the news, I expect. English breakfast this morning, or would you prefer something lighter?"

"Just toast, please," I said. The idea of sausage or eggs turned my stomach.

"Certainly," she nodded, then brightened as another couple entered the room. "Good morning, Mr. and Mrs. James," she chirped, ushering them toward a table by the window.

The girl looked barely sixteen, a tiny thing with a pixie face and no makeup. Her new husband wasn't much older, his wispy mustache doing little to age him. A slight bump at her waist explained their early marriage.

I looked away and retrieved my camera, scrolling through the morning's shots. The sunrise over Snowdonia was as breathtaking in pixels as it had been in person. But when I reached the photos from the beach, the pleasure drained from my mood. Even on a two-inch screen, the girl's still form stirred something icy in me.

Sometimes my imagination got the better of me. I could almost see her struggling, choking, pulled out to sea by an unseen undertow. A shiver crawled down my spine.

I sipped my tea, grateful for its warmth. Sympathy wouldn't bring her back.

When my toast arrived, I forced myself to eat and focus on the afternoon ahead. I had plans. I always had plans. Mrs. Linton returned with more tea and a sly look.

"My nephew's about your age," she offered brightly. "Coming up from Kent this weekend. I think you'd like him, love."

I gave her a polite smile. This was attempt number three in her matchmaking campaign. First, the nervous gardener who'd stuttered through our five-minute conversation before bolting. Then, the grocer—thirty something and clearly uninterested.

Now, a nephew named Eddie.

She must have thought I needed company.

"That's lovely for you, Mrs. Linton," I said. "I'm sure you'll enjoy the visit. Will he be here long?"

"Just three days. You must meet him, though. Someone to chat with, you know." She gave me an encouraging smile before gliding off to check on her other guests.

I smiled into my tea. As well-intentioned as she was, I didn't need her help.

As it happened, I had a date of my own.

After breakfast, I headed up for a quick shower, rinsing off the last traces of salt and sand. I dressed in a soft, pastel summer dress—loose sleeves, nothing fancy—and chuckled to myself at her matchmaking antics.

She wouldn't need to worry.

Chapter Two

"...a son of the earth..."

A path cut across the cliff face from the hotel to the main road leading to the castle. Thick bracken and trees lined and surrounded the paved, easy paced sloping path, giving a forest feel to it. It ran about three hundred yards from the back garden to a gate before it let out onto the street.

From there, a steep climb up the road led to the top of the bluff. I took a deep breath and tackled the ascent for the second time in the four days I'd been here. Midway up, the backs of my calves began to feel the strain of the steep climb, and I paused to rest. I only had about a hundred yards to go, but it felt like miles. Harlech could use a cable car, I reflected, but then I couldn't quite picture a San Francisco trolley chugging up the hill to a castle in Britain.

As I started up again, someone called me, and I turned to look down at the way I'd come. The man who half-ran up the slope towards me waved and grinned broadly. I returned the wave and waited for him. He was my own discovery—not Mrs. Linton's.

I'd met him on the train coming down from Porthmadog on the first day. A ticket-collector for BritRail, Toby Morgan was one of the fair-haired men I tended to favor.

"Miss Donahue... Kat'leen," he gasped, slightly out of breath from the sprint up the hill. "I was afraid I'd miss you."

He paused as he came even with me. Toby was only slightly taller than my five-foot-six, and as I met his bright blue eyes, I grinned to see the warm greeting in them. His longish, dark blond hair framed his charming, oval face.

"Well, you haven't," I pointed out.

He caught my hand as we resumed the walk up the hill. "I have tomorrow off," he announced. "I can take you to Dyffryn then if you like."

"I'd love it," I said without hesitation. I wanted to see the burial cairn there so it would be splendid to have a guide.

Toby squeezed my hand, an almost shy look on his face. "Good. I'll bring along some pasties and fizzy lemonade, and we'll make a picnic of it."

"Sounds great. What shall I bring?"

"Just your pretty self, luv," he said with that irrepressible grin again. "What're you up to now?"

I held up my camera. "Photos of the castle and some more research."

His eyes shifted towards the building. "I suppose castles are a bit of a novelty for you Americans."

I laughed. "In a way they are. We have some amazing buildings and even a few castles, but nothing on the scale of the ones here. And it's the history that makes them so fascinating."

He shrugged, accepting my superior knowledge on the subject with a grain of salt. Not that I was an authority. He wasn't well traveled himself; more of a son of the earth in the land where he was born, and he accepted things as they were. That was one of the qualities I liked about Toby.

10

"So you say. It's just the past and these things—" He paused to sweep a hand towards the old buildings ahead of us. "—are part of the landscape."

We climbed the rest of the distance in silence. I couldn't vouch for Toby, but I needed all my breath for the hill. He seemed to be in much better shape than I was. He wasn't even breathing hard by the time we reached the level of the castle while I was puffing like a steam engine. Goodness, one could get out of shape just standing or sitting all winter.

Like the rocks of the walls of Harlech Castle, the houses and businesses of the old town were built of the same blue-gray stone and looked as medieval. The overall impression was to sweep one back through time to the fifteenth century when this was a thriving town. Even by then, the Irish Sea would have retreated a considerable distance from the postern gate of the castle.

I gazed out towards the water, taking in the vista of the bay and the line of dunes that formed a natural barrier inside that. Once, the sea had occupied everything above the highway and the row of houses nestling above it. At the time Harlech was constructed, the waters came all the way up to the bottom of the cliff where the lower gate of the castle allowed access to the sea. I'd seen the illustrations of the castle from the twelfth century, so it was easier to visualize how it had looked then.

At times, I felt a touch of sadness for those lost times, almost as if I'd been a part of them. It may have shown on my face for Toby touched my elbow and asked, "Is something wrong, Kathleen?"

I shook my head, returning reluctantly to the present. "No. No, Toby. Just lost in the past for a bit."

He looked a little sheepish. "I guess these old castles affect visitors more than the locals. I've grown up with them, you know. I don't see anything except an old building."

"Ah, but you're one of the local experts on Dyffryn Ardudwy," I countered, a touch of surprise in my voice. I hadn't expected the casual disregard of the historic castle.

Candidly, his eyes met mine, the intensity in them belying the lightness of his tone. "Well, now, that's different, isn't it? These—" He paused, stepped back to gaze at the twelfth-century relic, and shook his head. "—these are recent compared to Dyffryn. That really represents the old ways, the old culture."

"You mean the old religion?"

"I mean a civilization that predates anythin' man has done here. Not just their religion, but their whole way of life." He grinned again, looking charmingly boyish all at once. "Now, *that* I find interesting."

Laughing, I said, "You're a bit of a paradox, Toby Morgan. But I like you anyway." I turned my attention to the photo I wanted to take. The sun slipped past its zenith, and the light on the castle glowed with a perfect glimmer.

While I moved along the edge of the cliff seeking the ideal photo, Toby leaned against a post and waited with an amused smile creating an impish expression. I found a spot that showed all four towers rising majestically with the now glistening grassy knolls behind it highlighted by the sun. I took a few shots from several slightly different angles. In the back of my mind, I entertained the possibility of one or two of my photos from this trip finding their way into a magazine or photo contest. I liked to believe myself a talented amateur photographer.

By the time I'd finished, the mood of the earlier conversation had vanished. Now, we chatted about music as he escorted me to the entrance at the main gate. At the door, he caught my hand once again, gave it a quick squeeze, flashed a shy grin, and said, "I have to get back now, but I'll see you tomorrow."

Turning to go back down the hill, he stopped and peered towards the coastal road, a frown crossing his forehead. Two police cars remained although the ambulance had departed. I could see that a small group of people had gathered near the cordoned off area where a few officers still worked.

"Wonder what that's all about down there," he commented. "Looks like quite a buzz."

"A body washed up on the beach," I said softly.

"A body? That's odd. Were you down there?"

"On the beach, yes. I saw the woman when the police came," I volunteered, still hesitant to let anyone know of my involvement.

"Ah, that's sad," Toby noted and gave me a curious look as if he wondered what else I might know. But he didn't pursue it. "Now, I better get back to the train. Until tomorrow, Kat'leen." He winked and grinned, then hurried down the hill while trying not to get too much momentum on the steep angle.

A small smile played on my lips as I watched him go. He'd come a long way from our first meeting on the train and the subsequent cup of tea when he'd gotten off work that evening. Just getting him to call me "Kathleen" had been a major breakthrough. I admitted to myself that I'd first pushed the friendship with him because he seemed an everyday type of Welshman, raised in the spirit of the new revival.

Part of my thesis had to do with this resurgence of the Celtic people that had begun in the mid-seventeenth century, which seemed to be growing more with a strong identity emerging in the people of the seven Celtic nations. Nonetheless, I did like Toby as a person and not just an information resource. I found his shyness and reserve refreshing.

Turning, I showed my admission pass to the ticket taker at the castle and went inside to get a better look at this magnificent piece of architecture.

After the tour and about a hundred more photos, I stopped in for dinner at a pub in the village area of the market before making my way back to the gated walkway. By now, only a hint of light remained on the horizon. The path lacked any brightness to make it easier to traverse the dark tunnel of foliage. It felt creepy, and any rustle of leaves or ferns made me uneasy. I pulled out my phone and used the flashlight option to light the way until I glimpsed the glowing windows from the hotel ahead.

I decided a glass of wine before bed would be relaxing and help me to sleep without my mind mulling over the dead woman anymore, so I headed for the dining room. At the three-seat wet bar tucked away in a corner, I slid onto a stool and glanced towards the entrance. John Linton, the proprietress' husband and business partner, kept a watchful eye on it and was already on his way to serve me.

For the most part, the little hotel was a two-person operation although they had two local girls come in daily to do the housekeeping. Sarah Linton handled the serving chores in the dining room and sometimes helped with the cooking, but Mr. Linton ruled there. He was an excellent chef–had, in fact, made his living at it before he and his wife purchased this hotel. They both manned the desk and did their best to see to the comfort of their guests.

I gave Mr. Linton my order, which he fetched promptly, then asked, "Which way did you go today, Miss?"

"Up to the castle. There was a nice view from there," I replied.

Linton liked to inquire about what splendid vista his guests encountered each day. He may not have been a native Welshman, but he certainly loved this area as much as anyone could. It was a feeling I understood well.

"There was a lovely view from the beach," Linton commented. "It was a glowing sunset. In fact, I took my camera down to get a few shots."

"It looked stun—" I started before someone interrupted.

"Yes, it was quite nice, John."

A deep voice rumbled in a smooth purr, a seductive quality to it.

I turned to face the man who'd just come in. Shocked, my heart leaped, thudding against my ribs. Stunningly handsome, his light green eyes caught my attention at once, as they flashed my way briefly. I shifted my view to my drink on the bar, but not before taking in his high cheekbones and appreciating the tendrils of thick black hair that lent a feral look to his features. Dear Lord, no one should be that gorgeous. I ventured a sideways glance at him, trying not to seem too obvious.

He barely glanced at me as he took the seat at the end of the bar, leaving the third one open between us. I turned my eyes away, my heart still thumping with the sudden burst of hormones just from seeing him. He had that magnetic quality that beautiful people seem to possess in abundance.

"Good evening, Mr. Thomas," Linton said. "Welcome back. Sarah told me you'd come in this evening. What brings you back to Harlech?"

I sipped my wine as I avoided looking towards the man at all. I pulled my wits together as I considered the newcomer. Men as handsome as that could have any woman they wanted and, in my experience, admittedly scant, tended to be real assholes once you got to know them.

"A bit of a working holiday," he answered. "An assignment for beach photographs and a chance to relax for a few days. You know I never turn down an opportunity like that." He chuckled, a warm, throaty sound.

My stomach lurched at the underlying sexiness of his voice. Without a word, I nodded at Linton, picked up my wine, and retreated to the lounge. The hairs on the back of my neck prickled and I wondered if his eyes had followed my withdrawal.

As I settled in a chair, I risked another glance at the bar and noticed, from the glass and color, that he'd ordered a whiskey. Unable to stop myself, I watched him from the corner of my eye, noticing the natural grace in his movements. He carried a camera, so I presumed he, too, had been taking photographs on the beach. Of course, that *was* his apparent profession.

Tearing my eyes and thoughts away from the man, I settled back in the overstuffed chair to watch a few minutes of television and sip my wine. An amusing British comedy was on, and Sarah Linton was already chuckling over the story. Other than Sarah and myself, no one else enjoyed the coziness of the lounge. Although the show was entertaining, it failed to hold my interest this evening as I kept wondering why the man at the bar commanded my attention. Something about him made me uneasy; something I couldn't quite define.

After the show, the local news cut in with a brief piece about the woman found on the beach, an apparent victim of drowning. No details yet on the identity and police continued to investigate the circumstances. They asked anyone who might have seen her on the beach the previous day or evening to contact the authorities. As they put up the photo of the woman, I caught my breath. I hadn't seen it when I'd found her, but it struck me now. She could be my sister we resembled each other so much.

Mrs. Linton turned her eyes towards me, then back to the screen before returning them to me. "You look quite a lot like her, Miss Donaghue. She's not a relative, is she?"

I shook my head slowly. "No. Not that I'm aware of, anyway. I don't have any family over here."

Unnerved, I gulped the rest of my wine, said goodnight, and went upstairs to my room. I pulled out my laptop and unloaded my photos to it. Pulling up the photo program, I paged through the pictures until I got to the ones I'd taken on the beach.

Her hair was dark, almost black, her eyes were closed, but the shape of her face and her nose looked like mine. The chin was a little sharper with a dimple in it, and her forehead appeared a bit wider. Still, she could have been a relative. Since I had strong Irish bloodlines, it wouldn't be too unusual to find lookalikes in Ireland. Many had migrated to Wales, so that would be just as probable here. A coincidence.

Dismissing it, I turned my attention to the photos I'd taken at the castle, feeling pleased as I paged through them. Even the information signs had come out clear enough to read. I shut the computer down and readied myself for bed.

Tomorrow would be a busy day, and I wanted to get an early start.

Still, as I drifted off to sleep, I wondered about the woman on the beach. Who was she and how did she end up drowning?

Chapter Three

" ...in stillness, the spirits wait..."

There's no great art to catching trains in Britain, and it's a splendid way to travel. I'd come to love trains. I liked the rocking of the cars and the steady chug of the engines. I regretted that mode of transportation was not as prominent in the United States, but with a country so vast and widely populated as America, the trains struggled to provide comparable convenience and economics.

On this island nation, trains were the primary means of transportation, whether it was the underground transports of London and Edinburgh or the engines and cars that rolled through the countryside connecting the cities. From London's main stations, trains—many of them charging down the rails at up to 125 miles an hour—whisked people to all parts of the island. With stops at the various cities and towns along the routes being brief, they made excellent time.

The BritRail line along the north Welsh coast was not one of the speedier trains, but it was somewhat reliable to its published time schedule. That schedule didn't allow for lengthy stops at any of the small stations, so one had to hop quickly on or off when it halted.

Toby Morgan jumped through the open door with the ease of an experienced train-catcher and offered his free hand to help me aboard. His other hand held a wicker picnic basket with a folded blanket on top. Once I stood safely beside him, he led the way into the car and selected two empty seats on the seaward side. A moment later, the train jerked to life and began chugging south.

"Usually, the cars are packed pretty heavily with students and tourists this time of year," Toby commented as he gazed around and noted all the unoccupied seats. "This really is a bad year for tourism with the terrorist threats and many Americans afraid to travel in Europe."

"Well, you really can't blame them," I replied. "It is kind of scary with all that's been happening."

"You came," he stated flatly.

"Yes, but then I don't think a lot of people think the same as I do. I'm a fatalist—if it's your turn to go, it won't matter where you are."

"Good philosophy. Sort of like, whatever your destiny is, you'll find it."

"Kind of like that," I agreed as I gazed out the window. "It looks like it could rain."

Heavy dark clouds hung on the horizon, threatening, and I wondered if a picnic today was such a good idea after all. I'd dressed warmly and practically in jeans, a short-sleeved shirt, pullover sweater, and tennis shoes with thick socks. I tended to chill easily even on the "warm" eighty-five-degree English days, but if it started to rain, the temperatures really cooled down.

With a grin on his face, Toby leaned to look past me to the sky and observed, "Could be, but I think it will be clearing soon. The weather changes a lot around here."

"I hope you're right then," I replied. Despite his assurances, I had some reservations about it.

At that point, the ticket-taker came into our car, and I pulled out my rail pass to show to him. He barely glanced at it, but he stopped to talk to Toby for a bit before moving on. Typically, their conversation was in Welsh and excluded me. In my short time here, I'd discovered that most of the Welsh, at least in this area, spoke their native language amongst themselves.

Toby chuckled as his friend left, then said, "I told him we wanted off at Dyffryn Ardudwy station—that we were picnicking at the ruins. He asked if we brought enough for the spirits."

"Spirits?" I asked, wrinkling my brow in puzzlement.

"We are going to a grave, Kathleen," he explained patiently, stressing his words. "Perhaps their spirits are still there... Or maybe we'll just have the goddess for company."

A partial smile spread to my mouth, an indication of my slow understanding. I had to keep reminding myself that quite a few people of this country still believed firmly in apparitions and ghosts. They considered places like the burial cairns to hold those spirits still. Although troubling to many modern people, lingering souls didn't bother the Celts; they just accepted them as natural and even joked about them. Yet underneath, there was a healthy respect for the unknown. I had to admit that Toby's casualness about it didn't leave me feeling at ease but reminded me that we were about to visit the graves of some very ancient people.

Four stations down the line to the south, the train pulled in alongside the old, deserted platform at Dyffryn Ardudwy. It stopped long enough to disgorge a pair of pre-teen boys, Toby, and myself before chugging out again. To the west, on the seaside, a broad flat meadow bloomed with dozens of orange and white beach tents obscuring the view of the bay. The boys ran off in this direction, their giggles and shouts fading from our hearing quickly.

The other direction, to the east, a road led up towards the hills and into the town. Toby caught my hand, pulled me along with him across the railroad tracks, and up this small road. From the look on his face, I felt like I was being escorted to the town social function by my best beau, and he was proud of it. In truth, I was pleased to see it since Toby seemed reticent to show any attachments. I was definitely making headway.

The road curved through a quiet and neat residential area then came to a T-stop with the main highway. A typical seacoast town, Dyffryn boasted a small public park across the road along with a few businesses lining the highway. Toby turned to the right, heading south again.

"It's only a few hundred yards down this way," he informed me. "Then we climb up into the hills a couple of hundred more."

We passed by a small general store and a gasoline station that were about the only shops open at this point. When we reached the local school, we crossed to the east side of the road. Toby opened a gate that ran alongside the schoolyard, and I wondered if it was a shortcut until I noticed the small sign on the gate that announced it as the path to the Dyffryn Burial Chamber.

The climb turned out to be a mild slope, easy walking, and we soon reached the gate to the monument. Certainly, I knew what burial cairns were like, but the sheer beauty of this particular site stunned me.

Two bluish-gray cromlechs rose majestically from the slight slope of the hill, seeming to grow out of the rubble of the smaller stones that surrounded them. A tall, slanting oak tree stood guard on the southern edge of the rocks and cast protective shade over both although it seemed to favor the back cairn, the larger one, more. Above the fenced-in area of the monument was a large field of green grass and wildflowers with a low line of trees and bushes just up the hill beyond. The cromlechs themselves were huge, splendidly balanced monoliths that resembled large, uneven tables.

Even as I reached for my camera, the clouds broke, and the sun streaked through casting a beam of golden-white light into the area. I snapped the picture, then I turned to find Toby watching me with that tolerant look of amusement on his face. Without a word, he motioned me through the gate and onto the grounds. Stillness spread through me, almost like I was walking into a sacred area. A sense of timelessness radiated around me as if the energy poured from the stones.

"The archeological dig took place in 1962," Toby said as he set the picnic basket down next to the gate and walked onto the pile of stones surrounding the western chamber. "Before that, all these smaller stones were piled on top of the two cairns and were covered with dirt and grasses, much like Bryn Celli Ddu —only not as large, of course."

That was an understatement, I reflected, as I thought of the massive tomb at the site he referred to on Anglesey. I hadn't been out there yet, but I'd read about the unusual mound. I suspected this one only bore a vague resemblance to that one. Still, it was amazing enough given the age of some of these monuments. To think there was still something here after maybe three or four thousand years was a sobering revelation of a human life's insignificance in the long range. The people who erected these burial cairns were long gone; essentially unknown, yet this remained. What, if anything, would still be standing for archeologists to find of twenty-first century humans?

Unaware of my thoughts, Toby edged around a bit and continued, "Probably there were a lot more stones, but local people often raided these cairns for building stones. Come on over here and look, Kat'leen..."

He motioned with his hands then reached to help me across as I stumbled over the rocks until I stood beside him facing the opening of the nearest cairn. He indicated the broad supporting stones and the heavy slab of rock across the top as he talked. "These are called portal dolmens. See how the capstone slopes across to form the door."

Giving him my full attention, I followed Toby from point-to-point as he showed me the details of the site. My archeological knowledge was slight, but it increased rapidly in the twenty minutes he took to tell me about this one place. Then he pulled me about thirty feet further up to the eastern chamber.

This one was larger, more elaborately built, and included an area Toby referred to as the portico. As much as I tried, I couldn't see it, but it impressed me anyway. Like seeing Stonehenge, I marveled in seeing incredibly heavy stone monuments that primitive men had constructed.

"What did the archeologists find when they excavated?" I asked as I recalled reading the accounts of rich finds in old tombs.

"Oh, not very much," he admitted ruefully. "Just some pieces of Neolithic pottery and some stone pendants. Not even very many bones were in them. The researchers think they might have been looted over the years, and quite probably, there was a great deal in them at one time. Of course, some of the people around here will swear lots of gold and bronze items were found, but they just want to make the find seem more important."

A light breeze came in off the ocean creating an eerie whistling sound as it echoed through the chamber. It was like a sad call, mournful in tone. Toby's eyes narrowed a little, the dark blue irises getting deeper. "Do you hear the spirits, Kat'leen?"

"It's just the wind," I said softly. Nonetheless, I found I was unconsciously tracing the sign of the cross.

Toby noticed and he, too, traced a sign before him, but his was not a cross. When I asked him about it, he replied, "It's an ancient symbol, like a circle from a religion older than Christianity."

"Your pagan group," I acknowledged and started back towards the gate. I was more than ready to leave this site. Maybe there were no spirits in these cairns; however, I was not prepared to find out. I'd learned enough about them today.

Basket in hand, Toby set the pace up the hill towards the trees and shrubs. As we climbed, he told me about a clearing in the trees where a standing stone made of the same rock as the dolmens stood guard.

As we climbed a little further up the hill, I turned and glanced back towards the ocean. I grinned at the splendid view that even the little orange tents couldn't block. How beautiful it must have looked several centuries earlier when nothing marred the landscape.

True to Toby's prediction, the sun had chased away most of the clouds leaving only a few lingering ones now. As my spirits lifted more, that unsettling moment by the cromlechs might never have happened.

The upper grove consisted of oak and ash trees, ferns, bracken, hawthorn, and other shrubs that I couldn't keep track of as Toby named them. I felt we were blazing a trail to get through them, but he had no trouble finding his way. Soon we came into an opening that was not entirely free of the wild growth that Toby called a clearing. Within this was a fire ring of small stones and at the easternmost edge, an upright standing stone dominated the area.

It was not a plain, unmarked pillar as the dolmens below were, but had a distinct rounded shape above the oblong lower half to resemble a man. This impression was reinforced by the eyes, nose, and mustache carved into the rounded section. I crossed the clearing to get a better look.

"The early Celts carved these stones around here," Toby said. "Actually, you don't find too many of them, but at one time there must have been hundreds. Archeologists have found them all over Europe where the Celtic tribes were."

"No spirit in this one?"

He laughed. "I don't think so. Not if the Celts carved it. They believed spirits inhabited stones, waters, and certain groves, but I don't think anyone would have carved up a stone they believed had a spirit in it. We often use this grove for our worship without repercussions from that fellow."

"He certainly doesn't look friendly," I commented as I studied the fierce expression carved into the face.

"Well, he was probably placed to protect so you wouldn't want a welcoming face, would you?" He winked at me, a teasing look in his eyes.

"I guess not. After all, the Celts were warrior tribes." I took a photograph catching a spray of light through the leaves as it streaked the face.

Grabbing the blanket he carried, Toby began to spread it on the ground. I joined him, helping to smooth it out before I dove into the picnic basket. He had brought quite a feast with pasties, fresh fruit, cheese, and two bottles of hard cider.

"No fizzy lemonade?" I quipped.

He laughed. "You'll like the cider better."

He settled at the edge of the blanket, leaned back on his elbows, and stretched his legs out in front of him before commenting on my earlier observation. "That they were. All you have to do is look at the Picts in Scotland to realize how fierce they were. I suppose they had to be, but the stories about them indicate that they really enjoyed a fight."

"Somehow, it's hard to think of being descended from them. I mean, the Welsh seem like a very peaceful race, and you have the Irish, who love music and poetry and philosophy." I found it hard to think of coming from a bloodline of warriors, but it was true, the Irish, too, were fierce fighters.

As I listened to him, I tried to imagine what it would be like to have all my life experiences confined to one little area of the world. Not that I was a world traveler exactly. In addition to my two European trips, I had been over most of the western United States, so I had been around some.

Yet here was a young man whose realm had consisted of a small section of a medium-sized island in the North Atlantic. How peculiar that in this day and age, people should be so isolated. Yet it wasn't that uncommon. Many countries had people who'd never traveled beyond the few square miles that constituted their reality. In fact, there were underprivileged in American cities that were in the same category—young people who had no idea what green countryside looked like.

It was odd, I thought without amusement, how encountering something in a different setting made you aware of it in your own neighborhood, so to speak.

Then it was my turn to entertain Toby as he pressed me for details of my life. A privileged American upbringing must have sounded very elegant to him. Even the very ordinary act of going to college seemed beyond his grasp.

"But Britain has many good colleges," I pointed out.

"Sure enough," he agreed "but not everyone can go, Kathleen. Some people, like me, are not university material and without a great deal of money, it is out of our reach. I don't mind that, though. There are additional ways to gain knowledge."

Our conversation drifted to other subjects. As I suspected, Toby's lack of a college education and thick local accent did not mean he wasn't intelligent. He could speak knowledgeably on politics, music, the arts, and many other topics. As we feasted in that sacred circle on the hillside, we chatted about a good many subjects.

What he didn't mention included the specifics of his religion, a revival of ancient druidism, and how this circle played into it. Perhaps it was secret, or he didn't feel ready to share it with me.

Eventually, Toby glanced up at the sky and consulted his watch. "Oops! We better get going. I want to catch the next train in 20 minutes." With that, he began gathering up the glasses and utensils and stuffing them back into the basket.

Within five minutes, we had the area cleaned up and were heading back down the path to the street. It was about 3:30, still early by my reckoning, but Toby seemed in a hurry. When I asked him about it, he explained he had an appointment at five.

We waited alone in the train accommodation at Dyffryn Ardudwy. While only a little shelter with a couple of benches beside the track, across from it a closed down building had been the train station in more prosperous times. Tony gazed anxiously down the track, occasionally walking over to the edge of the platform, and glancing at his watch. "It's a little late," he announced at last.

I tried to conceal my disappointment as we waited for the train to make its appearance. While the day had been delightful, I'd hoped we could continue it with dinner together, but it seemed he had other plans. Was it a girlfriend? A pang of jealousy crept through me at the thought.

Then the train rolled into view. Toby grinned, stepped to the edge of the platform, and waved his arm broadly to let the engineer know he had passengers. With a hiss of the pistons, the train slowed to a halt, and we hopped aboard again.

This carriage packed in more people than the one coming down, so I ended up with an end seat while Toby stood to give an older woman his place. Impressed that he had good manners when so many people didn't these days, I leaned back as the train jostled away. At Harlech Station, Toby hopped off long enough to give me a hand down and say goodbye, then he mustered up enough courage to kiss my cheek.

"I'll talk to you later, Kat'leen," he assured me, then hopped back on the train.

I waved to him until the train had chugged a good hundred yards down the track before turning towards my hotel with an amused smile on my lips. I'd had a good

time, enjoyed his company quite a lot, and the little peck of a kiss offered encouragement. Yes, that relationship was definitely progressing. A grin of satisfaction spread across my face, and I might have skipped a little as I headed back to the Thornhill Hotel.

*S*omething about the sea, about the primal sound of the waves pounding against the shore, fascinated me. It was a constant lure, like a lover calling my name. Almost of their own accord, my feet made the short trek across the dunes to the bay. I slipped my shoes off and ambled along the edge of the water where it could lap against my ankles.

No indicators remained to mark where the body had been the previous morning. The tides had cleared any evidence left behind leaving the beach looking smooth and fresh. She'd been identified, Mrs. Linton had informed me when I'd gone in for tea before heading to the beach. A woman from Cardiff, who had been visiting, she'd said, but the police didn't reveal any details of what had happened.

"Very tragic," she'd added, then asked if I'd seen the new guest who'd come in the previous evening. "His name is Owain Thomas. He's a photographer from Pembroke, and he comes here a couple of times a year. Although this visit was a surprise one. He's such a handsome fellow."

"Handsome, indeed," I'd agreed as I recalled the man from the bar the previous night. Absolutely, stunningly so. He'd seemed distant and aloof, untouchable. More than that, something about him suggested I should steer clear of him; he'd be trouble.

"But not my type," I'd added in case she had any ideas of matchmaking.

"Your type?" she'd challenged. "How can define what your type is until you know the person?"

"My instincts are pretty good."

She'd shaken her head, casting a disapproving look at me.

Now, I shrugged my shoulders and brought my attention back to the beautiful bay. Far more crowded now than the previous morning, dozens of people walked, ran, and played in the water as I strolled a few yards beyond where I'd found the woman.

While my thoughts rambled, I gazed across the sea towards Ireland. The island was around a hundred or so miles away at an angle from the North Wales shore. Technically, this was Tremadog Bay, a very sheltered inlet at the top of Cardigan Bay. The hook of land easily visible directly across the water and to the north was the Isle of Anglesey with Holy Island just off the tip of it. From there, a ferry could whip you across to Dun Laoghaire harbor just south of Dublin in less than four hours. But from this point, there was no sign of the Emerald Isle, just a haze on the horizon that gave no indication the ocean did not go on forever.

Slowly, I became aware of someone watching me— that prickly feeling you get when eyes are on you. I cast a quick glance over my shoulder and up to see him. He was standing on one of the sand dunes to my right— towards the hotel. How long had he been there?

And he was staring at me.

Even as I gradually turned around to face him, he continued to gaze directly at me. Just what was Mr. Thomas' problem? He didn't even pretend he wasn't watching me.

Whatever it was, I decided I'd have to face him on this. I took a deep breath and walked towards him.

As I approached, he didn't move, nor did he even look that uneasy about his obvious attention to me. I stopped at the base of the dune and gazed up at him.

Casually dressed, he wore an almost white short-sleeved shirt that made his darkly stunning features stand out even more. As I peered at him, my mouth was like sandpaper, dry and rough. With an effort, I found my voice. "It's very rude to stare, Mr. Thomas."

A moment or two passed before he blinked and seemed to register that I'd said something to him. "What?"

He made his way down the dune to come level with me, and I repeated my statement. "I said, it's rude to stare. You were staring at me."

For the first time, he looked a little uneasy. "Have I been? I'm very sorry. I assure you it wasn't intentional, Miss—? Have we met?" He cocked an eyebrow at me as he paused.

That set me back a little. "Sort of. At the bar in the hotel last night, but we weren't introduced."

"Ah, yes, the young lady at the bar." His luscious lips, perfectly shaped with a bow at the center, formed a slight smile that brought a spark of amusement to his eyes.

That annoyed me. He found me funny. I nodded, my own expression more serious.

After a moment, he said, "I actually wasn't staring at you. I was looking at the general area where my cousin died. I was lost in my own thoughts. The police told me it was right about where you were standing."

"Your cousin?" I echoed, shocked at the revelation. The woman was his cousin? That was why he came in unexpectedly last night. "I'm terribly sorry, sir. I misinterpreted that totally."

He glanced down, as if organizing his thoughts, then looked up again. His eyes met mine with clarity and frankness I'd seldom seen. "I do apologize. I was looking at you also. You resemble her somewhat. Of course, you don't look at all like her up close. Do forgive me."

"Ah, so you were staring," I replied, vindicated. "Well, take a good look, Mr. Thomas, so you won't have a problem anymore."

A half-smile touched his lips. "Touché. You don't like me, do you? Why?"

"I don't know you. There's neither like nor dislike. Now, excuse me." I started to go past him to return to the hotel.

Unexpectedly, he caught my arm. An unnerving fierceness glistened in his eyes. "Be careful along the beach, miss. It could be unsafe for a girl like you." His voice didn't sound threatening, more of a soft-spoken warning.

Aware at once of his tingling touch that sent waves of shocks through my arm, I caught my breath, inhaling the earthy scent of his masculine cologne while my heart thudded against my ribs. After a couple of moments, he released my arm, turned, and strode towards the beach with long, purposeful steps.

I pivoted in slow motion to follow his retreating back with my eyes. There was a sense of unreality about the whole encounter. Why the warning? And what did he mean, "a girl like you?" He didn't even know me, let alone comprehend what I was like.

Owain Thomas continued down the beach, heading far to the south, not towards the place where his cousin had washed in. I hadn't expected that. Why?

I tried to shake off the uneasy feeling he'd left behind, but there was more than the memory of the look in his eyes. I heard his voice, with its sultry, appealing quality and the delicious roll of the "r" that was common among the Welsh, murmured seductively in my mind. He would, I reflected, be a most persuasive man if he chose to be. And one it would not be wise to trust.

A shiver shot through me although I was not cold. Turning, I started back up the sand towards the main road and the hotel. I wanted to know more about Owain Thomas and trusted that I would find something on the Internet.

Chapter Four

"...gamboling in a fanciful village..."

I hopped off the train at Minffordd and hiked the one-and-a-half-mile path towards Portmeirion, a rather unique village that was more tourist attraction than an actual town, although a few people lived there.

Sometimes described as an Italian Renaissance Village, the hamlet nestled artistically in the hills along the coastline. Designed by Sir William Clough, a well-known architect in his day, it blossomed with a multitude of unique buildings in an assortment of colors. He conceived the place to demonstrate that a colorful, functional community could be built anywhere without detracting from the natural beauty of the area.

Whether he was successful at this or not is something that might well be up to the viewer, but no matter what one may or may not think of it in that respect, it was certainly different. In some ways, it reminded me of a storybook village at Disneyland although much of it seemed to be a mixture of styles.

As I wandered along the various walkways, I snapped dozens of photos. Along the main pathway inside, various shops offered an assortment of pottery, clothing, souvenirs, and other unique items. Other buildings housed private residences not open to the public, but all appeared beautifully maintained and groomed.

One of the small stores had a sign for "The Prisoner," a British television series that had been filmed at Portmeirion several decades earlier. I'd seen a couple of episodes a few years back, but I couldn't exactly say I was a fan. Nonetheless, I stopped in and browsed through the souvenirs of the series.

As I started to leave the shop, I spotted the tall, lean figure of Owain Thomas across a pavilion area near the hotel. He walked alongside a stunning, model-perfect blonde. Just the type of woman I expected to see him with, I thought, exonerated in my opinion of him. Yet, I just couldn't tear my eyes away from the smashing pair.

So, who was staring now? I looked away but kept glancing back towards them. I lifted a brochure in front of my face, so it didn't look like I was spying on them as I sauntered towards the fountain in the center.

They paused outside the main door of the hotel. Whatever they were discussing, it seemed intense with occasional hand gestures and glances towards the bay. Mr. Thomas appeared to pay strict attention to the woman's words, only responding occasionally. At the end of the conversation, he nodded to her, then turned away to go down the stairs.

For just a moment, he paused, and I stood directly in his view. Hastily, I diverted my face, turning my attention to the nearest building to study the ornate trim. To add to the deception, I reached for my camera and focused on the flower design. When I glanced again, I didn't spot the photographer anywhere. I breathed a sigh of relief. I didn't want him to think I was spying on him.

I backtracked down the path to the statue of Atlas and took the short climb down the steps to the observation platform where I discovered a splendid view of the bay at the river's mouth. Turning to look up the ravine, I caught my breath at the vista of wild-looking vegetation and tree-covered hills rising higher and higher into the mountains of Snowdonia. As I ran my eyes across this panorama, I thought again just how beautiful this country was, so rich and vibrant with life. I wished that Toby had been free to share it with me this day, but I hadn't even seen him on the train when I caught it from Harlech this morning.

"Beautiful, isn't it?"

I stiffened as I recognized the voice and made a slow turn to face Owain Thomas. He stood three steps above me, hands thrust in the pockets of his dark gray slacks. I hadn't heard him approach at all.

"Portmeirion is an unusual place—very picturesque," he continued. "I did a photo article about it a few years ago. Now a few more tourists find it than before, but it's still not a major attraction." Pausing, he studied the expression on my face. I felt certain it wasn't a pleasant one as I wasn't happy to see him.

"Look, Miss Donaghue, I want to apologize again for being rude. I didn't do it intentionally. Won't you join me for tea and we can get properly acquainted?"

"I see you've learned my name," I replied curtly. "However, I have other plans today, Mr. Thomas, and I have no need to get better acquainted with you. You've apologized more than once, and that is sufficient. Please excuse me." Without waiting for him to say anything more, I hurried past him to go back up the steps.

"I really do need to speak with you," he said before I'd barely passed him.

I halted, turned my head back towards him.

"Why?"

"As I told you my cousin's body was found on the beach and the local constabulary informed me a young American woman found her. I believe that was you."

"And if it was, what of it?" I couldn't see where this would go anywhere.

"I just want to talk, ask you a couple of questions. Is that so unreasonable?"

"Why did you warn me about the beach last night?" I said, not willing to trust him.

His eyes met mine, a gentle look on his face as if he was trying to be a friend. "Please. Let me take you to tea at the hotel, and I'll answer your questions. Then I hope you'll answer mine."

I made a show of glancing at my wristwatch, then nodded. "Very well. One cup."

"Splendid." He stepped beside me and offered an arm for support as we started up the steps.

I declined and continued up them with him trailing behind. I would not get involved with this man, especially if he thought I might know something about his cousin's death.

As we made our way to the hotel, I mentally reviewed the small bits of information I'd found on the web. He was thirty-one, unmarried, and a well-known photographer who'd done cover photos for several magazines and wildlife periodicals. He didn't give interviews and remained a bit of a mystery man. Although he'd been born in northern Wales, he lived in Pembroke, according to Mrs. Linton. On the surface, he seemed to be a legitimate professional photographer and, if not an upstanding man, at least one who hadn't gotten any bad press.

The hostess seated us near the windows with a view of the central square and the fountain. I ordered just tea, no biscuits, or anything, and he nodded once to the server indicating the same, I presumed. While we waited, I cleared my throat and asked, "Did the local police give you my name?" If they did, I would have a word with the constable after he told me they wouldn't release it to anyone.

"No. They just said young American, and there aren't too many in the area right now. I'm afraid you'll have to blame Mrs. Linton for that divulgence as she mentioned you at breakfast this morning." He leaned back in the chair, looking relaxed.

"In what context?" My voice sharpened. I would definitely have words with her.

"She just told me your name, and that you're a school teacher from California. She mentioned you are a guest staying for a few weeks and perhaps I'd like to chat with you since we both were interested in photography. She meant well." His voice carried a soft purr that made everything sound sexy. "What else do you want to know?"

Well, damn the woman and her incessant matchmaking. I almost spoke it aloud but caught myself in time. I gazed down at my hands to give me time to cool my anger. I noticed a couple of chipped fingernails and tucked them into my lap.

Just then, the tea arrived, and I took a relieved breath as the server poured for us. As I added sugar and a bit of cream, I said, "Back to the question I asked earlier. What did you mean by that warning?"

He gazed at me a moment or two, then said, "The shore there can be dangerous in more ways than one. First, there are the tides to worry about. They can creep up on you, and there is a strong undertow when they go out. People often aren't aware..."

"I grew up on the coast," I cut in. "I know how tides work. What else?"

"Sometimes smugglers use the easy beach access to bring in illegal items. You wouldn't want to get involved with any of them."

"Why would I?" I asked, confused by this statement.

"Perhaps involved was the wrong word," he said smoothly. "It's more a case of being in the wrong place or getting inadvertently caught up in something. Just a warning not to get too curious about anything you might see on the beach."

I laughed. "Really? You think I'm going to cross paths with smugglers? Do you warn all tourists?"

"No, just ones who might be vulnerable."

"You don't know me, Mr. Thomas," I replied curtly, setting my cup onto its saucer with enough force to rattle it. "I am not vulnerable nor am I likely to get involved in anything. I'm here to do research for a paper; that's it. You needn't concern yourself about me."

He dipped his head in a short nod. "Good. Will you answer my questions now?"

"Depends on the questions." I frowned daring him to ask anything personal.

He disappointed me.

"When you found Madlen, my cousin, how did she look?" He spoke softly, and the name rolled off his tongue with a gentle tone.

I looked away from him, thinking it an odd question to ask. How did she look? Dead. Her face was pasty and blue-tinted, but that surely wasn't what he was asking. I thought about her, picturing the woman and I remembered the photos on my camera. He wouldn't want to see those. Not if he cared about her.

"She didn't look scared. Her eyes were closed, and she looked as if she slept. Is that want you want to know?"

His eyes flickered, a sadness touching them. "She didn't look like she'd been abused or injured? No one harmed her?"

I shook my head. "None that I could see. Didn't the police show you her body?"

"No. Not yet. They have her at the morgue and haven't released her body yet." He turned his gaze to the table as if composing himself. Then he reached for his tea and sipped a little.

As I connected with what he might be implying, I asked, "Are you thinking it might have been something other than accidental?"

He shrugged. "Like you, Madlen grew up on the coast... *this coast.* We often came here when we were children and teenagers. We knew the currents and the tides. She wasn't caught in the tide by accident. I don't believe the constables think it either."

Silence settled between us as we each followed our own thoughts. For my part, I wondered how else his cousin could have been pulled into the sea to drown. Could she have been on a boat that capsized? But wouldn't it have been found?

At last, he broke the silence. "One last question, please. Was Madlen wearing a necklace?"

I blinked and brought my attention back to him. "Yes, a Claddagh locket. Her left hand clutched it. I guess she held it as she died."

He nodded. "Good. She treasured that." He paused and noted that I'd finished my tea, then offered, "Would you like another cup or a biscuit?"

"No, thanks. I have to be going. Thank you for the tea. I trust you have all the answers you need."

"Yes. Thank you, Miss Donaghue. Again, I caution you to be careful around the bay."

All the sympathy I'd been building over his loss vanished in an instant. I didn't appreciate him talking to me as if I was a child. "I'll be fine." Rising, I picked up my handbag and left without another word.

My pace didn't slow until I was nearly out of the main entrance to the village; then, at last, I let my irritation go and slowed to a more reasonable stroll. How dare Thomas make assumptions about me! In a moment, I realized I was reacting irrationally. Why did I get so defensive and upset around Owain Thomas? He hadn't done anything to me except warn me against possible danger, yet he irritated me enormously.

I sighed, wishing I could understand why I reacted so strangely to this man. I reflected on it as I started the long walk back to the train station. Perhaps it was because I instinctively knew he was not a man to trust and one to stay clear of, I argued, almost convincingly. But there's a strange attraction about fire, and that man was far more than a mere candle flame.

Still, I hadn't lied to him—not exactly. I did have plans for the rest of the day, although another cup of tea was included in the scheme.

That I got, along with a couple of scones, back at the hotel before I set off along the upward path to hike in the hills above Harlech.

Chapter Five

... when the storm clouds roll in...

I picked my way up the hill with cautious steps, not that there was much to hinder walking, but a few shallow gullies in the land and outcroppings of rocks here and there could trip you if you didn't pay attention. For the most part, the gradual grassy slope amounted to an easy climb.

Despite the coolness of the day, I worked up some sweat, but when I paused, I cooled off in minutes. I pulled my scarf from around my neck, rolled it into a smooth band, and tied it around my hair to keep the long strands from sticking to my face.

As I turned around, my heart swelled with joy at the magnificent view behind me. About a mile or so down the slope, Harlech castle stood proud and defiant on its bluff of rock, daring anyone from the sea to threaten it. Beyond it, the waters of Tremadoc Bay pounded against the shoreline, no longer a threat to the mighty fortress that dominated the stretch of land but now a haven for bathers from all over England and the world.

"Lord, I do love this land," I whispered with unbridled emotion. I turned around with tiny steps, my eyes lapping up the magnificent view with an effect akin to drinking champagne. I felt giddy.

Wales grew lush with trees, shrubs, and ferns making it a green land, very like Ireland except there were more woods in Wales than I'd seen in Ireland. Of course, once trees had covered the latter until the English had arrived and cut them down. But not here. A sizeable portion of North Wales fell in Snowdonia National Park, preventing the destruction of this beautiful countryside.

Off to my left and a little way uphill, a small hut or lean-to perched at an angle. I reckoned it belonged to a sheepherder although I didn't notice any of the animals in this area.

Rested now, I shoved the sleeves of my lightweight sweater up my arms and resumed climbing. Another mile or so up the hill, a grove of trees represented my immediate goal. I'd spotted them halfway up and decided they were as good a destination as any. Within another thirty minutes, I'd reach them, huffing and puffing once again. I paused to catch my breath and gave thanks that the way back would be downhill.

When I reached them, I gazed at the trees, identifying most of them as mountain oak. It appeared to be an old grove, but then I didn't know enough about horticulture to determine if they were a few years or a few hundred years in age. What I did know is that they were beautiful and the breeze cascading through their leaves gave them a voice that appeared to whisper magical incantations. At any rate, they totally charmed me into fanciful thoughts.

Finding an almost flat rock, I sat cross-legged, then opened my tote and pulled out a chicken salad sandwich and a canned orange soda leaving the rest—another soda, a bag of crisps, two scones, and a pack of shortbread cookies—for later. I couldn't find a more ideal spot for lunch. I spent the next hour listening to the seductive voices of the leaves and letting my imagination run free.

Perhaps a band of knights had camped in this grove once. English knights, of course, waiting for the ideal time to strike at the castle below. Or maybe it was a meeting place for young lovers. After all, the legends of Tristan and Iseulte and King Arthur were Welsh tales. They were a very romantic race of people.

I grinned at my own foolishness. The Welsh certainly didn't have the market on romanticism– Their Irish cousins were as bad. I tidied up the remains of my lunch, closed the tote bag, and climbed to my feet. From this point, I went on a casual stroll to the southeast following the belt of the grove. It wasn't exactly a path, but it did seem to be an unencumbered route through the wood.

Just ahead, I noticed the trees thinned somewhat opening into a small clearing. I continued that way and stepped from the wood into an open meadow dominated by a ring of rocks. Surprised, I stopped to study the stones in silence for a few minutes.

Seven of them stood spaced an equal distance apart in a circle to form a dance. While they were far from the scale of Stonehenge or even the smaller cromlechs of Dyffryn, the stones still rose to my waist and were placed with such purpose that I concluded they were not a natural occurrence. Yet, I'd heard nothing about a Neolithic monument above Harlech–not in my research or any of the materials distributed by the Welsh Tourist Bureau.

Letting my breath out, I took cautious steps to the nearest stone of the dance. Like the relics at Dyffryn, I approached these with a sense of reverence. I laid my hand on them, skimming my fingers across the cold surface of the stone to explore its crown. It felt smooth, worn by years of wind and rain, but if I expected to sense anything else from it, I was disappointed. No mystical sensations, no feeling of power or holiness about it, just the cold hard touch of stone.

Then I noticed the fire pit in the center of the dance that had not been visible until I'd moved into the circle. Curious, I knelt by the depression to see its contents. Several pieces of half-burned wood thrust up through the ashes filling the center. The ashes felt moist and stuck together giving me the impression it had been used recently, not that there was any way to tell with any certainty.

Straightening up, I brushed the ash from my fingers then turned to survey the ring from this central point. Yes, I'd been right that the stones were too evenly spaced, convincing me that this dance was a recent addition to the Welsh hills, possibly within the last few years. I could see they'd been here long enough for them to settle into their earthen cradles and for the grass to build sturdy skirts at their bases, but the dance was not ancient. Not in this location anyway. The stones themselves may have been as old as the cromlechs, but they'd only found this configuration within the last decade.

So, the obvious question was who and why had someone erected this dance? Who had recently used it?

Oak groves and stone dances often figured in ancient cult worship. Some theories held that Stonehenge was once a druidic worship site although most authorities denied it. Druids were more often associated with groves of trees than with stone circles, yet modern worship groups might seek the combination.

Perhaps Toby Morgan could shed some light on this place, although I would have expected him to tell me about it if he knew it existed. This was part of what I wanted to know about the modern people of this country. While most of them were Christians, some reverted to the old beliefs.

And there were those with a foot in each door, so to speak. Those people enjoyed the traditions of their ancestors, whether as a way to honor them or to make sure that any important spirits wouldn't be forgotten.

I was familiar with this concept as my Irish father and his sister both kept some of the old traditions even though they were born and raised Catholic and had lived the majority of their lives in the United States. A Bridget's Cross hung above the entry and back doors of their homes; they still put out an offering for the fairies on certain nights; and in so many ways the ancient customs worked their way into their lives.

Aunt Maeve often spoke of the banshee that would come to warn of an approaching death in the family. She even swore she had heard one when my grandmother had passed.

Whatever the purpose of this small ring of stones, a distinct feeling of unease wormed through me as I stood in the center. There was something dark about it; something that made my skin crawl. The hairs on the back of my neck began to rise as my discomfort mounted and the air appeared to grow heavy, thickening like a dense fog.

I whipped around expecting to face someone or something behind me, but I only saw the blank faces of two more stones and an empty stretch of meadow before the trees started again. I let my breath out, face flushing at my imagined threat.

Without warning, a sharp crack cut through the stillness of the day. I jumped, startled like a wild doe as the sound echoed through the hills and grove. Wildly, I spun around in a circle, looking for the source of the noise, almost convinced a sudden crash of thunder caused it. I ran for the trees, away from the open area in the ring. Thunder and lightning go hand in hand, and I didn't want to be a lightning rod.

But as I gazed at the cloudy sky and waited for a repeat crack or a lightning flash, I began to think the noise sounded more like a rifle shot. With the echoes in the hills, I couldn't be certain what direction it had come from or how near it was. I took several deep breaths, realized that my hands were clinging to the nearest branch, and forced my tense fingers to relax. Nothing seemed out of the ordinary here.

"Talk about over-reacting," I mumbled under my breath as my heart rate settled down to its normal speed. I remained where I was for a few more minutes, listening for any additional rifle shots, but it was quiet. Probably a hunter who'd bagged a rabbit, I thought and turned away from the dance.

As I retraced my path through the grove of trees, I wondered about the uneasiness I'd felt while standing within the stone circle. I'd never really experienced the touch of evil or imminent disaster, but I'd definitely felt that something was not right about that dance. Whatever its purpose, it had not been used for good intent.

By the time I emerged from the trees and back into the open hills, the day had grown slightly darker and a sharp breeze bit at my cheeks. I pulled my sweater closed and buttoned it, then set a brisk pace downhill towards the town.

While the day had been overcast since early morning, I'd not thought too much about it except to grab my sweater before I'd started this trek. Now, the sky roiled with dark, ponderous masses of clouds that posed a very definite threat. I was still about three miles from the town with Harlech Castle a miniature version in the distance.

With the need to look for unexpected gullies and small stones on the way, I figured it would take at least an hour before I could reach the town and another ten to fifteen minutes to the hotel. I doubted the storm would hold off that long, but I aimed to make the best time I could.

Within ten minutes, I'd come over a rise and spotted the lean-to I'd noticed on the way up. For a moment, I wondered how much protection it would offer in a storm. Then a crash of thunder—the real thing this time—rolled through the sky, echoing in the hills and sounding ominous. A few minutes later, the first hesitant drops of rain, light touches barely felt on my cheeks and eyelids, followed.

I stepped up my pace, determined not to be stuck on this hillside in a rainstorm. Although only four in the afternoon, it looked much later as the darkness of the storm muted the light. The sun didn't have a peephole at all for as far as I could see.

Clouds appeared to boil in from Ireland, and even the hook of the Lleyn Peninsula wasn't visible now. But I could make out the rain beginning to pour on the sea and the churning of the waters as a wind whipped across them. It was going to be a nasty storm.

Illuminated by the lightning, the castle appeared eerily outlined against the backdrop of stormy clouds and the foaming white caps of turbulent waves hitting the beach.

Cold, heavy rain, driven by the fierce wind pelted me. I ducked my head and pressed on towards the castle, cursing my stupidity for even coming out here on a day like this. I should have paid more attention to the weather forecast. Within a minute or two, rain soaked my clothes even through my sweater.

I could barely make out where I was going, but I felt the slight rise of the land and I stumbled down the other side. I tripped as my foot caught something soft, an animal of some sort, and I pitched forward in a lurch. Off balance, I couldn't regain my footing and crashed to the ground, sliding on the wet grass with my legs sprawled akimbo over the beast that had tripped me.

As I twisted to shift my legs, I realized that the animal was not a furry creature but felt more like soaked cloth against the bared skin about my ankles.

And it was moaning... A very male, human moan.

Chapter Six

"...finding shelter from the storm..."

$\mathcal{H}$ ad some poor shepherd been hit by lightning? Never mind that I hadn't seen any shepherds or sheep on the hillside during the day. That kind of logic didn't occur to me at the time.

I flipped my legs off and crawled over the slippery surface to him. He was lying face down, sprawled next to an outcropping of rocks, but what caught my attention were the spreading patches of blood covering the left shoulder of his off-white sweater. I knew who it was before I even turned his face towards me—Owain Thomas.

He moaned again as I lifted his head. His half-open eyes held a dazed, unfocused dullness. I eased his head to the side as I looked for an injury and barely saw the dark purple of a bruise at the base of his skull a little below the hairline. I figured he'd struck one of the large, scattered rocks in the meadow as he'd fallen.

Moving my hands with care, I started to check him over, feeling for any other obvious injuries. Apart from the shoulder and the bruise, he appeared to be sound.

I caught his face between my hands and asked, "Mr. Thomas, are you all right?"

He blinked but didn't answer.

"Mr. Thomas? Owain? Do you hear me? Answer me!" I spoke louder to be heard over the storm.

The rain flooded down, soaking our faces and hair. Owain seemed oblivious to it, then his right hand locked on my wrist, and he pushed my hand away from his face before releasing me to run his hand across his eyes, wiping the water away.

"I'm... all right," he said, his words slurred a bit and drawn out as if he had trouble connecting them.

"We've got to get back to town," I said, not at all convinced he was all right. "Can you walk?"

He tried to focus on me. "What?"

"Walk," I repeated. "Owain, can you stand?"

"Sure," he said, drawing it out and closed his eyes.

"Oh, great!" I muttered then tried to get an arm under him to lift him to an upright position. I succeeded in eliciting a sharp yip of pain followed by another groan from him, but his eyes popped open again and he seemed a little more alert.

Even with his cooperation, I struggled to get him to his feet, pulling his arm around my shoulders, and lifting as much as I could without causing any more damage to the wound. After two false starts that almost had me tumbling on top of him again, I managed to get him to his feet, even though I was supporting more of his weight than he was.

At this point, with my hair sticking to the sides of my face and my blue jeans squishing uncomfortably against my legs, I had a firm hunch that we'd not make it back down the hill. I couldn't support his weight for very far, and if he collapsed on me, I didn't think I'd be able to get him to his feet again.

The lean-to I'd passed a short time earlier was the closest shelter. If I could get Owain back there, I could leave him in a place out of the storm and go for help.

Determined, I pulled him along, taking the climb up the hill with caution. Several times, I felt his body tense as an uneven step jarred his shoulder or sent a lance of pain into his skull. For however dazed he was, he, at least, understood the necessity of getting out of the open and he struggled to make the climb under his own power.

It felt like it took an hour, but within fifteen minutes, we had staggered up to the lean-to. After a quick look, I decided it wasn't a shepherd's hut, but a stone and straw construct of a way station, a little resting place. The doorway faced up towards the hillside indicating that most of the elements the builder hoped to avoid came from the west, from the sea. But it was clean inside and, most of all, dry.

Against the western wall was a thin straw mattress spread over a flat board on the stone floor. Another pile of straw was in the north corner and next to it was a small stack of wood. A wooden box served as a table where three pillar candles sat along with a tin to contain the melting wax. Other than that, the hut held nothing else.

With no grace at all, I lowered Owain to the mattress, stumbling in the process, then eased his legs around to straighten him out as much as possible. His long legs dropped off the end of the flat mattress.

"Well, it's not made for a tall man, but I guess it'll do," I said in a voice cheerier than I felt.

Owain was indifferent at this point. He'd passed out, perspiration beading on his forehead, and his breathing sounded ragged. A man in shock was something I didn't need. "Damn it, Owain," I muttered. "Don't you dare die on me!"

I steeled myself to get a good look at his shoulder. The light in the hut was poor, but it was enough to see the rips in his sweater... and in his arm a few inches below the shoulder. There were two ragged holes, one at the front and one at the back as if some object had passed through. It wasn't hard to figure out what. Even though blood had soaked his sweater, it had now slowed to a gummy-looking ooze.

Taking care, I lifted his head, turning it to get a look at the bruise. A little larger than a quarter and a bit to the right side of his neck vertebrae, the skin didn't appear torn. While it would no doubt be sore, it didn't seem like anything too serious. No, the main worries were the bullet wound and shock.

I ran my fingers through my wet hair, my hand brushing against the soaked silk scarf.

"Oh, what the hell!" I muttered, under my breath and pulled the scarf from my hair. It was ruined anyway, so a little blood on it would hardly make any difference. I had to bind the wound with something and, contrary to the movies, it was not all that easy to tear off a shirttail.

I tried to be gentle, but it was necessary to bind it as tightly as possible if it was going to do any good. Owain groaned, wincing with the pain as he gained consciousness. He turned his head to watch me and caught his breath with a sharp gasp.

"Sorry," I said, then raised my voice a little to be heard over the storm. "You've lost a lot of blood. What happened?"

He turned his head back, staring at the straw roof. "This is the hut?"

I nodded as I finished up on his arm. "It was the closest shelter. Owain, what happened? How did you get hurt?"

He didn't say anything for so long that I thought he'd passed out again. Finally, he spoke, straining to make his voice heard over the wind. "I want you to get back down the hill, back to the safety of the town."

I gazed out the door at the torrent of rain that poured off the roof and ran into the gutter cut into the dirt next to the opening. "I'd be drowned if I went now. When the rain lets up some, I'll go for help."

"No! Don't bring anybody!" His voice was sharp, insistent. "Miss Donaghue, I want you to leave me. I can manage."

"Like hell you can," I retorted. "You wouldn't even make it ten feet."

The look of frustration was evident on his face as his eyes met mine. "Please. When the rain lets up, get to safety. I'll be all right. Really. I'll get down okay. A little slower maybe." He forced a smile as if that would make me believe him.

I shook my head in slow motion as a thought occurred to me. "What kind of trouble are you in?"

He mumbled something I couldn't understand and tried again to rise to a sitting position. I knelt beside him and leaned across to push against his right shoulder with my other hand.

"Lie back," I said with authority. "You're not going anywhere right now, so just take it easy."

His eyes shifted to me, his right hand rising to touch my hair. His breathing was hard, and I could tell he was not at all well. With a lurch, he reached for me, mumbling something in that jumble of words that was Welsh. While I had no idea what he said, the tone of his voice carried an undeniable gentleness and affection. Unsure what to do, it seemed easiest to keep him down by holding him.

I shifted my weight onto the mattress so that I was sitting with my back against the wall. Lifting his head and shoulders, I eased him into my lap all the while talking to him and offering reassurance. The fingers of his right hand laced through mine and closed getting a firm grip. He squeezed and looked into my eyes. I stroked his temple, my fingertips going through his hair much as I might pet a cat. He settled down again, falling into a deep sleep.

I shifted the blanket back over him, tucking it up around his shoulders the best I could with one free hand. He felt feverish. With the loss of blood, the shock, and the lack of proper attention to the wound, the fever wasn't surprising, but I never felt so helpless in my life. I had nothing that would help him, not even aspirin.

Over the next hour or so, I continued to hold him as I drifted off into a light sleep. Little by little, I became aware of a lack of sound. To be specific, the thudding sound of hard rain against the roof and walls had stopped. Disentangling myself with as much care as I could so as not to disturb Owain, I climbed to my feet, feeling stiffness in my back and legs. Crossing to the door, I opened it and peered out. The rain had almost stopped, only a light mist coming down, but it was pitch black outside. Thick clouds concealed the moon that might have given me light and visibility beyond the two feet I could make out.

I would have to be insane to try to get down in the darkness, I decided. The gullies would be flooded and without a decent light, I could stumble into one. Beyond a doubt, Owain couldn't make it down, and I was reluctant to leave him behind.

I shivered, feeling the coolness of the night in every bone in my body. I gazed over my shoulder towards him. His breathing still sounded ragged, easily heard in the small hut. Well, if I needed to wait for daylight, I'd have to do something about keeping warm myself, and there was only one blanket.

Closing the door, I returned to the mattress and crawled over Owain to the side next to the stone wall, slid under the blanket beside him, and pulled the warm wool up to my neck. With silent thanks to whoever had built this hut and left this little bed, I sighed and closed my eyes.

He shifted in his sleep, turning towards me. In a smooth, natural movement, he wedged his right arm under me as his head rolled onto my shoulder with his face buried only inches from mine.

His touch was warmth, a welcome sensation. I inched a little closer, putting my arms around him, one arm covering his left one so he couldn't shift it too much and cause it to start bleeding again. As we lay snuggled together, warmth spreading through me like a wave, I once again realized how physically attractive he was, the sensuousness of his body.

I gazed at the face close to mine and tried to tell myself he was not a man to trust or get involved with. But it was too late for that; I was already involved.

I dropped my head against the mattress, aware not only of the discomfort of the straw, but of the uneven breathing next to my ear and the heat of his body against mine. Yes, indeed, it was going to be a very long night.

I drifted off in twilight sleep for a time, then woke to check on my patient. He'd shifted away from me, his head now resting the other direction and he no longer held my hand. Concerned about the blow to his head, I worried that he might have a concussion, yet I didn't want to wake him when he slept without apparent discomfort from his wound.

I eased myself off the mattress, crawled to the door of the lean-to, and opened it partway. Rain still drizzled down, and a wash of moonlight slipped through a break in the clouds allowing a little illumination to the hut.

With a bolt of realization, I called myself an idiot and pulled out my cell phone from my back pocket. I could have called for help hours ago. Then I sighed as I realized it was almost out of battery power. I hadn't charged it the previous night. Worse, the bars indicating a signal were at the very bottom. No satellite connections up here. Using the flashlight mode to look around the hut, I noticed Owain's wallet had fallen on the dirt floor, likely while I'd struggled to get him onto the mattress.

I wondered if he had a phone and made my way back to him to check his pockets. He slept on his side giving me limited access to both his back ones and the left front. Nope, they felt flat, nothing inside either back one. I felt something round in the front, but not big enough to be a phone.

With a couple of blinks, the phone's light went out and the indicator to charge it came on. So much for that light source. I sat down next to the mattress and picked up the wallet.

Too curious for my own good, or so my mother had often told me, I opened his wallet, thumbed through it, and found two credit cards, a driver's license, a bit of money, and a newspaper clipping. Holding the paper up, I tried to make out the words but the light was too low and the printing too small. Setting it and the wallet aside, I began a quest for matches to light one of the candles.

This required more stealth than I usually had, but I didn't want to disturb the man who still slept soundly on the mattress. Although he had a fever and was pretty well out of it, digging through his pockets might pull him out of his slumber. I eased two fingers into the front pocket of his slacks and moved them around with light movements seeking the edge of a matchbook.

I didn't find one, but my fingers touched the rounded object, a tubular shape, that I pulled out. A grin spread across my face as I identified it—a butane lighter. As good as matches, or maybe better since those might have been wet.

Things were looking a little brighter, all puns aside. We had light, some warmth and I still had an orange soda, chips, and cookies in my bag. I nuzzled the butane flame to the wick of a candle, pulled the wooden door of the hut shut, and turned my attention to the clipping.

The story related to an Irish woman named Sheila Malone, who had drowned while visiting in Harlech the previous summer. The article insinuated the local constables had suspected foul play and were investigating, but the article didn't go into any details. The quoted constable said they had information indicating the woman's death might not have been an accident, but he was not prepared to give out any more details at that time.

There wasn't a lot more than that. I replaced the clipping in Owain's wallet, set it back beside the mattress, and sat back on my heels staring at Owain Thomas with my curiosity burning for answers.

Why was he carrying this particular clipping? Who was Sheila Malone? A girlfriend, maybe? And who shot him and why?

I had no doubt in my mind that his shoulder injury was from a rifle. Probably the *rabbit* I'd suspected someone had shot while I was in the stone dance. Owain Thomas was mixed up in something. That much was certain, and I had no idea what or which side he was on.

In the glow of a candle flame, his face looked young; the defining lines softened by the shadows. His long, black lashes stood out sharply against the paleness of his skin. Unfair that they were longer and thicker than mine. In that moment, I'd ceased to be unnerved by Owain and began feeling a different, more tender, emotion towards him, in spite of all the logical reasons I knew I shouldn't.

He shifted in his sleep, groaned at the movement, then his eyes opened, unfocused, and he tried to sit up. Without thinking, I pressed a hand to his shoulder, just above the injury.

"Owain, lie still," I ordered in a low voice. "Don't move around." Even through his still damp sweater, I could feel the heat around the wound.

Chapter Seven

... with the coming of dawn..."

aking with a start, I wasn't sure what had disturbed me. Not warm sunshine streaming through the windows since the windowless hut was almost as dark in daylight as at night with the door shut. And it wasn't an early morning chill—I was warm and cozy as I still snuggled close to Owain, who was producing enough heat to warm the whole hut.

I didn't need to touch him to know he was still feverish, but I did anyway. At least his breathing was even and steadier now as he slept. I pressed my fingers against his throat, feeling for his pulse, noting that it was strong. Beyond that, I knew nothing about nursing.

Moving at a snail's pace, I shifted my arm, lifting it up to get a look at my watch. I pressed the button to illuminate the face—five-forty-eight. I hadn't expected to be able to sleep at all, let alone to sleep so many hours undisturbed. I stretched, shifting my now stiff body from the cramped position I'd occupied for the past few hours.

Owain mumbled in his sleep, rolled a little closer towards me, but I managed to vault over the top of him to crawl off the mattress. As I forced my muscles to respond, I reflected that I would never again believe anyone who tried to tell me that straw mattresses were comfortable. Feeling like a fifty-year-old woman instead of a twenty-eight-year-old, I got to my feet and staggered to the door, pushing it open to face whatever nature had delivered this morning.

Pale light greeted me, not bright and warm, but welcome nonetheless, for it revealed a non-rainy although still overcast morning. At least, I could get down to the town and find help. I stepped outside, compelled by a certain necessity that demanded my attention and located a discrete thicket of bushes.

Even though a light fog layered the hillside and the bay, I could still see the welcome outline of the castle and a few projections of the stone buildings of Harlech. Beyond that, the sea continued to roll, and like the night before, whitecaps crowned the waves hitting the shore.

I shivered, chilled by the morning mist, and glanced down at my clothes. Muddy smudges coated my jeans while dirt and wrinkles sullied my cotton shirt. I could imagine how matted-looking my hair must be. Well, what did I expect under the circumstances?

One thing was certain; I needed to get down the hill right away. I suspected more rain was in the day's forecast. As I headed back to the hut, my thoughts turned to the scones and soda in my purse. Without warning, my stomach decided that it had missed dinner and now demanded feeding.

I had dropped my tote bag to one side as I'd staggered into the hut under my burden the previous night and that's where it still sat. Picking it up, I started over to reclaim my sweater when I became aware that Owain was awake. I suppose it was the feeling of his eyes on me for he hadn't made any noise. I turn my gaze his direction.

I hadn't been wrong—he was watching me. Now he coughed to clear his throat.

"What are you still doing here? You should be back at the hotel. Safe. I told you to go." His voice was hoarse but stronger than I'd expected.

I picked up my still damp sweater and slipped it on, frowning at the chill feeling of it, before I answered him. "It was too wet and too dark last night. I decided it was safer to stay the night here and wait for daylight. As you can see, I've come to no harm during the night. Besides, I didn't want to leave you alone."

He looked cross. "I'm all right. You didn't need to stay on my account. You could have been in danger—"

"Danger?" I pounced on the word like a cat on a mouse. "What kind of danger?"

Once again, he chose to ignore me. Instead, he concentrated on shifting most of his weight to his right elbow in order to force himself to a sitting position, but he winced with pain as soon as he lifted his left arm. As I watched him bite at his lower lip, I fought back an urge to help him. With exaggerated care, I turned my attention to removing the food from my bag.

Owain twisted himself around until he leaned against the wall and eased his sore arm across his lap. He breathed hard from just that little exertion. I exercised prudence in not remarking on it, but I felt justified in my position to remain with him.

I broke the scone in half and offered him a part. He shook his head, then asked, "Do you have anything to drink?"

With a nod, I pulled out the orange soda, popped the cap, and handed it to him. He took a couple of sips, grimaced, and forced down another swallow before giving it back to me.

"Too sweet. How do you stand all that sugar?"

"Years of practice," I replied and poured a hearty gulp into my mouth to wash down the biscuit. Grinning, I explained my plan. "Look, as soon as I finish this, I'm going down to the hotel and will return with help. It shouldn't be much more than a couple of hours—"

"No! Don't bring anyone. I can make it down on my own."

"Not without help, you can't," I stated realistically.

"Please, Miss Donaghue—," he started to say. His eyes held a pleading look.

"Kathleen," I interrupted. "Call me Kathleen. After spending the night together, Miss Donaghue seems little formal."

"Kathleen." He acknowledged, my name sounding somehow different when he said it—more musical and with a slight lilt. He glanced down at his poorly bandaged arm, then at me again. "Please, Kathleen. I don't want anybody to come up here. I appreciate what you've done, but I can't take any more chances."

"Then we'll go down together."

He started to object, but I continued before he could get anything out. "Owain, I'm not going to leave you to try to get down without help. You're feverish. Whether you want to admit it or not, you have a serious wound that's going to need attention soon. Do you truly believe you can make it by yourself?"

For a moment, the stubbornness in his eyes and the set of that obstinate jaw made me think he was going to argue it, then his shoulders slumped and his mouth tensed as he sighed. "No." His voice was soft, an overtone of defeat in it. "But I don't want anyone else involved."

"Okay," I agreed. "Let's get going before we get rained on again."

I still had dozens of unanswered questions, but right then I wanted to get back to the hotel, a steaming hot bath, and a comfortable bed—not to mention breakfast and hot tea.

Owain forced a smile. "Well, at least, you're talking to me now." Then he started to push himself to his feet. I got an arm around his waist before he was even halfway up so he would have my shoulder to use for additional leverage. A moment later, he was on his feet, but he was undeniably unsteady.

The almost two miles to the hotel shouldn't have taken more than forty-five minutes, less if I had gone alone. However, with Owain leaning heavily on me—more than he intended, I was sure—it ended up taking over an hour. My watch showed seven-thirty-two by the time we struggled down the path to the hotel. I had to credit Owain's stubborn streak that he was still on his feet. He was a chalky white that would rival the Cliffs of Dover and perspiration covered his face. Worse than that, I could see fresh blood oozing from beneath my silk scarf.

"It's only a little further," I stated, feeling exhausted. I'm not sure if the encouragement was for Owain or myself.

We were almost to the hotel door when John Linton hurried out, rushing to help us. He must've spotted us through the front window of the lounge. His face wore a blatant look of alarm.

"Good heavens, Miss Donaghue!" he exclaimed. "What on earth has happened?"

I swallowed, trying to catch my breath again before gasping out, "Mr. Thomas had an accident yesterday afternoon, and I found him. We spent the night in a hut to avoid the storm."

Linton had already assessed the situation and moved to shift Owain's weight to his slightly-larger-than-mine frame. I slipped out of his way, relocating myself at Owain's left side.

"We'll get him straight up to his room," Linton said, taking control.

Having given over my burden, I more or less kept pace, thankful the ordeal would end soon. As we came in the door, Linton called to his wife, and Sarah hurried in from the dining room. A glance that way showed me that only the newlyweds, the James couple, were down to breakfast. Good. Fewer people to explain to later.

Sarah Linton's eyes widened, but before she said anything, her husband ordered, "Get Mr. Thomas' key, Sarah—room sixteen."

Bobbing her head in hasty acknowledgment, she darted behind the desk and pulled the key from its slot. Although I held out my hand for it, Mrs. Linton hurried back out and preceded us up the stairs. Like her husband, she was ready to take control of the situation. To be honest, I was beginning to feel unnecessary, but a glance at Owain's troubled expression assured me that he, at least, didn't feel they had taken over.

Mrs. Linton opened the door, then dashed ahead to turn the bed covers back while Linton helped Owain onto the bed.

His wife's eyes rolled up and down before she spoke again. "You look a right mess, love. Why don't you get a hot bath and I'll bring you some breakfast up? John and I will take care of Mr. Thomas."

I had to admit, a hot bath sounded good. Owain's sharp intake of breath drew my eyes his direction. Linton had removed my scarf, along with stuck, dried blood and was now dropping it into the wastebasket. So much for my silk scarf.

Owain's eyes were closed, and I thought he'd fainted until I realized he was biting his lower lip against

66

the pain while Linton peered and pulled at the wound as he tried to see through the fresh blood and the mixture of caked blood and mud on his sweater.

"Sarah, get me some scissors -- and call Dr. Evans," he instructed.

"No!" Owain objected loudly. "No doctor!"

But Sarah was already out the door and would no doubt handle the task. In sympathy, and to feel I was doing something to help, I stationed myself at Owain's right side and caught his hand.

Keeping a calm voice, Linton talked to him as he began removing Owain's shoes. "Just relax, Mr. Thomas. Doctor will have to take a look, you know. Your arm looks slightly dodgy. There could be an infection."

"I don't want a doctor," Owain said through tight lips.

Linton continued to try to reason with him. Whatever he was involved in had him determined not to allow anyone else to get caught in it—even at the risk of his own life.

As he talked, I could tell Owain knew every word Linton was going to say, and he knew it was true, but his eyes darted with a trapped animal look. Something had him very scared. And that sent a shiver of fear up my spine. He was not a man to frighten easily.

Sarah returned with the scissors and handed them to her husband. She studied the whole scenario, then added, "Doctor will be here soon. Miss Donahue, why don't you leave this to John? You look exhausted."

I shook my head. "I'm staying until the doctor arrives." I turned pleading eyes on her. "But if you could bring up a pot of tea—"

"Of course." The reluctance in her eyes seemed to belie her reply. I suspected that being the curious sort, she wanted to stay and oversee the operation as her husband began cutting at Owain's sweater but she only hesitated a moment or two before she left again.

Linton clipped through the sweater from bottom to top alongside the left shoulder and used care as he cut around the wounds leaving a patch attached to the injury, front and back. He tried a tentative pull at the remaining patch of material, but stopped as Owain failed to suppress a yip. "I'll get water and washcloths. Be back in a few moments."

I nodded, but I couldn't drag my eyes away from Owain. I let them wander over his broad shoulders and the trim torso that narrowed to a slim waist. Under normal circumstances, I would appreciate a man in such good physical condition a great deal more than I did just now. I was more concerned with the nasty dark purple of the bruising around the wound that just showed at the edge of the stuck patch of the sweater.

Linton had partially covered him with the quilt on the bed. I reached to pull it up around his chest, anxious that he should keep warm. In an instant, he grabbed my wrist. He looked agitated, and he spoke in a harsh, low voice.

"Kathleen, I need your help. First, tell me, what were you doing in those hills?"

"I was hiking," I answered, curious where this was leading.

"Did you hear or see anything out of the ordinary?"

I lifted my right eyebrow. "You mean aside from an injured man on a hillside?"

"Kathleen!" he hissed, flashing me an irritated look.

"All right! I heard a noise that sounded like a rifle being fired. I thought it was a hunter."

"It was. Where were you when you heard it?"

"Farther up the hill. There's a stone dance up there, and I was looking around it. I have an interest in history—" I stopped as I realized what he'd said. "What do you mean it was a hunter?"

"Just that," he said, his voice softer as he grew more tired.

"Hunting for you?"

"Rabbits. Listen to me, Kathleen," he hurried on after the unlikely remark. "I don't want you to tell anybody where you were—only that you were hiking in the hills when you found me. Not anyone. I don't want you to go back up there."

"Why? What difference does it make where I was?" Besides, I wasn't about to let him dictate where I could and couldn't go.

With a surge of strength, he pushed up on his right elbow, a look of real worry on his face. "Please Kathleen. It could make a difference for you. Don't tell anyone—no matter who it is. And for God's sake, don't let on that you heard anything. Promise me!"

Concerned with keeping him quiet, I tried to get him to lie back down. His face was flushed, and I was beginning to think the fever was giving him delusions, but I spoke to reassure him. "All right, I promise. I won't say anything, but I don't understand. Now, lie back. You are in no danger from me, although I suspect there's someone out there who means you harm. Rabbits, ha! You were the target of that hunter, weren't you?"

As alarm flashed in his eyes, I assured him. "It's okay. I've already told you I won't say anything. But you owe me one, Mr. Thomas."

He nodded, relieved, then dropped back against the pillows, perspiration beading on his forehead. He took a deep breath and admitted, somewhat grudgingly. "Yes, I owe you one." He was quiet a moment, then added, "You understand, Kathleen that you can't tell anyone—not even the authorities?"

"Now, wait a minute! I can't lie to the police," I objected. Somehow, I hadn't expected my silence to extend that far.

"Especially the police," he said in an urgent tone. "Please, Kathleen. Please trust me on this."

I hesitated, then a look of worry crept back into his eyes. "Okay, I'm a dummy to the police as well. But at some point, I want an explanation, Owain"

"At some point, I'll tell you." He closed his eyes, yet he still fought the exhaustion he must have felt. After a quiet few moments, he sucked in a breath as if he was going to say more.

At that moment, Linton returned with a basin of warm water and half a dozen hand towels curtailing anything that Owain might've added. Linton soaked a towel and laid it on top of the wound. Owain clenched his jaw, squeezing my hand.

Linton shook his head, a look of sympathy on his face. "Doctor will be here soon. We'll just leave it until then."

As if on cue, the door opened, and Mrs. Linton popped her head in with an update. "I just saw Dr. Evan's car in the lot, so he'll be up in a few minutes. I'll go down and bring him in." She turned away, then faced back around after a moment. "Oh, I put the tea in your room, Miss Donaghue.

A not-so-subtle hint that I should go there now?

Linton stared at me, studying my tired-looking face. "Why don't you go clean up, Miss Donaghue? Mr. Thomas will be fine now, and you look about ready to collapse yourself. Doctor doesn't need two patients here, you know."

I hesitated even though I knew he was right. I could do nothing more here, yet I was reluctant to leave Owain. As if he knew my thoughts, he squeezed my hand once more, then released it, giving a sharp nod.

"All right, then," I told them as I stood. "Be sure the doctor looks at that bruise on the back of his head."

Owain shot a sharp glance my way, as Linton said, "Bruise? What bruise?"

I cast a brief smile of encouragement to the patient, then said, "I'll see you later on."

Out of the corner of my eye, I glimpsed the amused look on Linton's face, aware that something had changed the status quo. I stepped out the door, glancing back to see Linton circling around to look for the bruise.

Chapter Eight

"...refreshing and reflecting bring some clarity..."

$\mathcal{N}$othing else in the world could have felt as good as a long soak in a hot bath did as it warmed and relaxed me.

When I'd returned to my room, I'd poured a cup of tea, gathered up my robe, slippers, shampoo, and other personal items then trundled down to the bath at the end of the hall and locked myself inside.

One of the disadvantages of this bed-and-breakfast hotel was that guests had to share the bathrooms. This hotel had two baths and two toilets on each floor, which simplified matters considerably. I'd stayed in places where the bath and toilet share the same room and a luxurious soak such as this wasn't possible.

As I merged into the bubbly warm water, I sipped at my tea and pondered Owain's request—nay, demand—that I remain silent about the rifle shot. The why of it escaped me. After all, he was the victim. Why didn't he want the police to know? But I had given my word although I wouldn't have been so agreeable if I hadn't been so concerned about keeping him calm. I'd stumbled on a mystery and, to be honest, I didn't care much for the kind of intrigue that had a key player so worried.

My thoughts shifted to the man himself. I thought about the look of him, the extreme physical attraction that drew me in, and I recalled how he talked—the phrasing, the sexy deep voice that almost purred, and the way he dropped the "g" on certain words. An indefinable quality about Owain Thomas made him extremely attractive—apart from his obvious drop-dead-gorgeous looks and athletic body.

Something deeper in his soul made me want to trust him, to be foolish enough to promise him my silence. From the start, I didn't want to get involved with him, but somehow, I couldn't help myself. Every instinct I possessed warned me there could only be trouble, as indeed there already was, and the smart thing to do would be to leave him to go about his business and do the same myself.

Yet, Owain was compelling. Even if he warned me to stay out of it, he seemed to want help as if something more insistent within him was reaching out. And there was that unnerving way he'd watch me with an almost haunted look in his eyes. Why? Did I remind him that much of his cousin?

As the soothing bath waters worked their magic, I began to feel quite relaxed, my limbs feeling weightless and limp. If I stayed much longer, I figured I would drift off to sleep. Slipping under the water, I drenched my hair, surfaced, and reached for the shampoo.

Thoroughly cleaned, hair dried, and clothed in comfortable jeans and loose shirt, I headed downstairs. One cup of tea and a granola bar did not a dinner and breakfast make. My growling stomach made it quite clear that I needed the real thing.

The newest couple in the hotel, the Stoners, was eating when I came in and glanced at me before turning their eyes away. I figured a rumor had already spread the tale of Mr. Thomas and that American girl. Lord knows what embellishments it already had. Within seconds, Sarah spotted me, hurried over, and asked if I'd have the usual.

"English breakfast, please. Better make it double," I replied as I took my seat. I glanced out the window. A slow drizzle had started as the darkening clouds promised yet another storm.

Sarah confirmed this when she brought my breakfast, a double order of eggs, bacon, bacon, bangers, and juice with a whole rack of toast. "Nasty weather, love. Thank goodness you and Mr. Thomas were able to get in this morning."

"Yes, it was," I agreed then asked, "How is Mr. Thomas doing?" I chomped down on a piece of toast and washed it down with a gulp of tea.

Mrs. Linton hesitated then replied, keeping her voice low. "Doctor's still with him. What happened up there, Miss Donahue?"

I kept it brief, only telling her I'd been caught in the storm and had stumbled across Owain, who'd been injured. "Luckily, that little lean-to hut was nearby. We would have drowned trying to get to town last night."

"I'm sure it would have been difficult," she agreed, and shook her head. "It was quite lucky for Mr. Thomas that you found him. I wonder how he got that injury."

I shrugged, indicating I didn't know, then attacked my eggs with enthusiasm. Mrs. Linton seemed hesitant to leave, but Mr. Stoner motioned her over. She hurried to address him, allowing me to enjoy my breakfast in silence.

Over my third cup of tea, I began to worry a little more about Owain. Dr. Evans had been with him for what seemed like a long time. Was he all right or was it more serious than I thought? At the point where I'd begun to convince myself that it was something bad, I heard John Linton's voice and another man's on the stairs. I sprang to my feet, dashing into the hallway before they made it all the way down.

"... pretty serious. You'd better call the constable on it, John," the doctor was saying as I came around the corner. A smallish man, Dr. Evans looked to be a good-hearted, country doctor. Behind thick glasses, lined and tired-looking eyes peered at me with a look of appraisal. "This, I suppose, is Kathleen Donahue."

"Yes," Linton said, going past me to the telephone behind the desk. "Miss Donahue, this is Dr. Evans."

I acknowledged him with a nod, then asked. "How is Owain?" I wasn't pleased Linton was calling in the constable. Nor, I was sure, would Owain be. Still, we'd both expected it given the nature of his wound. My concern right now centered on him.

Dr. Evans studied me for a moment as if he might learn something from my face, then spoke sternly. "He's a stubborn man, young lady. He should be in hospital, but he refuses to go. Other than that, he's doing fine for a man with a bullet hole through his arm, who spent the night in a rainstorm."

"Bullet hole?" I hoped I sounded surprised. "I thought he injured it in a fall against a rock or something. You mean someone shot him?" Careful, I warned myself. Don't overdo it.

The doctor's eyes never left mine, and he didn't question my reaction although I didn't think he believed it.

"So it would appear," he stated in a flat tone. "But I don't guess you have any idea about it."

I shook my head.

"I thought not. Anyway, I stitched Mr. Thomas up and gave him antibiotics and painkillers; and that's about all I can do here. With rest, he should be okay. If you hadn't found him, he most likely wouldn't have survived the night. The man owes you his life."

Relief washed over me. "Then I'm glad I was there. Can I see him?"

A tiny smile graced his lips, simply a hint of one suggesting he was amused by something but trying to keep it to himself. "For a few minutes only. Rest is most important now." He stepped out of my way, and I hurried up the stairs.

Owain slept with his head turned to one side on the pillows. I stood by him for a moment before I pulled a chair over near the bed. I only intended to stay with him for a few minutes, long enough to assure myself that he was okay.

Thick layers of white gauze covered his upper left arm and came all the way over his shoulder. With the curtains closed, his skin appeared quite pale in the dim light that slipped in. But his breathing seemed fine. He looked almost boyish instead of a man in his early thirties, an illusion that made him seem young and vulnerable. I wanted to reach out and hold him close.

"Oh, stop it!" I murmured to myself in irritation. It would be too easy to be taken in by him, I realized. He was in big trouble.

A bullet wound would not be ignored in Britain any more than in America. Whoever shot him knew who he targeted and had left his victim for dead on that hillside. His mistake was not checking to see the bullet had actually hit the target's chest.

Or maybe it was meant as a warning. Either way, I definitely didn't need to get mixed up in this man's business.

Unbidden, my hand brushed against his forehead. He still burned with the fever, but the antibiotics would work on that. A lock of his hair hung down, plastered against his temple and I gently pushed it back, letting my fingers slip through his thick mane and thinking some quite unladylike thoughts as I did.

He grunted, shifted his head, and looked up at me, his eyes focusing after a moment. He tried to smile but seemed too tired for it—or too drugged.

"Hi," I said in a low voice. "I'll bet you're feeling sore, but from here on, it'll get better."

He half-nodded, all the effort he could manage.

I caught his right hand in mine, stroking the back of it and continued in the same voice. "Now, don't worry about anything. It's going to be okay. I know you're in some kind of trouble. I don't know what it is, but if you need to talk to someone, I'll listen. No—don't say anything right now. Try to sleep. The doctor says you need rest."

I released his hand. Unable to resist, I skimmed the tips of my fingers down his cheek. "Don't fight the medicine. I'll see you later."

He blinked once, mumbled something I couldn't make out, then drifted off again. With reluctance, I pulled my hand away, acutely aware of the tingling sensation in my body. I sucked in a shaky breath, rose, and crept from the room.

Chapter Nine

"... count the fruits of harvest..."

I know you're very tired, miss, but could we go through it just one more time?"

The speaker was a pleasant-voiced, dark-haired man with the same quiet manner so many of the Welsh seem to have, a handy quality for the local constabulary to possess. Nothing seemed to disturb Tom Bowen. I had the distinct feeling he could persist and wear at something until he had the whole truth of it.

I'd been through my story twice already. I'd kept it brief, careful not to embellish it any. I smiled at him now, my face showing an open and, I hoped, earnest look. "Certainly, Constable Bowen, but I don't think I can add any more."

He nodded. "Are you quite sure you didn't hear any noise—like a rifle firing, perhaps? It would sound very much like an auto backfiring, a loud crack of noise."

I shook my head. "No, I'm sorry. Maybe I was just so caught up in my own thoughts that I didn't notice it, but I don't recall hearing anything like that."

How I got the words out without them sticking in my throat surprised me. I'd always been an honest, law-abiding person and this little denial of facts made me feel guilty. If it hadn't been for my promise to Owain, I'd have told him of the whole incident without hesitation. As it was, I felt I was getting myself in deeper with each non-statement.

Bowen's face showed a touch of disappointment. "From what Dr. Evans says, Mr. Thomas was shot with a rifle. The sound would have been heard easily in those hills. Those thoughts of yours must have been pretty heavy if you didn't notice, Ms. Donahue."

"I'm a history teacher, sir. The hills around Harlech are filled with history, and it was simple for me to stand out there and imagine events taking place. It is possible I heard the sound and simply didn't associate it with the present. You know, I might have incorporated it into my imaginings of the past, made it the blast of cannon on the castle–that sort of thing." I thought it sounded like a possibility. I only hope the constable would agree.

As we sat for a few moments in silence, I added, "Although I could have mistaken it for thunder. I did hear a bit of that when I started back to town."

"Yes, I see," Bowen replied, although I felt he did see past my fabrication. He closed the little notebook he'd scribbled in as I talked and looked across at Dr. Evans, who sipped tea during our conversation. I'd wondered why the doctor had remained, but I'd settled on the idea that Bowen had wanted a witness there.

Linton had closed off the little lounge for our privacy, so only the three of us occupied it. Outside, rain poured down the windows making it seem like the room sat behind a waterfall.

Although we hadn't been talking for long, it felt like forever. I realized now how tired I was, how little sleep I had gotten the night before, and how much the strain of all this was adding to the fatigue. I'd given Bowen a little more information in that last round, slipping up a little with the remark about the thunder, but I hoped the constable was through with the questions.

It seemed he was as he cleared his throat and said, "Well, I suppose that is all for the moment. I appreciate your cooperation. I would like to catch this bloke—can't have someone shooting at our visitors, you know. Bad for business."

"I certainly hope you do," I agreed and pushed to my feet. "If you'll excuse me then, I am quite exhausted."

Bowen rose with me, nodding his head as a signal of dismissal. As I started from the room, Bowen turned back to the doctor. "Well, Edward, what is the possibility of talking to Mr. Thomas now?"

"Not at this time," the doctor's gruff voice replied. "He is not to be disturbed. The man lost quite a bit of blood, there was shock, and he needs to rest. Perhaps later in the day."

I closed the door quietly as I left, an amused smirk on my face. At least, Owain wouldn't have to face the constable for a while. I suspected he would have a harder time keeping the truth from the man than I did. And that brought back the question of why? Why did Owain want to hide the truth?

I was too tired to think anymore. Instead, I pointed myself up the stairs and programmed my mental computer to disregard anything except bed and sleep.

𝓛ight flickered from a bonfire reflecting shadows on the barren faces of the monoliths. They were huge stones, taller by far than I. With a growing sense of combined wonder and fear, I gazed at them in awe, as a shadow dancing on them grew larger and larger. Soon the shadows multiplied. Three horned figures advanced on me. Each one looked the same, twisted rams' horns on the side of a human head that sat on a quite human-looking body. I didn't need the pounding of my heart against my ribs to know that I feared the shadows and the reality they represented. Frozen in place, I couldn't turn from the horned men. I couldn't run from them. As much as I feared, I also seemed to welcome them. The apprehension built in me as one shadow grew bigger. My heart pulsed against my ribs as blood raced through my veins. With heightened anticipation, I spun to face the ram-like man thing!

Shock shot through me as I faced an ordinary bearded mountain goat!

Gasping for breath, I bolted up in my bed. It took a few moments before I oriented myself. The afternoon shadows danced through the rain-misted windows, but behind them, a half-visible sun peeked out through the clouds. In muted outline, Harlech Castle guarded the coastline as it had for hundreds of years.

Christ, what a dream! I rubbed at my eyes as if I could wipe away the images. So much for an overactive imagination and a visit to a curious dance of stones in the hills.

I reached for my watch—three-seventeen, almost teatime. I admitted that afternoon tea was one custom I considered quite civilized and looked forward to with relish, especially the delectable scones.

Despite the odd dream, I felt somewhat refreshed. I paused for a moment outside Owain's door and thought about checking on him before going on. No, I decided, if he was sleeping, I didn't want to disturb him. As Dr. Evans said, he needed his rest, or at least, it sounded like a good excuse.

I arrived a little early for tea, but Sarah was prepared anyway. She had just baked a batch of scones and brought out a plate with thick clotted cream and a pot of tea.

"Did you have a good sleep, love?" she asked. "I thought you'd be a little longer, but it's probably best, or you'd never get to sleep tonight."

"I'm sure you're right. Honestly, I feel quite well now—fully recovered. It's too bad Mr. Thomas can't say the same. How is he doing?"

She raised an eyebrow as if she had a question of her own, then answered, "He is well enough, I expect. Sleeping soundly the couple of times I checked on him. Just to see if he needed anything, you know."

She ceased talking but remained by my table, lingering like a lost chick. A curious woman, she felt inclined to chat but seemed reluctant to broach whatever was on her mind. Perhaps she might help me as well, I decided. "Why don't you join me for tea, Mrs. Linton? May I call you Sara?" I asked with a genuine smile. "After all, I've been here several days, and I feel as if you are a friend. And please call me Kathleen."

"I'll fetch another cup," she said with a quick grin and disappeared the minute or so it took to get one. As she pulled up a chair, she chattered. "I can't take long, Kathleen, but it's nice to visit for a few minutes. We had three guests come this afternoon—a whole family—and I'm expecting another couple this evening. Still, I'm glad to see business picking up. It's been so slow these last few weeks."

She paused to sip her tea, then her eyes met mine squarely, ready to register my reaction to whatever she had to say next. "A young man called earlier for you— Toby Morgan."

I felt my eyes widen in surprise. "Toby called? Did he say what he wanted?"

"He said he was worried about you, just wanted to know if you were all right."

"How did he know?"

A little smile crossed her mouth. "News travels fast in these rural areas. Anything makes news and Toby would be among the first to hear, working on the train, you know. Anyway, when he heard one of the people caught in the storm was an American girl, he figured it was you. He said to tell you he'd be by after dinner to see you. I didn't realize you knew Toby."

With a slight smirk, I said, "Well, I can meet someone on my own now and again. I ran into Toby on the train the first day I was here and started chatting with him. He seems to be a nice fellow."

"Yes, he is," Sarah replied, but she seemed somewhat hesitant. "Although he is a little different–"

"I know. He told me about his beliefs."

Reassured, she nodded once. "Ah, well. So long as you know. What about Mr. Thomas then?"

I broke off a piece of scone. There it was. "What about him?"

"You like him, don't you?"

"He seems nice enough, although I haven't been with him under the best circumstances." I hesitated, then plunged ahead. "I'd like to know a little more about him, Sarah. Didn't you say he was a photographer with a magazine?"

Sarah nodded, her dark blonde hair bobbing about her shoulders. "Oh, yes. He's a well-known photographer, but he's not with any specific magazine. He works on a commission basis, I believe, doing different jobs at various magazines."

"You mean he freelances?"

"Yes, I guess that is the expression. I suppose that allows him to do a variety of assignments. It would probably get boring doing only one type of photography, don't you think?"

"I would imagine," I agreed. "Did Mr. Thomas mention what magazine he was on assignment with?"

She sipped her tea before answering. "I think he said *Travel World*. He's done some work for them before. Let's see. He said he would be photographing interesting tourist sites in North Wales, and that's the sort of thing *Travel World* would want."

I made a mental note of the magazine's name then asked, "You wouldn't happen to have a magazine any of his photos are in, would you? I'd like to see some of his work."

Sarah brightened. "As a matter of fact, Kathy, I do. Wait here a moment."

She was on her feet and headed towards the lounge before I could say anything more. I felt somewhat irked at having my name reduced from Kathleen to Kathy so fast. I should have been used to it by now, but I hardly allowed friends to call me that, let alone acquaintances. Ah well, no point in fretting over it, I reasoned and poured another cup of tea.

A group of three came into the dining room, husband and wife, along with their teenage son, it appeared. These must be the new arrivals. They didn't wait for anyone to show them to a table and selected one in the middle of the room. The man and woman were what might be described as a handsome middle-aged couple, neither particularly outstanding nor noticeable.

Their son, on the other hand, wore his hair shorn almost to the skin on the right side with longer locks dangling on the other, the most extended strand colored bright pink. He was clad in a tee shirt and blue jeans, both garments properly adorned with the minimum required number of holes. From the scowl on his face, I suspected he and his parents had exchanged words over his fashion choice.

Just then, Sarah returned, deposited a small stack of magazines in front of me, and excused herself. "Our new guests," she mumbled to me. "Back on the job for me. You'll find a few photos in these." She left the books, winked at me, and hurried to her new customers.

I watched her as she hastened to serve the trio before turning my attention to the magazines. As I flipped through them, I noted several issues of *Travel World*, a couple of volumes of *National Geographic*, a copy of *Back Roads of Britain* and two copies of *Photographic International*.

Taking a sip of tea, I opened the first magazine, hunted for the photo credits and ran my finger across the columns until I spotted his name. He had photos in four successive pages in this issue, so I turned to them. The article featured a photographic journey of Moorish Spain. My first impression concluded that Owain Thomas possessed an excellent photographic eye indeed. Next, I became aware of the depth and angle of his photographs. He had an instinctive, yet innovative feel for his work and the unusual view of places and things.

The next issue of *Travel World* featured the rousing Bahamas from sun and surf to the cosmopolitan nightlife. Again, the depth and angles set the photos apart, adding a sense of excitement to the photographs. I open the *National Geographic* and found he was one of two photographers who had done work on an article about the Lapps across the frozen tundra of Norway and Finland.

Back Roads of Britain was like a love letter to Scotland, incredibly beautiful photographs combined with poetry about and by Scots. A particularly striking and poignant photo of an old Scotsman clad in his traditional clan kilt, leaning on his walking stick and gazing out over the heather decked fields made me feel as if I gazed into an era long past.

I turned to *Photographic International* and found not only several photo credits for Owain but also a brief biography that included a photo of him. I read this with deep interest. He was, the article said, "a native of Wales, making his home in Pembroke, and had begun his career as a photographer at sixteen. He enjoyed riding horses, reading, sailing, and fishing when he wasn't visiting exotic locales on assignment."

The biography photo showed him casually dressed in a cable knit sweater and jeans seated before a fireplace. The pleasant smile on his face was one I'd not had the pleasure of seeing. It transformed his whole face, lighting up his eyes with warmth.

Overcoming the desire to tear this page from Sarah's magazine, I turned to his photos. These included a series of shots of Dartmoor ponies, fishermen, a Cornish village, and two portraits done in shadows. The first was a small boy with a look of wide-eyed innocence as the glow of sunlight through stained glass provided the lighting. But the second portrait almost caused me to drop the magazine.

The woman was in three-quarter profile; her mouth parted as if to speak. Her long hair had been brushed to a smooth sheen, pushed to one side, and even in shadow, showed a golden auburn. Wide, rounded periwinkle blue eyes dominated her almost perfect, oval face. Freckles sprinkled her tipped up nose and rounded cheeks. An Irish-looking face. And, except for the color of the eyes and the fact that my nose was a little bit smaller, it could have been my face.

No doubt, *this* was the woman I reminded Owain of; he hadn't made that up. I took a deep breath, then scanned the article to see if there was a name, but the text covered only the technical details on exposure, lighting set up, and that kind of thing. My hands shook a little as I closed the magazine. I'd been told I had a typically Irish face, but this was the first time I'd encountered anyone who resembled me close enough to be my sister. My resemblance to Madlen paled in comparison.

One thing was clear—Owain was most definitely a photographer. He clearly had a fan in Sarah Linton. I wondered if she'd seen the resemblance between the girl in the photo and myself. After all, she'd seen the similarity with the drowned woman, Owain's cousin, and mentioned it. This one was even more so. Come to think of it, Sarah hadn't mentioned anything about his relationship to the victim. Could it be she didn't know?

Well, I had to admit that I also had a certain admiration for his work, detecting a sensitivity and awareness of his subject matter that I would never have suspected. All right, so I had underestimated him, and he was a talented and perceptive man, that didn't help to explain why someone had shot him, and why he didn't want to talk to the police about it.

The only clue I had to anything was the newspaper clipping about Sheila Malone. Why would he carry it around? Of course, he knew her and maybe he liked her. She died around Harlech, an accidental drowning, but there was some doubt. With a little investigation, I might find out more about that.

Sarah paused by my table interrupting my contemplations. "Did you find the photographs, love?"

"I did. He's very good."

She smiled. "Yes. I became familiar with his work a couple of years ago. Listen, Kathy, can you do me a favor? I have a tray of soup and tea for Mr. Thomas, but I'm a bit busy right now." She motioned with her head, and I looked around her to discover the James couple had now come down. Sarah looked apologetic as she continued. "Would you mind awfully taking the tray up to him? I mean, I hate to ask—"

"Of course," I interrupted. "It's no problem. I wanted to see how he's feeling anyway."

"Thanks, love," she gushed then scurried away again.

Chapter Ten

"...seeking the truth within the story..."

T he room was dark, only a slight haze of light making its way through the heavy curtains on the window, but it was enough to make out the shapes of the furniture, and the person-sized lump in the center of the bed. I set the tray down on the table next to the bed and pulled the curtains open to let in more light. Along with the sunshine, I noticed the dull gray blue of the sea. Owain had a splendid view of it from his room.

As I turned around, I spotted a stack of books on a chair in the corner. Curious, I picked up the first one– *The History of the Celtic Race*, then another, *Stone Dances and Monuments Around Britain*. One by one, I read the titles and found they were all on the same subjects, the Celts and ancient religious sites. I set the books back in order, wondering why he had them. Was he doing some research for his photo expedition?

While these would no doubt be interesting sites, what about the other places of interest like the many castles along the coast, Portmeirion, or the resort cities that have such charm? It seemed to me they should also be included in any photo trip to North Wales. I decided I would ask him about it later.

I pivoted toward him, noted from the steady rise and fall of his chest that he still slept unhindered. When

I pressed my hand against his forehead, it felt cooler, only a bit warm instead of hot with fever. A positive sign.

For a moment, I thought back to my childhood and playing at being a nurse. I had one of those little medical bags with a toy thermometer, hypodermic, and stethoscope along with small bottles of candy pills. I could cure all my patients with those. The reality was much different, and it would take more than a candy pill to heal a rifle wound, but I guess that deep down, a little of the nursing instinct or desire was still there for the right person.

I watched his face for a minute, studied the defining lines of his jaw, the fullness of his mouth when it was relaxed, and the long eyelashes I so envied, ink black against his pale skin. I wouldn't call it a pretty face, but Owain's handsome features followed classical lines and showed strength. I found myself wondering how he kissed—what his lips might feel like against mine.

I pulled my gaze away from his face, going to the tray of soup, scones, and tea, still hot in their containers. I hated to wake him, but he needed to get some nourishment. He hadn't eaten anything since yesterday morning, assuming he had lunch after I left him at Portmeirion.

I called his name and shook his right shoulder a little. While it didn't take much to wake him, it did take a few moments before he became fully aware and coherent. The first few phrases had been Welsh—I thought—then he focused in and realized where he was. "Hello," he said in a low voice. "Have I slept long? What time is it?"

Grinning at him, I replied, "It's teatime. And a bowl of creamy barley soup, homemade, of course. It's time you got some food into you."

"I'm sure you're right." He didn't sound enthused, but he pushed up on his right elbow, trying to sit up without moving his left arm too much. A look of pain crossed his face indicating he wasn't very successful.

I slid my arm under his shoulder as I spoke. "Here, let me help you."

Even at that, he still winced against the pain of movement, and I hurried to stuff all four pillows behind him so he could lean back against them for support.

The touch of Owain's bare back against my arm was warm, smooth, and electric, sending tingles of desire coursing through me. As my stomach muscles tightened, I held my breath. Seeking more, I slid my fingers along his right shoulder as a strong urge to touch him more overwhelmed me. Catching my breath, I forced my hand away. My heavens, why was I reacting like this?

He sank back into the pillows, closed his eyes a moment, and seemed to be drifting off. "Well, nurse," he said at last, "that was a stimulating experience—new adventures in the technique of pain."

Hurt by the remark, I glared at him. My feelings tumbled from ecstasy to annoyance. It showed as I narrowed my eyes and frowned in disapproval.

Seeing that, he spoke again before I could say anything. "No, don't get upset. I wasn't blaming you. I likely wouldn't be around at all if not for you. You saved my life. I owe you that debt."

That acknowledgment took a considerable bit of sting out of the earlier remark. With a sharp nod, I reached for the tray as I said, "I suppose your whole shoulder is quite sore."

His mouth shifted to a sheepish smile, as a gentler look altered his face. "Actually, it's the stitches pulling that are hurting the most. Yes, it's a bit sore, and it throbs some, but I'm all right, Kathleen. You needn't worry."

I didn't say much while he ate turning my attention to reviewing some messages on my phone and replying. While he took a while, Owain persisted, determined to do it without any help, and managed to force every bite down. As I poured him a second cup of tea, he finished off the last scone, then said, "That was good. I hadn't realized how hungry I was."

"When did you eat last?"

He thought for a moment. "Breakfast—yesterday. Since you refused to have cakes with me at the hotel."

"So, it's my fault you didn't eat lunch?"

His eyes sparkled, and he tilted his head in a simulated shrug as he said, "Well, it would have helped."

"Right. It would have made a huge difference." It seemed like the perfect opening, so I asked, "What were you actually doing in those hills yesterday, Owain?"

He sipped the tea then gazed at me, his intense light-green eyes meeting my questioning stare head-on. "I was exploring. I'm on a photo assignment and I was looking for interesting picture locales. There are many of them above the castle. Wales is very scenic."

"You didn't have your camera with you—or did you lose it?" I was looking for the obvious flaws in his story, knowing full well that wasn't why he'd been there.

Once again, a flash of a quick, amused smile. "I was *looking* for locales, not photographing them. I like to look around before I began working in earnest. That camera equipment gets heavy to cart around. Once I know what I'm going to shoot, then I go back with the cameras."

I nodded as I removed the tray. "So, then, what's your assignment, Owain? Anything specific?"

"You're fishing," he said without accusation, but he answered anyway. "I'm doing a photo expedition of this area of Wales, a guide to the interesting places to see, for a travel magazine. I have enough of a reputation that most magazines give me a lot of leeway on an assignment, so it's my decision what I photograph."

Nothing newsworthy in that. About as much as Sarah had told me. I brought my eyes back to his to see them as I asked, "Who shot you?"

His eyes didn't give away a thing. "I don't know. A hunter, I would imagine."

"On an open hillside? A hunter could have seen you with no hindrances." My tone of voice reflected sarcastic disbelief.

Unfazed, he said, "I was kneeling down, seeing if a lower vantage point would improve the shot I had in mind. A hunter wouldn't have seen me that well. He probably thought I was a rabbit. He might even have seen one, and I straightened up at the wrong time. It was an *accident*."

"Is that your story for the police? I don't believe you, and I don't know that Inspector Bowen will either. Something or someone scared you. You know who it was, don't you?"

For the first time, the amusement left Owain's eyes, and a steely look banished away any hint of warmth in them. "This is my affair, Kathleen. No one else's—*mine*. Stay out of it. You've already gotten more involved in it than I like. Don't complicate it more."

I felt my mouth tighten with anger. I bit my lower lip to delay the sharp words that boiled on my tongue.

In a swift motion, Owain pressed his hand on top of mine, and the warmth returned to his face as if he had turned on a switch. He spoke with a soft, gentle voice.

"Please, Kathleen. I appreciate your concern. Honestly, I do, but it would be dangerous to have you involved."

With a lift of my fingers, I indicated the bandage on his arm. "It's already dangerous."

"Yes," he said in quiet agreement as he squeezed my fingers for a moment in his free hand. Then his voice lightened as he changed the subject. "What do you do to earn your keep in America?"

The sober moment gone, he was ready to move to another subject. Did he honestly care what I did, or did he want to steer the conversation in another direction? "I teach history to seventh graders."

"A teacher? I would never have suspected. You're far too pretty to be a teacher."

"Oh, come on," I groaned at him. "There are a lot of pretty teachers and some very handsome ones, too. They don't all look like bookworms, you know."

"Yes, I know," he acknowledged. "But it's funny how we never think so when we're in school. I don't recall any of my teachers as being particularly attractive, and memory has most likely made them worse than they were."

He laughed, his eyes twinkling and for that moment, I did see the Owain Thomas, whose photograph had been in the magazine. This was a man with nothing sinister or threatening about him; a man I wanted very much to know.

"So, what brought you to Wales?" he asked next.

I told him about my project, the enthusiasm for it growing in my voice as I went on, and he encouraged it by expressing an honest interest in it. He asked questions and volunteered some background information now and again, as I mentioned some detail or another. "I have some friends who might be able to help you with some of it," he suggested. "I know several people at the

University of South Wales. I can introduce you if you like."

"That would be wonderful." I paused, then laughed. "I guess I have been going on about this though. I hope I'm not boring you."

He shook his head. "No, I'm glad to see outsiders showing an interest in my country. It helps keep us alive."

It seemed the ideal moment to ask him about something that had piqued my curiosity. "Owain, when you were half delirious yesterday, you said something to me in Welsh–"

"What was it?" he interrupted.

"For crying out loud, it was Welsh!" I stated in surprise. "I can't begin to tell you what it was."

"I mean, how did it sound? What were the words?"

I had the feeling it wasn't a casual question; that he was concerned about what he might have said. I shrugged. "I couldn't repeat it even if I could recall it clearly. Welsh is totally beyond me. The point is, you spoke in Welsh then, and you spoke in Welsh when I woke you a little while ago."

He looked puzzled. "Yes?"

"Why?"

"I'm Welsh. It's my native tongue."

Now I was perplexed. "You mean, you honestly use Welsh as your first language—not English?"

"Of course," he said with amusement in his eyes. "My family was Welsh speaking. Many people in the smaller towns and rural parts of Wales speak it as the primary language. We truly are a different country from England, you know."

I studied his face, uncertain as to whether he was serious or putting me on. He might have been teasing, but I didn't feel he wasn't laughing at me. Of course, I knew the Welsh often spoke their own language amongst themselves, but it had never occurred to me that English really was their second language. "You're not putting me on?"

He shook his head. "No. Not everybody speaks Welsh as a first language, but many of us do. I think you see it less in the South, in the big cities like Cardiff and Swansea where the English influences are stronger than in the north. At any rate, it's my first, and unless I consciously think about it, I speak in Welsh."

"I'll have to talk to you about this more," I said as I noticed him trying to shift his left arm a little. His eyes dropped to half open, his shoulders slumped a little, and he looked tired. "Is your arm bothering you?"

He nodded. "Some. I think Doctor left some pills..."

A quick search of the table soon yielded a small bottle of pain pills that had hidden next to the lamp. "One every six hours as needed," I read, noting that at least, the instructions were in English. "Guess it's been that or more."

Pouring a glass of water, I handed first the pill then the water to him. After he'd taken it, I started re-adjusting his pillows, encouraging him to lie down. Once he had settled again, I pressed my hand against his forehead to assure myself he hadn't overdone it.

He looked amused. "Well, nurse?"

I offered a tolerant smile. "You're fine, patient. Now, go to sleep."

"Those are pain pills, not sleeping pills," he objected.

"You still need to rest," I answered, smoothing the loose lock of hair back from his forehead. I liked the thick, smooth feel of it and my hand lingered longer than needed as my fingers fanned out to comb it into the rest.

His right hand shifted back over mine, feeling warm and gentle. With a light touch, he rubbed against it with his thumb. His touch teased with intimacy, sending prickles of pleasure up my arms. My blood pressure rose, heating my cheeks and other, more intimate, parts of my body.

His mouth curved into a closed-lip smile as he noted the flush on my face, and I turned my head away. Damn! I didn't need him to see what his touch did to me.

Although he didn't swallow sleeping pills, the effect was almost the same. He soon grew drowsier, his eyes fluttering shut for a few moments before he forced them open again and gazed at me with a curious look like he was trying to piece something together. When he spoke, his words came with hesitation, as if difficult for him to say. "Thank you, Kathleen—for everything. I do appreciate it."

Spurred by a bold desire, I leaned forward to plant a light kiss on his cheek. Speaking in a whisper, I said, "I'm your friend, Owain. Remember that."

His head nodded once, then he closed his eyes as he allowed the dulling effects of the medication to take hold. Almost as good as candy pills.

Outside the room, I leaned against the wall and pulled in a deep, steadying breath. This attraction to Owain was something I'd never encountered with any man before. He was not a man to be trusted, I repeated over and over to myself. At the same time, I knew I wanted to trust him, wanted to believe there was a rational, honest explanation for why he was involved in something he couldn't seem to tell the police—or me—about.

I stepped away from the wall. No matter what, his story was something I had to confirm for myself.

I went out, wanting to get out in the fresh air and to get away from any listening ears in the hotel. I hurried down to the path through the woods and pulled out my phone, lifting it in search of a signal. I walked forward waving it around like a beacon as I hunted for a spot that would give me at least three bars,

Under the still overcast sky, moisture from the rain glistened everywhere in drops on leaves and puddles. Most likely, a lull in the storm, I figured and hurried on while I breathed in that sweet, flower fresh fragrance that comes with rain. Like the trees and plants, I felt renewed by it. I almost skipped down the path dodging the muddy patches.

A few minutes later, I reached the road, located a signal, and looked up the number in London for *Travel World* magazine. I noted the time, a little after six. There might still be someone there. What the heck? With a shrug, I placed the call.

The number rang four times before the recording answered. A pleasant, but precise male voice informed me the office for *Travel World* magazine was closed, but I could call any time between 10 a.m. and 5:30 p.m. Monday through Friday. I hung up, added that call to my list of things to do the next day and put the phone away.

Above me, Harlech Castle watched the coast with ever-patient vigilance, a great stone sentinel built at the orders of a king, who was now little more than decaying bones in the earth and a few dozen impersonal lines in history books.

On that hill behind it, someone had tried to kill Owain yesterday. My lord, had it only been one day ago?

Chapter Eleven

"... whispers in a conversation..."

W ell, young lady, it appears you had quite an experience last night," Harry Stoner stated, tapping his pipe in preparation to lighting it. He was a portly man, about five-foot-six in height with a tummy that was almost as round. His wife Louise was the opposite, a couple of inches taller than her husband and thin as a reed.

"Nasty weather we've been having here," Stoner went on. "But it seems the weather is getting worse every year, don't you think, love?"

"Oh, most certainly," Louise agreed. "I remember when June was a splendid month to be on the coast. Now it seems to rain a great deal more."

"Caused by the climate change," Wendell Osterberg offered. He was the father of the punk teenager, the new arrivals that afternoon. "At least that's what most folks are saying. Businesses using dirty technology and shooting rockets into space. How could it not have affected something?"

Stoner struck a match against his shoe, jabbed it at the bowl of his pipe, and puffed until the tobacco sparked to life, then made a harumphing noise in his throat. "Yes, that might well be. Without a doubt, there has been a distinct change in the weather."

Echoes of the Past

With a fixed smile, I leaned back into the comfortable chair and half-listened to the conversation as Mr. Stoner and Mr. Osterberg exchanged opinions on the weather and the effects of modern technology on it. The lounge area was crowded this evening, the only missing guests being the James couple and the Osterberg teenage son—and, of course, Owain. The other guests Sarah Linton expected had not yet arrived although they called to say they would be late getting in.

Outside, the subject of the conversation had once again deteriorated to a steady drizzle, but at least it wasn't the hard downpour of the prior night. If it had been that slow, I would've tried to make it back down.

And ignored Owain's request not to bring help? I asked myself. Most likely, yes, I would have. In my opinion, he had not been in any condition to know how badly hurt he was. My conscience would not have allowed me to leave him there all night unattended.

"I should think that being caught in a storm on an open hillside with a hurt person would be frightening," Louise said, the thought coming from out of the blue. "Were you worried, Miss Donahue?"

I didn't want to talk about it, but I answered as briefly as I could. "Actually, it wasn't too bad. We were warm and dry. My only worry was for Mr. Thomas. It was rather dumb of me to go hiking in such doubtful weather, but I suppose it turned out a lucky thing I did."

"Most assuredly fortunate for Thomas," Harry Stoner agreed. "Imagine being shot by a hunter and simply being left there. What is the world coming to?"

"Bad luck seems to haunt the coast at this time of year," Louise commented. "Wasn't it about this time last year that a young woman drowned near here?"

Harry arched an eyebrow and thought for a moment, then said, "I believe it was, Lou. Caught in a tide

100

or some such, they said, simply off the shore. She was an Irish girl—Sheila Malloy; I believe her name was. There was a bit of a stir about it—some talk of foul play, and I don't think anything ever came of it."

Sheila Malloy, I thought, *or Malone? It must be the same one; there couldn't be two.* "What kind of foul play?" I asked, trying to sound casual rather than curious.

Louise answered, her eyes growing thoughtful. "Let's see... Harry and I were here when it happened, you know. We try to come every summer for a couple of weeks, and of course, we heard the stories, but I can't say how much of it is true."

Do get on with it! I wanted to scream, but I realized Louise Stoner was going to tell the story her own way, so I nodded my understanding.

"Well, as the story went, this girl, Sheila, had a fiancé somewhere in south Wales that she had a falling out with, so she came north to sort things out. You know, figuring a change of scenery might put things in a clear perspective.

"She found herself a place to stay at Aberystwyth, using that as a base, more or less, and began exploring the area. Eventually, she came up to Harlech and here's where the story gets interesting. According to the stories that went around at the time, she met someone in Harlech and enjoyed somewhat of a friendship with him."

"Friendship?" I questioned, wondering about the term she used.

"Yes, you know," Louise said coyly. "A relationship."

"Even though she had a fiancé?"

"Well, as I said this is the rumor. She'd had a disagreement with the fiancé, so I guess she felt the relationship was done. Anyway, she was visiting her new boyfriend, here in this area, when she turned up on the beach one morning, drowned. Talk went around that she was murdered, but I don't believe the constables were ever able to prove anything, were they, Harry?"

Her husband shook his head emphatically. "No, not a thing. They pulled a couple of people in for questioning, but nothing came of it."

"What about the local boy she was hanging around with?" I asked. "Was he a suspect?"

"That was a curious thing," Louise answered. "No one seems to know who it was. Sheila never mentioned his name to anyone, and she wasn't staying here, so none of the people in Harlech talked to her much. Of course, the police questioned her fiancé, but it was all hushed after the first flurry following the accident."

"What about her fiancé? Was he in the area?" I asked, leaning forward in my chair.

She shrugged. "I don't know about that. Like I said, not much more came out afterwards. I don't recall any mention of the fiancé's name or if the police had any evidence against him."

Harry Stoner looked thoughtful. "It seems to me he was a prominent person in the Swansea area. He arranged for her body to be taken back to Ireland, I believe. What was that peculiar group the girl was involved with?"

"It was an alternate religion group," Sarah Linton interrupted.

She'd been listening to this discussion from her post at the desk. I'd noticed she was working on a shopping list as I passed her coming into the lounge. "And it's all rumors. Nothing ever came of any of it. The poor girl drowned, that's all. Now, let the sleeping spirit lie, for goodness sake. Let's not be calling any of them up."

"But it's happened again," Louise interrupted, holding the newspaper from the previous day up with the story about the drowned woman on the front page. "A dead woman washed ashore. Can you believe it?"

Sarah's eyes narrowed, and she looked down her nose like a stern headmistress in a private school. "Let it be," she repeated and continued with her work.

Taking the cue from Sarah, the conversation shifted, this time to English politics and the upcoming wedding of one of the royals.

I rose and made my way out to the small bar. Sarah came in to serve me saying that her husband had gone out for the evening. I ordered a Gaelic coffee which, I discovered on my first visit here was the equivalent of an Irish coffee, and thought about the tale Louise Stoner had related.

When Sarah placed the drink before me, I asked, "What religious group was that girl associated with?"

She shook her head. "Oh, it was one of those nonconformist groups—non-Christian. I gather she'd been involved in it for several months at her home. There was nothing to that. I see no point in spreading rumors that accomplish nothing."

"Of course, you're right," I agreed, but it seemed to me there was more to this story than Sarah wanted to tell.

At that point, the front door swung open, and Toby Morgan hurried through it. He wore a rain slicker, but his hair was wet. I grinned and slipped away from the bar to greet him.

"The weather is very moist," he said in that no-nonsense way of his and pulled off his coat before he pulled me into a tight hug. "How are you, Kat'leen?"

"I'm fine," I answered, enjoying his embrace. It was nice to know he'd been worried about me.

He pulled back and gazed at me as if to assure himself that I was safe. "When I heard about you being stuck on the hill, I was afraid you might have gotten hurt."

"Just wet," I said with a laugh. "My fault for going out in that kind of weather. But I didn't expect it to turn into a roaring storm."

"What were you doing up there anyway?"

"Exploring the area," I replied. "You know me, looking for anything of interest."

Toby nodded and gazed past me to the bar where my coffee still sat on the counter. "I could use one of those, too," he said nodding at it.

As Sarah went about making another coffee for Toby, he caught my hand and led me off to a table in the deserted dining room.

"What's up?" I asked.

"I'll tell you in a minute," he said, then casually asked, "Did you find anything interesting in your hike yesterday?"

"A stone dance in the hills," I answered, not thinking about Owain's warning. "But it didn't look that old—more like it was constructed recently."

Grinning, he confirmed my suspicions about it. "You're right. A Wiccan group in the area built it a dozen years ago, but they seldom use it. I'm not sure what they were trying to do with it—heaven knows, there are enough monoliths and stone monuments around here already without someone erecting more. I'm surprised you found it though. It is rather off the beaten path."

As I attributed my finding it to the luck of the Irish, Sarah brought his Gaelic coffee over. She made polite conversation as Toby dug a few coins out of his pocket to pay for it.

When he was quite sure we were alone with Sarah well out of hearing range, Toby caught my hand. Whispering loud enough for only me to hear, he said, "Kat'leen, I've made arrangements for you to meet the head Druid of our sect. That is, if you're still interested."

"Of course, I'm interested," I said, keeping my voice low as well. I felt like a conspirator with him. There was no reason on earth why we should be whispering like this. "It's all part of my research, Toby. Anything that is going to add to the story of modern Wales interests me. When?"

"On Thursday. I'm off then so I can take you and introduce you to him. His home is in Tywyn so we'll take the train down. I've told him about you, and he's most anxious to talk to you. As he says, a lot of people have a misconception about the old religion, and what the revival groups are attempting to do, so he welcomes the opportunity to discuss it."

"Well, I'm anxious to talk to him, too. And I have an open mind although I have done a little reading on it. What time do we need to go?"

He thought for a moment. "If we leave here at one o'clock, that should give us plenty of time to get there. I'll call for you here, if that's all right with you, Kathleen?" It was a definite question.

I nodded. "That's fine. I appreciate your help with this."

He blushed slightly. "I'm glad to do it for you."

On an impulse, I reached across the table and squeezed his hand. Still a touch shy, he dropped his eyes to the table for a couple of moments, then asked, "How is Mr. Thomas? I heard he was injured."

"News does travel fast around here," I answered. "He's doing fine."

"It was nothing serious then?"

"Serious enough, but he'll recover from it."

"I take it he's in hospital?"

I shook my head. "No, he's too stubborn to go."

"How well d'ya know him?" he asked, his eyes narrowing a little.

I wondered if the look on his face was jealousy or worry.

"Not very well. I had seen him here at the hotel, but I didn't know him or even talk to him much." I left it at that. It was turning out to be harder to keep silent than I thought it would be.

Nonetheless, that seemed to satisfy Toby as he nodded his head once again and his eyes brightened. "Ah, I see. That's good, then."

He took another sip of his coffee, and we chatted slightly longer about the area. He told me about the Lligwy burial chamber on the Isle of Anglesey and said that if I had time, he would try to take me out there when he had a day off."

"The capstone on the cromlech there is most impressive. It's eighteen feet long, a massive stone," he added to tempt me.

I agreed it sounded amazing and assured him I would likely have time to go there with him. With a final swallow of his coffee, he set the cup down, glanced pointedly at his watch, and got to his feet. "It's time I was going."

I rose when he did. "I'm glad you came by, Toby. Thank you for your concern."

He paused, hesitated for a moment, and stepped towards me. He telegraphed his intentions, and I waited as he put his arms around me and pressed his face close to mine, his lips brushing first against my cheek, then finding my lips. Reflecting the uncertainty he felt, the kiss barely touched my lips. Then he pushed into it, pulling me tighter to him, and I felt my lips pressed against his teeth.

Only a short time ago, I'd wanted Toby to kiss me, to hold me like that, but now I found myself reluctant, not enjoying it at all. Relief washed through me when he withdrew and did not attempt another kiss. That had been awkward, but I plastered a slight smile on my mouth, trying to reassure him.

His eyes searched mine for a few moments, then he reached for his rain slicker. As he pulled it on, he avoided looking at me and said, "I'll be going now. See you on Thursday."

"Right," I agreed and walked to the door with him. "Take care going home."

"That I will. Well, good night." Then he ducked out the door, his shoulders hunched over against the rain.

I turned to find Sarah watching me. Even though she didn't say anything, her look definitely read as disapproving.

"He's helping me with my research," I heard myself saying as if I needed to explain.

"Of course," she said and went back into the lounge to watch television. I hesitated for a moment before deciding I wanted no more company tonight and started up the stairs to my room. Halfway up, I began to feel angry that I'd needed to justify myself at all.

Chapter Twelve

"...savoring the place and the time..."

I couldn't breathe; something smothered me. I gasped, desperately trying to pull air into my lungs. With a jerk, my eyes popped open, and I stared into the blackness surrounding me. My heart was pounding against my ribs trying to leap out. Perspiration coated my face and arms. What had happened?

I drew deep, long breaths in an effort to get my breathing under control. As I calmed, I adjusted to the fact I was lying on my bed in my hotel room, safe. I sat up and turned on the light, looking around to be certain I was alone. I glanced at the door, confirming that the safety lock, a simple slider with a chain, was still secure. Nothing looked disturbed, so it had to have been a dream.

Once my heart rate settled down, I dropped back to the pillow and tried to remember the details. It didn't come readily, and when it did, there were vague snatches of things. I recalled seeing faces, many faces, watching me and I felt threatened by them although I didn't know why. Even though I couldn't remember it distinctly, I was sure of two of the faces—those of Owain and Toby, but I couldn't remember what they were doing in the dream. I only knew I felt fear in connection with them.

Was it fear of them or for them? I didn't know.

I picked up my phone and checked the displayed time. Barely two—I'd only slept for a few hours. Tossing back the covers, I got up and opened the curtains at the window. A three-quarter moon peeked out from the cover of a cloud, casting light across the castle on the hill. At least, it looked like the storm was clearing.

Still unsettled, I dropped into the chair facing the window and gazed at the sky, watching the moving glow of moonlight across the castle. When the clouds danced around the moon's peephole, the shadows shifted on the castle, making a moving picture of medieval beauty that I watched while I let my mind drift.

I conjured flashes of the nightmare again but could make no sense of it. After an hour or so, I grew chilled and crawled back beneath the bedcovers for warmth. I'd never cared much for terror-filled dreams. Although I didn't think I could go back to sleep, I soon drifted off.

Waking much later, around nine, I recalled no other dreams from the night and nothing more of the one that had frightened me. By the time I showered and dressed, I decided the bad one was the result of the excitement of the past two days and the strange conversations I'd had with Toby about the revivalist religion he practiced. Clearly, I possessed an overactive imagination.

I hadn't expected to sleep so late, but like my grandmother often said, I must've needed it. At least, I felt fully rested as I slipped out the door and down the hallway to the stairs.

At Owain's door, I paused, thinking I would pop in to see how he was doing this morning. I tried the handle, but it wouldn't turn; locked, it seemed. Even though I thought it odd, I guessed he'd locked up for the night, so I knocked softly, not wanting to wake him if he was asleep. When I got no response, I assumed this was the case and continued downstairs.

Since I was late, the hotel appeared almost deserted except for John Linton. He was outside sweeping the patio in the bright morning sun and looked up when I called a greeting to him. With a cheerful smile, he waved, laid his broom aside, and set a brisk pace back into the hotel.

"It's a splendid morning, Miss Donahue. It turns a brooding coast into a playground on a day like this. I expect the beach will be crowded later. Might I get you some tea? I'm afraid Sarah's had to go shopping since we are a bit low on supplies, but I can get you some toast and an egg."

"Oh, simply toast would be fine," I replied and followed him into the dining room.

Within a few minutes, he brought a pot of tea, a rack of freshly toasted homemade bread, and an assortment of jams. I gushed appreciatively over it, then asked, "Has Mr. Thomas had breakfast yet?"

"No, I don't believe so," Linton replied. "When Sarah checked on him earlier, he was sleeping soundly, so she didn't disturb him."

"Oh, I thought maybe he'd been up," I said, thinking about the locked door.

"No, and not likely to be up and about much yet. Doctor says he's to stay in bed a couple of more days, let that shoulder heal some and gain some of his strength back. That's a nasty wound. Truth is, I rather wish he'd gone to the hospital. Sarah doesn't need an invalid to be taking care of."

I looked sympathetic. "You're right about that. Look, if you could fix a tray with more tea and toast, I'll run it up to him now. He's probably ready for breakfast."

"Yes, of course," Linton agreed. "That's very kind of you. I'll see to it right now."

While he went about getting a tray ready, I enjoyed two cups of the fine tea and an equal number of toast slices with blackberry jam. I pulled out my phone and called up my to-do list to organize my day. For one thing, I wanted to replace the candles we burned in the hut with a few more and a decent candleholder. I figured it was the least I could do.

Then there was the magazine I still wanted to call. Next, where would be the best place to start looking for information about Sheila Malone?

As I was pondering this, Linton returned with a tray. "I'll need the key," I told him.

He looked puzzled. "The key is in the room."

"But the door is locked. I tried it on the way down."

"How odd," Linton muttered. "Well, I'll simply get the spare key then."

I was beginning to feel a little uneasy about Owain. Why was his door locked? It must have been open when Sarah had checked on him, so when had he locked it?

Tray balanced in one hand, key in the other, I managed to get the door open. In only a couple of moments, I ascertained he wasn't there, a fact that didn't surprise me. I set the tray down and looked around the room. Nothing much had changed from the previous day, even his wallet still sat on the bedside table. A book now lay beside it, the one on The History of the Celtic Race. I picked it up, flipping through it, but Owain hadn't placed a marker in it leaving me no wiser.

With a sigh, I replaced it on the table and turned to the window and peered towards the beach. The figure crossing the dunes was barely visible, certainly not identifiable, but I was positive who it was. Call it instinct or whatever; I knew it was Owain.

"Damn," I muttered, then hurried downstairs, out the front door, and ran, at a breakneck pace down the hillside towards the beach. I cut across the Royal St. David's golf course; it was quicker than going down to the other public access path.

Signs warned bathers to watch for golfers on the green where the path cut across, but I paid very little attention to them this morning. Golfers, if there were any, could wait for me this time, and luckily, none were hitting balls across the open fairway. Within a few more minutes, I was climbing the first of the dunes, my feet sinking into the still moist sand making it harder to hurry.

About ten minutes later, I emerged on a broad flat beach that looked like glass. Gentle waves lapped the shore with a soothing whisper and the air carried a salty seaweed aroma. I followed the sand lightly marked with tiny ripples, leading to where he stood unmoving, staring at the sea. Not hurrying so much now, but thinking about what I would say to him, I approached silently.

Off to my right, at the edge of the shore, was a log, standing upright, washed in by the storm. It teemed with hundreds of mussels that had lodged themselves to it while it made its home in the sea and now protested being out of the water. For a moment, I wondered if it would be pulled back into the sea by the tides or if the stranded shell creatures would eventually meet their death only a few short yards from their life-giving waters. Not so different from drowning, I reflected. Both were a lack of oxygen even though the surrounding elements to the body contained all the air necessary if the animal in it is equipped to use it.

I paused for a moment, studying the log, marveling at the mass of creatures. Any other day, I would have gone closer to inspect it in more detail, even gone back to get my camera for a photo, but now I had other concerns on my mind. I glanced back down the beach where Owain stood, unmoving and somehow indifferent to the world around him.

I resumed my progress until I came within a couple of yards of him, and I halted, waiting for either acknowledgment or until I decided the best approach to him. He seemed to be completely unaware of me, his attention locked on something in the distance, well beyond the range of anyone's vision, I imagined. Perhaps he was looking for the island that lay across the Irish Sea. In any case, I certainly didn't see anything on the horizon. Yet Owain seemed so intent on it that I was reluctant to disturb him. Whatever his thoughts, they seem to have shut out any reality around him.

Decision made, I quietly slipped beside him, repeating his name a couple of times until at last, he turned to face me. It was a moment or two before his eyes focused on me and his face registered recognition. He looked paler than before.

I flashed a small smile and said, "How long have you been out here?"

He shrugged his right shoulder. "A while. I needed to walk and think. I came out for a bit, went in for coffee at a shop on the road, then came back. How did you know?"

"I saw you through the window from the hotel. I brought your breakfast and found you weren't in your room." I was careful not to sound too accusatory.

He shoved his hands into his jean pockets, moving his injured arm a little gingerly, and stared down at the

113

waves rolling up on the sand. "Well, I needed to move. I can't stand lying around."

Understanding the feeling, I nodded, "Yeah, I get that. But you don't want to overdo it."

"Yes, I know." He stared at my face, his eyes roving from feature to feature, eyes to nose, to lips, like he was cataloging them.

Intrigued, I asked, "Owain, who do I remind you of?"

His eyes dropped to the sand, perhaps with guilt since I'd called him out, but I thought it might be something more.

"Tell me," I repeated.

When his eyes came up, they met mine, and I glimpsed the look of pain in them. Not the physical discomfort from his injury, but emotional distress. With a slow shake of his head, he turned away from me, gazing back at the water, question unanswered.

I had a decent hunch about it and decided to take a chance. "It was your fiancée who died here last summer, wasn't it?"

His head whipped sharply toward me, surprise evident on his face.

"Do I look like her?" I continued. "Is that who I resemble? Do I look like Sheila?"

He stared hard at me. His lower lip trembled then he took a deep breath before speaking. "Somewhat—the red hair and the Irish-looking face, but that's about it. I told you, up close, you're not the same. From a distance, it's a resemblance, but she was much different—blue eyes, more freckles, a slightly crooked nose." He laughed, a brittle sound, bordering on a sob.

As the pained expression remained on his face, I guessed he'd held a lot inside over the past year; that he hadn't spoken to anyone about her.

114

I touched his arm gently, a slight contact to convey sympathy. "Tell me about her."

He hesitated, looked away from me again, then turned back. "What's to say about Sheila? She's dead. Just like Madlen. Both drowned here. Why?" The last came out in an anguished cry while his eyes filled with tears. He turned to look the other way, not wanting me to witness his loss of control.

I said and did nothing, simply waited for him to continue when he was ready.

Recovering, he looked down, focusing on the beach. "Sheila was a lively girl," he said in a low voice, more to himself than to me. "A girl who should have had a long, full life with a large family. She had four brothers and a sister in Ireland. I met her in Galway about three years ago. I thought she was the loveliest girl I'd ever seen. God help me, I can't help but feel her death was my fault." His voice broke and he whipped his head back toward the sea.

I ached to hold him, to put my arms around him and pull him free of the pain he was feeling. A lover and a cousin both lost to him on this beautiful shore. What could I do to ease that anguish?

I looked where he gazed and saw open water, gentle waves. What did he see out there on the foam and ripples? In some way, he was haunted by Sheila and Madlen, tied to this spot.

Wetting my lips with the tip of my tongue, I took another chance. "Is this where her body washed up?" It seemed such a callous question, but I could think of no other way to phrase it.

His head dropped towards his chest, slumping a little. I saw the muscles of his jaw tighten, answer enough even though he didn't speak. After a hesitant moment, I reached for him, caught his right arm, and pulled him towards me. As he responded, I urged him to the dunes, away from the beach. This could be doing him no good.

"Let's sit," I said and looked for a reasonably dry place on the sand. The sun had managed to bake the top layers. I lowered myself down on a likely hump, pulling at his hand until, with reluctance, he settled down next to me.

"Now, why do you blame yourself for Sheila's death?"

He hunched over, his vision focused on some point between his legs and spoke without emotion. "We'd had a disagreement. Sheila was a headstrong girl, and I'm a stubborn man. We both had our ideas about how things should be. If I hadn't fought with her, she wouldn't have come here at all."

"You can't blame yourself for that," I said, the sensible me trying to reason with him. "Even if you hadn't argued, she might have come anyway. You can't know any differently."

Slowly, he shifted his head to face me, his eyes seeming to bore into mine, but his voice sounded mild, almost gentle. "Why are you bothering with me anyway?"

A good question and one for which I didn't have an adequate reply. "Maybe it's simply because I feel a responsibility for you after what happened."

A sardonic smile flashed on his lips, then changed to more of a sneer. "Oh, of course. You saved my life, so you accept responsibility for it. I believe that's the accepted practice in some cultures."

"That's not what I meant!" I retorted, anger flaring at the way he twisted my words. But what had I actually implied? Why was I worrying about him? I cared about

116

him, and I was undeniably drawn to him, but I wasn't about to tell him that.

Unexpectedly, Owain touched my cheek, lightly running his fingertips along it, stroking from my ear to the edge of my chin. The movement jolted like an electric charge through my nervous system, and I felt I must be trembling like a leaf. Ever so slowly, his face moved towards mine.

Mesmerized, without resistance, I leaned into the approaching kiss. His lips touched mine delicately, feeling like a brush of wind against them, then he pressed closer, the masculine scent of him tickling my nose and sending signals of intense desire through my body. Now, I understood why I was so concerned about this man.

He pulled back, his lips breathing at my ear and with that sexy Welsh accent, he whispered, "I don't want you to only feel responsible for me, Kathleen. Isn't it truly the same attraction I feel for you?"

I didn't answer him exactly, but I pulled back a little, realigned our lips, and I returned the kiss, letting that speak for me. It was enough.

Yes, I felt a definite attraction for him—and concern. His lips found mine once more and he pressed insistently against me. All I could think was that I wanted to spend forever on this sand dune with him holding me, even with his one-armed embrace, and feeling the passion of his touch. I never wanted to let him go.

Abruptly, Owain pulled his mouth from mine, his face only inches away, and cast a searching gaze on me; a look that seemed to ask many questions. He straightened up, swallowed hard. "I can't let this happen. Not yet."

Bereft, feeling the sudden loss of intimacy, I replied, "Is it Sheila? Are you comparing me to her?"

"No!" The answer was quick and sharp, then more honestly. "Yes. Yes, that's part of it. But I'm not comparing you to her. Believe me." He stopped, took a deep breath before going on. "There's something I have to do, to lay the ghost to rest before I can get on with my life. Please trust me, Kathleen."

"What is it?"

He simply shook his head and looked away from me, his eyes going back to the lonely stretch of beach where a copper-haired girl had washed to shore a year earlier. There was a wall between us here—one that I couldn't get through. Whatever it was that haunted Owain, be it Sheila or something else, I was not a part of it, and he wouldn't let me be.

Placing my hand on his shoulder, I squeezed it a little. "Whatever it is, don't let it destroy you."

His hand went to my hair and his eyes softened, turning gentle. For a moment, his fingers played in my hair, twisting through it, then he kissed me again, lightly and without the earlier passion. "I won't. I have too many reasons to survive, not the least of which is you."

I hugged him as tightly as I dared and felt him tense when I pressed too hard against his sore arm. "I'm here if you need me," I murmured.

Then, when I loosened my hold on him, I noticed the exhaustion on his face and a touch of a bright blush on his cheeks that was not natural. I pressed my hand against his face, easily detecting a touch of fever.

"Come on," I said exerting my authority while I got to my feet and tugged at his arm. "Let's head back to the hotel. You've done enough wandering today."

"I'm all right," he stated emphatically, but he allowed me to slide my arm around his waist to offer support, and he dropped his good arm around my shoulder.

I turned my gaze to meet his, putting an official look on my face, much as I would address a stubborn seventh grader. "Now, see here, mister. As your nurse, I'm going to put you back to bed, and you'd better stay there until Dr. Evans releases you. He says you need to rest."

Owain shot a sharp look at me, like he was ready to argue, then he grinned, a bright full smile that I hadn't seen on his face before. His lips sought mine again in a long, firm kiss that left me breathless and trembling. When I kissed him back, I inhaled the distinct scent of his musky cologne and feared I would never know this moment again.

"Owain, please," I whispered. "Please let me help you. I'm so afraid for you."

His fingers came under my chin, tilting my head up to look in my face. Warmth and passion shone in his eyes, but he shook his head slowly. "You can't help me with this, love. I have to do it."

*O*nce I got Owain settled back in his room and had his promise he would rest, I felt free to pursue the tasks I'd outlined for the day. First on my list was a phone call to Travel World magazine.

I bounced down the stairs and out the door of the hotel with a heightened attitude towards life. Wales was beautiful, the world was beautiful, and Owain Thomas was the most special man in the whole world. I guess you could say I had tumbled head over heels, but not so topsy-turvy that I'd forgotten that someone had intentionally shot him.

Even as I hurried down the stairs to the town, I kept that foremost in my mind. More disturbing was that he seemed to know why someone tried to kill him but couldn't, or wouldn't, tell anyone about it. What would cause someone in obvious danger to continue to expose himself to the threat rather than turning it over to the police? The answer that kept presenting itself was that he was involved in something illegal; however, I could not accept that as a possibility. There had to be another explanation.

Finding a quiet spot, I pulled out my phone and made the call to the magazine, waiting with a flutter of anxiety in my stomach as the phone rang four times before someone answered. For my peace of mind, I had to know what Owain's assignment was.

Passed through to the editor, I made my inquiry as simple as possible under the pretense that I was an acquaintance trying to locate him. "I understand he's doing some work for your magazine," I concluded.

"Owain Thomas?" the editor repeated. "No, he's not contracted to us at the moment although he's done several pieces for us in the past. As a matter of fact, we tried to reach him a few days ago for a job in Austria, but his agent said he wasn't available. Have you spoken to his agent yet?"

"No. I... I haven't," I stammered caught off guard by this news. "I'm afraid Mr. Thomas didn't give me his agent's name. Perhaps you could? I truly need to contact him."

"Of course," the editor agreed. He paused for a few moments and gave me the name Caroline Marshall and a London phone number.

For another minute or so, I stared at the number I'd scribbled down. So, Owain wasn't on the job for Travel World; I acknowledged bitterly. Giving him the benefit of a doubt, maybe it was for another magazine. I chewed my lip a moment, decided, then dialed again.

His agent sounded like an older woman with a clipped, very proper English accent. In my business voice, I asked if it would be possible to reach Mr. Thomas about a photo assignment.

Caroline Marshall was polite but firm. Mr. Thomas was on holiday; however, if she could have my name, magazine, and a phone number, she would be pleased to get back to me in a few days when he was available.

I made a quick excuse and hung up with my emotions vacillating. First, I was angry because he lied about the photo assignment. Why hadn't he simply said he was vacationing? Then I was worried because he felt he needed a cover story to come to this area. Again, why?

For that matter, why did the Lintons not know of his connections to the murdered women, either of them? Apparently, Owain hadn't let anyone know, and the news hadn't reported it. That, in itself, seemed unusual. Wouldn't they have listed a fiancé in the obituary for Sheila? Maybe passing up a connection with a cousin was one thing, but the man she'd planned to marry before their breakup? Would that have made him a suspect at the time?

I glanced back towards the hotel, the irritation I felt making my jaw tighten. If he'd been near me, I would have punched him in his injured arm for lying to me. One thing was evident; he was not likely to answer the questions, and I felt those answers were important.

My plan now clear in my mind, I turned sharply towards the train platform, stomped down the street, and joined three other people waiting for the southbound train.

Echoes of the Past

Chapter Thirteen

"...following the trail south..."

I studied my small map of Wales, consulted the BritRail train routes and schedules for the same area, and contemplated the best way to get to Carmarthen. That would be my first stop. It was the largest city in Dyfed and was only a few miles from Pembroke, so I figured I would find out what I needed to know there.

The hard part would be transportation from Aberystwyth to Carmarthen, but there was sure to be a bus I could catch. The train would take me to Aberystwyth with only a few stops and one train change at Machynlleth. Getting there would take a while but at least, I had a spectacular scenic view all the way.

The railroad skirted along the shoreline through almost the entire route allowing magnificent views of Cardigan Bay. The fair weather that had prevailed at Harlech held all the way down the coast, although there was some fog at Barmouth. In the short time I'd been in Wales, I'd learned pleasant weather in one area didn't mean it would be the same a few miles down the coast. On one occasion, I played tag with a rainstorm, either arriving in one area shortly after it had left or leaving right before it hit and all in a matter of about fifty miles.

However, this day sparkled with clear skies and warmth. Calm and peaceful, Cardigan Bay beckoned bathers to play in her waters and bask on her shores.

Many British were doing exactly that. Beach umbrellas and cabanas blossomed along the shoreline and at every stop of the train, more people got off to join the throngs enjoying the sunny day.

The train stopped for a few minutes at Tywyn while a dozen more people scrambled off then it jerked forward again.

"Kat'leen! Where are ya' heading today?"

Surprised to hear my name, I jerked around to look behind me to see Toby standing a couple of feet from my seat. He was in uniform, so I gathered he was working.

A smile erupted on my lips. "Hello, Toby! I didn't realize you were on today."

He stepped up to my seat, delight at seeing me showing as his face lit up. "I only came on at Tywyn. So, where are ya' headin'?"

"I have some research to do so I thought I'd travel south for the day."

"For that paper you're writing." He nodded his understanding. "How far are ya' goin'?"

"I think Carmarthen," I replied with uncertainty, strangely reluctant to disclose my plans to him.

"Carmarthen, that's quite a ways south. The train doesn't go directly. You have to go east, and then backtrack. It'll take quite a while."

I tilted my head to one side in agreement. "I know. But I thought I could probably get a bus from Aberystwyth on." I slaughtered the name of the town, but Toby simply chuckled and knew where I meant and didn't correct me.

He pursed his lips thoughtfully. "Maybe. Or possibly I could arrange somethin'. I have a friend who might loan you a car or even drive you on down. She goes that way every once in awhile."

"Oh, don't go to any trouble for me," I protested.

124

He laughed. "It's not that much trouble. Just let me look into it. Besides, I want to make sure you're back by tomorrow afternoon."

"Tomorrow afternoon?" I repeated blankly.

"The meeting with the head druid," he said, his voice dropping and a worried frown wrinkling his forehead. "You still want to meet him, don't you?"

"Oh! Of course. I simply lost track of the days. Yes, I'll be back in time."

Toby's face cleared. "Good. Well, I'll let you know about the car then."

With that, he moved on forward in the compartment, checked the tickets of two passengers in front of me, and went through the connecting door to the next train car.

What a sweetheart of a guy! So thoughtful. A silly grin covered my face as I leaned back again. I truly did like him, but not in the same way I liked Owain. With him, I felt sparks and excitement I couldn't define. Apart from the obvious attraction, I feared it might stem from the sense of danger and adventure I felt when I was around him.

Within a short time, the train pulled into Aberystwyth Station, the farthest I could go on this line towards the south. Unfortunately, rental cars were not as plentiful in every little hamlet in Wales, and I'd already checked and found none available today. If Toby's friend wasn't able to help, my only resort was to locate the bus.

Almost as soon as I alighted, Toby hopped down by my side and urged me to follow him towards the telephones. "I only have a few minutes here, Kathleen, but it should be enough for me to reach my friend. If she's at home, it won't take more than a couple of minutes for her to get here. She lives close. Wait here."

I did as he requested and wondered why he didn't use a cell phone.

A good-sized town on the coast, Aberystwyth clustered on the banks of a wide river mouth that flowed into the bay. I'd been here long enough to know that the "aber" prefix on the town names indicated a river mouth, like the "inver" on Scottish names indicated the "mouth of " a body of water. So, following that logic, I could presume this was the mouth of the Ystwyth River.

I was still lost in these thoughts when Toby returned, laying his hand on my arm to get my attention. Startled, I jumped at the touch.

He laughed at my skittishness, and as I joined in, he said, "Sorry! It's all arranged. A historian for our group lives here. She says she'll drive ya'. It so happens she has to go down to meet with a couple of people from a Druid group in Swansea. She says she can drop you off on the way. Her name is Abigail Halsted. You'll recognize her right away—about five-foot-five, very small build, and light blonde hair. There aren't many of those in this area." He grinned, then pulled me into a brief hug. "I have to go now, but I'll see ya' tomorrow."

"Right. Tomorrow. Thanks, Toby." I barely managed to get my quickly spoken thanks out before he dashed back to the train.

I glanced at my watch, almost ten-thirty. I figured it would take at least two hours to get to Carmarthen then another couple of hours at the library there. If the bus schedule proved convenient, the return would take another two hours or more. With luck, I might be back at Harlech by eight this evening. With a sigh, I wandered over to look at the train schedules. The last train from the station to Harlech was at 21:10—nine-ten at night—

so I wouldn't have a problem there, but it was going to be a long day.

I recognized Abigail Halsted as easily as promised. She arrived within minutes, her eyes darting around the area, and scurried towards me giving me the impression of a rodent heading for cheese. As Toby had said, she was petite and her ash blonde hair cascaded down her back almost to her waist. In spite of that crowning glory, her deeply set cobalt blue eyes and sharp, pointed nose created a somewhat mousey appearance.

She stopped in front of me, looked me straight in the eyes as if she could read something in them, then said, "You're Kathleen Donahue."

It was a statement, not a question, but I nodded anyway.

"Yes, Toby was right about you. Well, come along. We have to get going." She spoke briskly as if she needed to hurry.

As I followed her to the small Metro, I digested the fact that her tight, clipped voice was English rather than Welsh. I wondered what Toby had told her about me, but I soon discovered I wasn't likely to find out. Not inclined towards conversation, Abigail deflected my first few tentative questions with terse, one or two-word answers. I abandoned the idea of drawing her into any chat, even though I wanted to learn where she'd come from and why she now lived in Wales. She did not impress me as the sort who was seeking the rural lifestyle this country offered.

The little car zipped across the hills on a route that went somewhat straight to the south. A little less than an hour and a half later, we arrived on the outskirts of Carmarthen.

In many ways, the initial view of the city shocked me. A large industrial center with factories and smokestacks rising into the skyline, it shattered the romantic image I'd long held of the town from the literature I'd devoured as a child. This was not the town where Merlin had wandered or where knights might've spent an evening in a warm, cozy inn. If any trace of that town remained, it was well-hidden in the maze of concrete and asphalt that now dominated the area.

Abigail Halsted navigated quickly and expertly through the city and stopped in front of an imposing, old-looking building. "The library," she said curtly.

With a nod, I climbed out of the car and paused to thank her.

"You should be able to get a bus back to Aberystwyth from here. Sorry I can't guide you around..."

"No, it's all right," I said, talking faster so I could get my thanks in before she pulled away. "You've been a big help. Thank you. I can manage my way back."

She didn't acknowledge and whipped the car back out while I stood on the sidewalk and watched the it disappear into traffic. I gathered she didn't particularly like me although I'd given her no cause to form an opinion either way. With a shrug, I turned to enter the library.

Fortunately, most libraries are set up virtually the same and have copies of newspapers and magazines on file. However, I did have to seek help in finding what I needed. Like many areas of Wales, the labels on walls and drawers were in Welsh and sometimes had English translations and sometimes didn't. I spoke with a librarian, hoping she spoke English. She perked up, eager to help the American tourist find the section where they stored newspapers from prior months and years. As she left, I settled myself down to read the English versions of a short stack of papers.

The death of Sheila Malone had not garnered much publicity in this area. In fact, after combing carefully through day after day of newspapers from the date of the initial report, I found only three brief articles that referred to the drowning. After that, nothing at all.

One of the reports matched the one I'd found in Owain's wallet; the other two pretty much repeated the same thing except the last one indicated that the suspect the police held had been released due to a lack of evidence. While the police had questioned her fiancé, he'd been cleared, and they had ruled the death an accidental drowning. Obviously, Owain had some pull to prevent his name from being revealed in the articles.

Disappointed, I replaced the last of the newspapers in the drawers and stretched. I'd been at this a little over an hour and hadn't learned anything more than I already knew except that Owain had been questioned. On an impulse, I asked my helpful librarian if they had any information on Owain Thomas.

Here, the articles were more extensive. It seemed Owain was somewhat of a local, although reluctant, celebrity. Again, the information proved repetitious covering his professional career and only revealing that he lived near Pembroke in a small farmhouse. There was no mention of his relationship with Sheila Malone.

I closed the last magazine. It was all too neat. How did Owain keep his name out of the papers in any connection with the dead girl?

I abandoned the library and hunted down a car rental. Once the clerk assured me I could turn the car in at a specified lot in Aberystwyth, then I headed west. To find out anything more about Owain, I needed to visit his hometown of Pembroke.

Chapter Fourteen

"...the mysteries in the southland..."

Pembroke was what I'd expected Carmarthen to be—a medieval town, small and old looking, much like Harlech. My first glimpse as I came into the outskirts cheered me with a view of magnificent stone towers thrusting into the sky.

In many places, the town walls still enclosed the old town along the long peninsula that formed the boundary. Wedged in on one side by a marsh, the city stretched to the Milford Haven, a waterway that curved around the head of the peninsula and connected with the Pembroke River on the other. The town of the same name languished further up the estuary on the other bank. Pembroke Castle, the head of the dragon, perched at the tip of the land bar on the Pembroke River where it met the Mill Pond.

I bypassed the first parking areas I came to, which were below the town walls, and followed the road into the city until I located a small car park near what appeared to be the market area. As I walked past the overwhelming towers of this magnificent castle, I gaped, astonished by the size of it. I knew it had figured prominently in the history of this area and that the walls, like so many castles, had been slighted by Cromwell in the sixteen-hundreds, but even so, it was still impressive.

For a few minutes, I continued to stare at it and wished for the time now to wander within the inner ward and along the walls. But I had other business here.

I continued down the hill from the castle and paused at the corner where the road turned across the Mill Bridge. I spotted a pub a short way down. Glancing at my watch—almost two-thirty, I started briskly towards it. If luck aided me, it would be open until three. Aside from getting a snack, it seemed like a good place to make inquiries.

Fittingly, the pub was named for the castle, and from its door, I enjoyed yet another spectacular view of Pembroke Castle with the huge keep rising well above the outer walls. Within the pub, the atmosphere reflected warmth and a welcome. My luck held as they still served pub lunches. I settled for a warmed Cornish pasty and a half pint of cider and maneuvered to a seat near the window.

As I glanced around the room, I noticed a man staring openly at me. His penetrating dark eyes stared out of a rosy, rounded face while a thick black beard hid the lower part of his face. As good a place to start as any, I thought and returned his look with a friendly smile. He left his spot at the bar and approached me, his gaze more intent than I expected from a casual pick-up.

Thumping his mug of ale across the small table, he said, "Do you mind?"

"Please do," I replied. "My name is Kathleen."

As he sat, he studied me a moment or two more, then grinned. "Pleased to meet you, Kathleen. I'm Llewellyn. Excuse my boldness, but you do resemble a girl who used to live around here."

Deep-voiced, with a quality that reminded me of Owain's sound, I found his accent harder to understand and it took me a moment or two to parse it in my brain.

"I've been told that before," I replied. "She was the girlfriend of a local man, wasn't she?"

Llewellyn nodded. "She was. You are American, are you not?"

"Yes. On holiday and doing some research for a paper. As I said, others have said I looked like the girl. What happened to her?"

"What kind of research?" He ignored my question, his eyes narrowing in suspicion.

"I'm a teacher and writing a thesis for my master's degree. So I'm basing it about modern Wales."

He smacked his lips together as he thought about that, puzzling if it seemed reasonable, I presumed. "Yeah, I 'spose there's somethin' to say about it. Not good for us though, these modern times."

"So, about the girl? I'm curious what happened."

He leaned in a little and huffed. "She's dead now is what. And he goes on as if nothin' had happened."

"Her fiancé? Do you know him?" I strove to sound interested without giving away any real concern.

"Oh, that I do. Ain't no one 'round here who don't know Owain Thomas." He almost spat the words out. "Brought that poor girl here then let her go off and get kilt."

"I heard it was an accident," I said carefully. I wanted to draw the information out without seeming too curious. Llewellyn didn't seem to notice anything odd in my interest.

"That's what everyone would have you believe, but there were rumors he had something to do wit' it. Constables simply can't prove anythin' on him."

"Ah, them's only stories, Llew," a woman's voice interrupted, and I shifted my gaze to the speaker. A plump woman of medium height approached the table.

She carried a tray in one hand and placed empty glasses off the table next to ours on it as she cleaned up. "Don't you listen to his prattle, girl. He likes to gossip."

"There's more to it than that, caru, and you know it," the man growled in answer. "Those two were always at it, weren't they? Always arguin' and bickerin'."

"And what of it? Aren't plenty of lovers? Those two had enough differences that it's a wonder they ever got along."

"Exactly the point!" Llewellyn said as his beefy hand hit the table hard enough to cause my drink to teeter. As I grabbed for it, he continued. "Some say he got rid of her. She was a sweet girl, wouldn't harm no one, and she was as pretty as this girl here."

"Sheila started more arguments than Owain," the barmaid replied sharply. "Besides, he was nowhere near the place where she drowned."

"You sound like a parrot now, girl. Was he able to prove it? No, not at all—off on a boat, all by himself, he says, and none to bear witness. A likely story, says I." He paused to swallow a large swig of his ale.

"But Sheila, she was a good swimmer and a cautious one besides, so how is it she comes to be drowned and washed up on the shore? And who else would have reason to want to see her dead?"

"Byddwch yn ddistaw!" The girl replied sharply—an expression I knew to be the equivalent of "shut up." Then she spoke to me. "Don't listen to him. He's speaking through his drink. Sure, there were stories, but aren't there always? The truth is Owain would never hurt anyone and certainly not a woman he loved as much as he did Sheila. It was an accident, nothing more."

"Oh yes, an accident," Llewellyn muttered and stared darkly at his drink. "But a very suspicious one, nonetheless. Aww, caru, I'll say no more. She is right—I talk too much when I drink. This must be boring for you, a visitor here and all, and not knownin' what any of this is about. Where do you come from?"

I told him California, then answered the many questions he had about the United States. The barmaid moved on about her task, but she glanced back at us occasionally. I wanted to ask Llewellyn more about the stories, but I didn't think I'd get him back to the subject without revealing more of my situation.

By this time, the pub was closing down for the afternoon and as I rose to leave, Llewellyn got to his feet to accompany me outside. For a minute or so, I feared I wouldn't be able to get away from him, but he stopped outside the pub and offered me his hand.

"Well, I have to be about me business, Kat'leen from California. Been good chattin' with ya'."

"I've enjoyed it as well," I answered with a smile and sincere thanks, shook his hand then watched as he walked eastward up the hill away from town. It had been interesting, but a slew of questions whirled in my mind about Owain. More now than ever.

Taking a casual pace, I started back to the central section of town. Clearly, Owain had been a suspect in Sheila's death; however, the police had been unable to prove he was involved. But what made them think it was anything more than an accident? I came south looking for answers, and all I'd found so far were more questions.

I stopped at a couple of shops in town, bought postcards, and asked a few questions about the area, but nothing directly about Owain. My resemblance to Sheila Malone didn't seem to influence anyone at these locations, and no one commented on it. At the newsstand, I bought a copy of the London Daily Mail and casually mentioned Owain in an obscure fashion.

"This is a lovely area," I said. "It seems very peaceful, an ideal place for an artist to work. Do any live around here?"

The news seller raised an eyebrow, shrugged, and replied, "Only one I know of is a photographer who lives near here. I guess you could call him an artist."

"A photographer? I'm a bit of an amateur one. Is he famous? Might I have seen his work somewhere?"

He tossed his head in dismissal. "Maybe. He's done work for magazines. Have you heard of Owain Thomas?"

"Owain...Thomas," I repeated, taking my time as if thinking about it. "It does sound familiar. And he lives near here?"

"Yeah. Has a little place a short way down on the Carew Road— calls it *Bwthyn Gwyntog*."

"Sounds lovely. What does the name mean?"

He chuckled, "Windy cottage, miss. It suits the location."

With an amused grin, I paid for the paper and turned back up the street.

Strolling towards my car, I paused now and again to glimpse in a window. As I debated whether to enter a teashop for a meat pie to take back with me, a couple of girls came out of a shop behind me. I heard an audible gasp then a sharp cry of "Sheila!"

I turned to face a girl about my age with black hair and a fair complexion. She looked startled, recovering quickly. "I... I'm sorry," she stammered. "You look like someone I knew."

"Sheila Malone," I said.

She nodded. "Then you know her also? You do look a lot like her."

"I've been told that a couple of times. No, I didn't know her, but I do know Owain Thomas." I don't know

136

why I volunteered that information; however, it seemed to have an effect on the girl.

She turned to her friend, another dark-haired girl who looked a little younger and mumbled something in Welsh. The other girl replied with a worried look on her face, then with a hard look at me, left us facing each other.

"Have you seen Owain recently?" the girl asked.

I bobbed my head in a positive response.

"Can we talk then?"

"Of course." I'd hoped she'd ask.

She pointed me into the teashop, waved at the owner, and led me to an isolated table at the back of the room. "My name is Awena. I'm a friend of both Sheila and Owain. He left here a few days ago, and I've been worried about him. He's been very moody lately and not talking much. Was he all right when you saw him?"

I hesitated. How much should I tell her? "He was okay. Very concerned about something, but he didn't tell me what. Look, Awena, I don't know that much about what happened with Sheila and Owain, but I do know he's in some kind of trouble. I'd like to help him."

She laughed at that, a brief, bitter snort of laughter. "Well, that's not easy to do. The man doesn't feel he needs help. Sometimes, I think he would prefer to die also. He holes up in that dreary cottage of his and doesn't talk to anyone. He hasn't truly done much work for months now. Damn his Welsh soul... the heart of a poet and the stubbornness of a goat. Sheila would never have wished to see him like this."

"I thought they weren't getting along too well when the accident happened."

"True, it was a bad time. Sheila decided to go up north to get away from him to think. He didn't want her to go, but she had a stubborn streak in her to match his. He couldn't have stopped her if he wanted to. Besides, he had a photo assignment in the south. Sheila was a priestess in a druidic worship group, and she wanted to meet with some other groups in the area. At least, she used that as an excuse."

"Then Owain was working when she died?" I asked.

"Well, there was some doubt about that. The authorities thought he might have taken a boat north. They believed he met with Sheila the night she died, but they can't prove it. And he denies it."

"What do you think?"

Awena looked at me strangely. "I honestly don't know, but I don't believe Owain would have intentionally killed her. He loved her very much, and he's never truly gotten over her death."

"Then you don't think it's a possibility?" I asked, my mouth feeling suddenly dry.

"Ah, anything is a possibility," she replied. "Including suicide. But I don't believe either was the case. Now tell me where Owain is."

"I can't be sure where he is now," I said, hedging on the truth.

If Owain hadn't told this girl where he was going, he must've had his reasons. Even though I didn't like what I was learning, I still didn't feel I had the right to tell her anything he didn't want known.

"He said he might be going up to Scotland for a few days, but I hope to see him again when he gets back."

"Probably fishing," Awena said. "If you do see him, tell him to get in touch with me, please. Will you do that for me?"

I nodded. "Yes, of course."

She rose, pausing to add, "Tell him I'm worried." She left quickly without a backwards glance.

With an odd stab of jealousy, I wondered who Awena was. An old girlfriend? Or a new one? Or possibly a relative? Somberly, I gazed at my half-empty cup of tea and tried to sort out everything in my mind. Various phrases and arguments kept running through my mind, but nothing I could settle on. I left the remainder of the cup and headed back to my car.

As I started out of town, I made an impulsive turn onto Carew Road. Many people in Britain named their homes; some marked it in bold letters on an elegant block or carving Celtic looking runes into an oddly-shaped stone while other names are held only in the hearts of their owners. Owain's home fell in the middle.

Not a large estate, Bwthyn Gwyntog, an old stone farmhouse, sat about a mile back from the main road. Owain had marked it with a wood nymph carved into a tree stump holding up the scroll on which the starkly carved Celtic lettering proclaimed the name he had christened the "cottage."

The front gate, also wooden, stood open inviting me to turn the car onto the road to the house. While not a huge residence, it looked to be a good-sized one, two-storied, and with a pair of fireplaces, if both chimneys rising above the roof were a correct indication. A pair of gardens ran from the side of the house down a shallow hillside. At the moment, they looked untended, overrun with wildflowers and grass. He hadn't done much with them this year.

A large gray cat wandered over to greet me and rubbed affectionately against my legs, the only sign of life I noted in the area. Kneeling, I offered my hand for it to sniff and scratched its head when it appeared to approve of me. "Do you belong here, kitty?" I asked, wondering who was taking care of it while Owain was away.

As I walked around the house, looking for who-knows-what, the cat accompanied me like a shadow at my back. A brisk breeze blew my hair against my face and made me feel slightly chilly, but the shiver that set my spine tingling was not from the chill. I couldn't pinpoint any reason for it, yet something felt foreboding about Bwthyn Gwyntog.

I wanted to run away, dash back to my car, and put as much distance as possible between this place and me. Instead, I forced myself to stay, telling myself it was only nerves and continued to walk the grounds surrounding the house. The cat ran along with me for a bit before it moved ahead along a narrow footpath leading up toward a clump of trees on a hill to the west of the house. Still nervous and ill at ease, I trudged up it. Tired of my slow pace, the cat darted back, trying to urge me along then scurried on uphill. Within a few minutes, I reached the trees and the summit of the mound where I turned to look behind me.

From here, the house looked rectangular and unremarkable, with the gardens forming a shape not noticeable when standing right next to them. Curved, each like a comma facing each other, they led to the hill path from the center where the two tips met through what looked like the outline of a third comma. Very odd, I thought, almost like a paisley pattern. What colors of blossoms might the flowers produce and did they contribute to the design? Did Owain construct this or was it here when he bought the place?

Turning back, I followed the path into the trees, emerged into a clearing, and froze where I stood. My stomach lurched, dropping to my guts in shock. A large, flat tabletop stone capped a trio of three squat pillars directly in the center of the clearing. The flat rock bore streaks of rusty-looking discolorations.

A sacrificial altar! The thought leaped into my mind as soon as I saw it. The rusty color could be dark, dried blood. As if to give credence to my deductions, I caught sight of the round circles and bars on some Celtic crosses a few yards away on the downward slope of the hillside. With increasing nervousness, I trod numbly past the altar and continued down to the row of three crosses.

The surfaces appeared old, discolored by the rains and worn out by the winds. The lettering on them seemed to be in Gaelic and was almost worn smooth in many places. Even if I'd been able to read them, I probably could not have made out the words.

At least they weren't new graves. I swallowed down my taut nerves with that bit of relief. What were they doing on Owain's property? Coincidence? Awena said Sheila had been a priestess of a cult. Was that a tie-in with these altar-like stones? But what about the crosses? How odd to see something that seems so pagan next to such strong representations of Christianity!

I didn't realize how much time had passed as I stood in that clearing on the hilltop until I noticed the sun had begun descending towards the sea. Now, it hovered above the tops of the trees, casting a golden glow and broken rays of light through the branches and onto the altar in a clearing. A shudder shook my body as I saw the illuminated capstone. A sense of urgency pushed me away, and I started to run back down the hill towards the house. All I wanted now was to be away from this place.

After I left the grounds of Bwthyn Gwyntog, I drove north, succeeded in getting lost no less than three times, and I eventually ended up, exhausted and frustrated, at a small town in mid-Wales called Machynlleth. By now, I was a score or more of miles northeast of Aberystwyth and in no mood to backtrack.

Finding a bed and breakfast house for the night, I grabbed a light meal at one of the pubs then turned in, dropping off into a deep sleep.

$\mathcal{R}$efreshed, I had a fortifying breakfast, backtracked to Aberystwyth, turned in the car, and, once again, caught the train north.

At a few minutes past noon, I got off the train at Harlech station and set a quick pace back towards my hotel and a change of clothes. I'd resolved nothing by this trip to the south and only raised more questions about the man I'd come to care about and his relationship with a woman who resembled me so closely she could be a twin.

As I walked, I was absorbed in my thoughts about everything I'd learned, attempting to piece it together. All the way, I'd tried to figure a way to ask him about the stones on his property. But that would be admitting I'd gone to Pembroke and his home. That I was checking on his story.

Coming to the parking area below the hotel, I noticed Owain's car was not in the lot. I frowned. Where the hell was he?

Irritated, I grumbled that he was gone and he shouldn't be driving anywhere, not with that wound in his arm. Cutting through my muttering, the tap of footsteps on stone approached from behind me, and I jerked to a halt, catching my breath. Whirling around to face the culprit, I stared into the relieved-looking eyes of Toby Morgan.

"Thank heavens, Kat'leen. I was gettin' worried about ya."

I let out the breath I'd been holding. "Oh, I'm sorry, Toby. It took longer to research than I thought it would. Then, I got lost on the way back."

He grinned. "Well, ya made it back safely, didn't ya? We'd better hurry. We don't have a lot of time."

I cast a quick look at my watch and pleaded, "Just give me fifteen minutes. I've got to take a quick shower and change."

Toby nodded, following more slowly as I bounded up the stairs into the hotel. Whatever my confrontation with Owain might be, it would have to wait for another time.

Chapter Fifteen

"... leading into the dance..."

We took the train down to Tywyn, a town that boasted one of the narrow-gauge railways that traveled up the deep green wooded hills rising a short distance from the shore. As we disembarked at the main line station, Toby pointed out the direction to the smaller railroad. I turned my head just in time to glimpse the pint-sized engine pulling out of the station with a load of tourists. I made a mental note to return and explore further.

For now, Toby pulled at my arm and urged me to follow him down the main street and across a small bridge to the seaward side of the town. A short way up the road, he ushered me to the front door of an unremarkable tract house, an ordinary square box-shaped home that resembled all the others around it. This sector reminded me of the houses I'd seen in the mining towns to the south.

However, the man who opened the door was anything but Welsh looking. Lean and of average height, his sharp gray eyes peered out of a long, narrow face dominated by a hawk-like nose. Silver-laced, reddish-gold strands of hair hung limply from a head balding on top.

"Kat'leen, this is Aaron McKay, the leader of our sect," Toby said by way of introduction.

McKay grinned, offering his hand to me as the gray eyes warmed. "Please be welcome in my home. We're always willing to have interested visitors. Toby tells me you've expressed a keen interest in the old religion."

The welcome was genuine, but I detected the distinct burr of Scotland in his accent. "You're a Scotsman?" I inquired to confirm it.

"Aye. Although, I've made my home along this coast for a good many years now. I shipped out a long time ago from Glasgow and ended up working on the Fishguard ferry. Here now, make yourself at home, lassie. This bonny lady is Edwina Morris, another member of our congregation."

The object of this introduction, a robust, mid-thirties woman offered a warm smile and her hand. Eyes crinkling, the laugh lines illuminated her face indicating she did it often.

"Toby tells us you are a schoolteacher in America," Edwina said.

"Yes—seventh grade," I replied and seated myself on the nearest chair.

"Oh, that must be quite rewarding. It's a great thing to be able to mold and shape young minds."

I laughed. "It's not quite as idealistic as that. Most of the minds I get already had plenty of molding and are barely receptive to my teaching. But I do my best, and occasionally, I find a jewel hiding in the pebbles."

Edwina smiled again. "It's still a noble effort. I only hope a good and decent teacher will try to do the same for my own two children."

"How old are your children?" I asked. It seemed the polite thing to do. I noticed it was now just the two of us. Where had Toby and McKay gone?

"My son, Dafyd, is just six and starting school this fall and my daughter, Merewyn, is three. I want them to have a good education, as I was lucky enough to have."

"Well, an education makes all the difference in the world these days. A person doesn't get a good job without an extensive background anymore."

She nodded knowingly. "That's the truth. I was telling my husband just the other day—"

"Well, here we go now!" McKay's voice rang out as he and Toby returned bearing trays filled with a teapot, cups, cream, sugar, and a plate of small, delicious-looking little cakes, which they sat on the coffee table.

"Edwina has a common interest with you," McKay went on as he began pouring tea. "She's a published writer and a celebrity of sorts hereabouts."

"Really? That's splendid—" I started to comment when Edwina interrupted.

"Ach! Aaron exaggerates. I've only had cookbooks published."

"Well, it's a start," I said and accepted the first cup of tea. "What I'm writing is a research paper for credit. It's beneficial for a teacher to publish in a journal and since I have a great interest in history, it seemed natural to do a paper on the people of this area and the rebirth of some of the Welsh customs along with the language."

McKay chuckled, passed a cup of tea to Edwina, and poured one for himself. Settling back in a heavy wooden chair, he took an appreciative sip of the brew before speaking. "Rebirth, is it? Well, it isn't exactly a rebirth, Miss Donahue. More a matter of fanning the embers of an old fire to give it new spirit. The customs and language have been here all along. The Celts don't forget their heritage easily, you know.

"Now, in Ireland, the Irish never gave up their backgrounds and customs. There are many places along the western coast where Irish is still the main language. In fact, some people don't speak English at all. Likewise, there are also pockets in Scotland and Wales, even

Brittany and Mann, where the old ways and words have a strong burning core as well."

"But what brought this forward in the last few decades?" I inquired, pulling out my phone and hitting the recording application. If McKay was going to talk about this, I wanted it to review. "Why now?"

"What else?" McKay replied with a depreciating grin. "A sort-of rebellion against English dominance, of course. The Scots and Welsh have been no happier than the Irish to be under English rule, and it's a way of expressing pride and individuality. A way of saying we're different from the English. You might call it a quiet rebellion."

I nodded and reached for one of the cakes before asking, "In the religion you all practice, is it also a rekindled spark of the old flames?"

McKay glanced at Toby who nibbled quietly on a honey cake but seemed to dip his head in a brief nod to the older man. "Aye, in a way, lassie. Again, the Welsh share a common background with the other Celtic countries, and the religious forms are very similar when going back to the earlier times. But the truth is, no one really knows much about the early worship of the Celts. Of course, there are volumes of material written on the deities and the symbols and other parts of the religion that can be discerned from the relics left, but as to the actual worship, that's another story.

"There are many variations on the ceremonies and those of us in this particular group practice our own version of the earth goddess devotion. You'll find it done differently all over the isles but based on the same background. What is practiced in Cornwall may vary considerably from the ritual we perform, but the deities remain the same."

McKay had a soothing voice with a strong burr rolling through his phrasing. At first, it had been difficult to follow, but my ear adjusted to it quickly and now the flowing cadence seemed quite normal to me. As he talked, I tried to picture this man in the garb of the pagan priest, but it was difficult to imagine. As he paused again to sip his tea, I interjected, "Toby mentioned something to me about the triple Goddess worship."

With a vigorous nod, McKay continued, "That's correct, Miss Donahue. But that's not entirely a Celtic concept. The Romans had the 'Matronae' or the Earth mother, and she was also portrayed as a triad. Part of the Celtic concept is of a merging of the spiritual, physical, and imaginative planes and perhaps this is part of the reason for the triple image."

Warming even more to his subject, McKay leaned more towards me, his eyes sparkling. "Now, since the earth religion was associated closely with nature, the most common worship places for druidic peoples were in the open or in the groves of trees where they would be surrounded by nature and feel a part of it. These groves of trees were called *nemeton* or sacred groves. Again, experts can speculate on what took place within these gatherings; however, no one knows for sure. There were no written records of these ceremonies.

"Indeed, there were no written records of any of the stories or customs of that time as it was the bard's job to retain that information and provide it wherever it was needed. A wealth of knowledge was lost due to being solely in bards' memories. We are lucky some have survived through people's recollections.

"The bards were the record keepers," Toby volunteered as McKay paused. "They held the stories of the people in the songs of worship. People respected the druids for their profound knowledge. They were the spiritual leaders of the tribes and spoke to the gods."

"Very true, Toby," McKay agreed and resumed his lecture. "The druids knew the rituals and the magic, but again, it is information that is lost. There is some evidence of sacrifice to the goddess or to the gods to ensure good crops and prosperity, but exactly what form this sacrifice took is not certain. In our modern worship, we use symbolic sacrifice, much as Christianity does."

While I understood what McKay was telling me about the history, I was a little confused. "But how did you end up with the ceremony you use now?"

All three of them laughed as if at some private joke, then McKay explained. "Well, that's most amusing, lassie, because the main part of the ceremony is the creation of a bard called Iolo Morganwg. Iolo formed the Gorsedd, a grand production designed to appeal to both the nationalists and romantics in Wales to spurn nationalism. He decided what elements to include in the ritual, and while parts of it may have historical credence, much of it is from Iolo's own romantic imagination."

I laughed with them. "So, what you do is really not a true form of the ancient worship?"

"It is, and it isn't, Kat'leen," Toby said seriously. "There are parts of it that have very old roots. Even old Iolo got some of it right."

"That's true. The essence of the ceremony is ancient enough, and Iolo did manage to get some of it right, but part of the pomp and ceremony of it is purely imaginative. Still, in these times, you need to have a bit of show for the congregation, don't you?" His face split into an amused grin as an eyebrow lifted into a quizzical arch.

"Of course you do," Edwina said, jumping into the conversation. "I think many of the members came because of the beauty of the ceremony and the ritual that makes them feel part of something ancient. In fact, we all take different names when we come into the congregation."

"Edwina is right," McKay interrupted. "But these names are all secret, power names." He'd cut in so quickly that I felt he'd had been afraid Edwina was going to reveal something she should not.

"You never tell anyone your name then?" I questioned.

"Only people that are trusted and a part of the congregation. Like the ancients, we believe there is power in the knowledge of one's true name, so to let others know gives them control over that power. Now, you have to agree, that's not a wise thing to do."

I found myself smiling at McKay's simple conclusion and murmured an agreement.

"Perhaps Kat'leen would like to see one of our ceremonies," Toby said, leaning forward to address McKay before glancing at me and adding quickly. "Wouldn't you like that?"

"I'd love to if it's possible." I set my teacup down and put on my most earnest look. "And if secrecy is necessary, I swear I'll tell no one about it."

"Of course, it's possible," McKay replied readily. "It's not all that secret and interested observers are welcome. In fact, we're having one tomorrow night in honor of the summer solstice. It will be a splendid revel, and I think it will show you a great deal more about our religion than trying to explain it."

"Oh, do come, Miss Donahue," Edwina gushed.

"You honor me with the invitation," I replied. "I'd be delighted."

Toby beamed at me, a big grin on his face. "That's terrific, Kat'leen. I'll be by to get you tomorrow evening so you won't have to find it on your own."

Satisfied with the arrangements, McKay set his cup down, poured more tea into it, then raised it to me as if in a toast, and said, "We'll look forward to seeing you there, lassie."

After that, the conversation drifted off to small talk about the weather and if it looked like they'd have a clear evening the next night. Edwina asked me some questions about life in California and what it was like to have so much sunshine all the year.

While I continued to be polite, I grew anxious to get back to the hotel. I wanted to know if Owain was back and what he'd been doing. I had so many questions after the trip to Pembroke. I still wasn't sure how to ask him about his home and the odd hilltop with its stone inhabitants without offending him. I had stepped over the bounds of our slight relationship, but I needed the answers.

Toby may have sensed my anxiety, or he glanced at his watch, for he said, "Oops. It's nearly time for the train. We'd best be going if we're going to catch this one back."

Within a few minutes, we'd said our goodbyes followed by a polite round of handshakes, then we were out the door heading back to the train station. His fingers locked through mine as he led me through the underpass again.

Through his broad grin, he said, "I'm glad you're coming tomorrow night. It's a beautiful ceremony."

"It sounds like it will be fascinating," I said then added as an afterthought, "Do you have a secret name, too, Toby?"

He stopped, turning to study me as if trying to decipher the reason for the question. "Yes, we all do."

"Will you tell me your name?" I didn't know why I asked, but it just slipped out. Perhaps I wanted to know if he trusted me enough to tell me.

"Not yet," he said softly. "But I will, when the moment is right." His hand rose to touch the side of my cheek. "You are lovely, Kat'leen."

Moving his hand to my waist, he swung me into his arms, pulling me closer to him in a tight embrace. His lips crushed roughly against my neck, along my jaw, and worked their way to my mouth. Surprised and unwilling, I pulled back from him, both hands pushing against his shoulders, reluctant to allow him the intimacy I had once craved. Puzzlement swam in his eyes.

"I can't, Toby. I think a great deal of you as a friend, but there's nothing more to it than that."

"But there could be if you'd give it a chance," he protested. "I thought you liked me, but suddenly you've seemed to shut me out."

I shook my head slowly, pained that I was hurting him, but I didn't want that kind of involvement with him. Two days ago, I would have welcomed it, but Owain had come into my life since then. All I could remember was the feel of his lips against mine, and his arms holding me. "Toby, I do like you, but not in that way. At least, not now. Please, let's leave it at friends."

Hurt shadowed his eyes as he stepped back freeing me from his embrace. His gaze searched mine, seeking the truth or reassurance, then he dropped his head forward, gazing at the ground. "All right—for now," he mumbled before he turned away and resumed the march to the station.

I sighed and followed him. Did I really love Owain, even after what I found so far? There were so many question marks about him. What if the answers proved I should have heeded my first instincts? What if he turned out to be a killer? Yet, the thought of him caused my stomach to quiver and the blood to pound in my temples. Even now, I was more concerned with getting back to Owain than about Toby's hurt feelings.

Toby stayed ahead of me for about a block, his pace deliberately fast. Eventually the anger that drove him died down, and he slowed to wait for me to catch up. I hadn't hurried to keep up with him. I thought it better to leave him alone with his thoughts. He stood at the edge of the walk, waiting patiently, hand shoved into his pockets and a sheepish expression on his face.

"I'm sorry, Kat'leen. I guess I expected too much out of your friendship. I thought we could be more than friends."

"Well, all good relationships start out as friends, Toby. And friendship is far more valuable than being romantically involved."

He sighed. "Maybe so. But—" His right hand slid from his pocket, formed a fist, and thumped it across his chest. "—it still leaves a gap here. I thought it would be different this time. But you're just like her."

"Like who?" I asked, confused by this twist.

Toby glanced towards the train station and resumed walking. "Come on. We'd better hurry or we'll miss the train."

I fell in alongside him. "Toby, who am I like?"

"A lady I knew last summer, a pretty Irish girl," he muttered. "She even looked a lot like you, red hair, and freckles. I was enchanted by her. I believed she loved me a little, but she was already taken. Pledged to another." Turning his head a little, he gazed at me from the corner of his eye. "Are you taken, too, Kat'leen?"

"No, I'm not involved with anyone. But I'm not looking for anyone either—not right now."

I spoke the words quickly, confidently, but I wondered at the truth of them even when I connected the girl from the previous summer with Sheila. Was Toby the boyfriend she had come to Harlech to see?

Arriving at the station, Toby led the way across the tracks to wait for the train. Already visible a short distance down the track to the south, it chugged rapidly, and within a couple of minutes, it slowed and stopped at the platform.

Once inside and settled, I returned to the previous topic. "Who was the girl, Toby? What happened with her.?"

He didn't look at me, just gazed out the window, and remained quiet. An oppressive silence, it felt like something I shouldn't break in on, as if whatever thoughts he pondered carried him a far distance from the train bench.

At last, he spoke, though his gaze, not moving from the ocean view, retained that faraway look, and his voice had a distant quality. "She was an enchantress—a fairy princess. If she had been free, I would have made her mine. But she was claimed by another. He came for her... From the sea."

Through dry lips, I asked, "Who came for her?"

Toby's gaze shifted to me, his eyes filled with a haunted look of the memory. "Her lover came for her. He took her with him to the sea."

Owain came to get her!

My mind cried out sharply, the voice in my inner thoughts shouting as loudly as if I'd spoken it. Like a blow to my whole system, Toby's pain-filled words shattered the hope I had for Owain's innocence.

154

"Did you see her go to him?" I asked in a raspy voice, the need to know forcing the question out of me.

Toby nodded.

"Are you sure of it?" Could Toby identify Owain?

Sadness overlaid Toby's face like a tangible thing that could be touched. "I loved her. She was so pretty and I—I had to watch her go."

"I am sorry, Toby," I said softly as I laid my hand on top of his. I regretted forcing the subject and dredging up these painful memories. He must've cared a great deal for her.

His eyes flicked down to look at my hand on his, studied it as if it was some odd creature that perched there, then he slid his from underneath and grasped it tightly. "Aw, Kat'leen, you're not free either. Like her, you are already pledged to another. That seems to be my ill fortune."

Even as I started to deny it, he shook his head emphatically and cut my words off. "No! Let's talk no more about this. Excuse me."

Before I could say anything, he lurched to his feet, made his way from seat to seat to the end of the train car, then stumbled through the connecting door.

For a few moments, I stared after him, stunned by the suddenness of his departure. I shifted my gaze to the window where the vast blue waters of Cardigan Bay glistened in the sun.

"From the sea—; to the sea—" The words seemed to echo in my mind. Could Toby have meant anything else except that Owain came on a boat to get Sheila and take her back with him? The references were vague, no names given. From what he'd said, they reunited under good circumstances, two lovers reconciling. So, what really happened that night?

By my reckoning, only Owain could answer that question. Did I dare confront him? And if I did, would he tell me?

Unbidden, the image of Owain standing on the beach came to mind, the look of pain and anguish on his face when he spoke of Sheila forming a poignant picture. I couldn't doubt that he had loved her. But did he kill her?

I had only the suspicions of a few people, a couple of cryptic newspaper reports, and Toby's account of seeing her go to him to base anything on. The police hadn't found more than that, or they would have arrested him.

But someone in this area knew more; knew enough to try to kill Owain.

What about his cousin? Was Madlen's death accidental or did someone kill her? If so, how did she tie into this?

Knowing what you should do doesn't mean that you will. Logic told me I should disentangle myself from this web of mystery, have nothing more to do with Owain. Even he didn't want me involved in whatever events were overtaking his life. But what my head said, and my heart dictated were two different things. No matter what the cost, I had to know the truth.

Toby didn't return to his seat next to me until the train pulled into Harlech Station. He managed a small smile; all the soberness of the earlier conversation had vanished like a departed spirit.

"Well, Kath'leen, I'll be seeing you tomorrow evening then. I'll come by around seven."

Hesitant, I acknowledged. "Yes, if the invitation is still good."

He bobbed his head, an affirmative.

"Tomorrow at seven then." The train slowed and chugged to a stop.

He caught my hand to help me off but stayed on the train. "You're not getting off here?"

"No, I have business farther up the line. Until tomorrow." With a squeeze, he released my hand, and I stepped to the platform.

Puzzled by his manner, I gave him a small wave before heading to the exit. Pausing, I glanced back once again as the train began to chug out of the station. I felt a definite change in our relationship. He'd become distant, much cooler towards me now, or was it only hurt showing for my rejection of his advances?

My shoulders drooped in regret, sorry for the pain I'd caused after I'd tried so hard to pull him out of his shell. I never thought he'd fall for me, and I'd never intended it to happen. I had just been looking for a friend while I visited here. I could try to clear that up tomorrow, but right now, more pressing matters troubled my mind.

As I approached the hotel parking area, I noticed the gray BMW sitting in the spot nearest the steps. I strolled past it, running my hand over the hood. It still felt hot. Owain hadn't been back for very long. Starting the steep climb to the hotel, I tried once again to order my thoughts before I talked to him.

I bypassed the welcome desk and started up the stairs to the second floor. At the top, I stopped, focused my eyes across the hall to the door of Owain's room and took a deep breath before approaching it. Steeling my nerves, I raised my hand to knock when I heard voices from behind it.

Two distinct voices, one Owain's and one I couldn't place, talked in garbled sounding words, probably

Welsh. I couldn't make them out, but I could hear the urgency and anger in them.

Just as I started to turn away, the other voice, speaking English, came through the door, louder than it had been, with exasperation evident in it. "Have reason, Thomas. You're in enough trouble as it is."

I recognized the voice now. It belonged to Constable Bowen.

Startled I retreated down the hall and slipped into the relative sanctuary of my own room. My stomach knotted as the constable's words added another negative to Owain's side of the ledger.

Bail out now, my inner voice whispered.

Chapter Sixteen

"... when the flames leap up high..."

*T*rust is a fragile thing—something not easily given, yet easily broken.

"Trust me," Owain had said, more than once. How could I when it seemed he hadn't been honest with me? Had he been truthful with Sheila, asking her to trust him also, then betraying her? If Toby had seen the Irish girl with him, I had to consider the possibility he had killed her.

I paced my room, a limited walk since it was not exactly large, and thought about this as well as Constable Bowen's remark to him that he was in enough trouble as it was.

Trouble and police business—

What could Owain be mixed up in that would bring that kind of warning on him unless it had something to do with Sheila's death?

Or Madlen's? He'd come north because of his cousin's death using a cover story of a photography job. No one here knew he was related to the dead girl I'd found.   Except for the police. They would have connected him to it. Were the two deaths tied together? Both died in the sea. Coincidence? Not likely.

I gnawed at my thumbnail and stared out the window. I needed to hear a perfectly reasonable explanation for all of this. I had to hear him tell me exactly what happened on the night of Sheila's death and why someone tried to kill him.

At the same time, I was afraid to ask him, fearful of the answer I might get. If he would answer me at all. Part of me was ready to stalk down the hall, knock on his door, and demand the answers while another part preferred to ignore it all, pretending that none of it was real.

Twice, I turned from the window, stared at the door, and debated if I should confront him. It might be a dangerous plan, I told myself. If he did kill Sheila, would he hesitate to kill me? Yet the idea of him being a cold-blooded killer seemed ludicrous. While he could be gruff, he'd shown a gentle, tender side. Could he intentionally take another person's life?

I didn't make it to the door either time. Eventually, I flopped on my bed and squeezed my eyes shut and tried to clear my mind of all the questions buzzing around it. Could I just not think about the whole dilemma for a while and try to gain perspective? Perhaps I hoped I could blot out the ugly face of reality, remove myself from the equation. I never found out.

A few soft taps on my door pulled me back to the present. My stomach lurched, and my mouth went dry. Ignore it, a small voice in my mind advised. But I couldn't. I knew who it would be even before I asked, "Who's there?"

"Owain."

Swinging my legs off the bed, I took a deep breath, rose, and crossed to the door. I hesitated at the last moment before opening the door part way and gasped.

He leaned with one arm against the wall next to the door, likely for support.

I stared at him.

He looked terrible. His eyes were dark with fatigue, circles of exhaustion underlining them, and a tenseness about him that suggested agitation. A wave of dark hair fell across his forehead in an untended tangle.

"Kathleen, I have to talk to you." His voice conveyed urgency, matching the distress on his face.

My heart, driven by fear or expectation, pounded uncontrollably. As much as I desired to talk to Owain, I didn't want to be alone with him, not in my room or his. "Downstairs," I said sharply, making my decision.

He looked puzzled, uncertain of me for a moment, and drew a breath as if to argue. He let it out, saying nothing, and nodded his agreement. Turning, he led the way to the stairs, pausing to allow me to go down first.

I declined and motioned for him to go ahead. He clutched the railing with his right hand, leaning into it for support.

The hotel lounge appeared deserted, not even Mrs. Linton taking an afternoon break with the telly. So much for having a witness near. At least, John Linton was at the desk in the outside entry, and he'd seen us as we passed. We continued across the room to a pair of chairs positioned near the fireplace, the spot farthest from the arched entryway. He took the chair with his back to the hearth where he could keep an eye on the entrance. Whatever he planned to say, he required it to be private.

Since it was nearly dinnertime, I figured most of the guests were either upstairs changing or had gone out for the evening. We had about twenty minutes before they might begin drifting in.

Owain sat hunched over, elbows on his knees as if he carried too much weight on his shoulders. Now that he faced me, he hesitated to talk, gazing at his clasped together hands. "I—I have to ask you something, Kathleen. Today, you were at Aaron McKay's house. Why were you there?"

Incredulous, I gaped at him. "How do you know that?"

A soft reply. "I saw you there."

"You *saw* me there?!" Anger tinged my voice along with the shock and disbelief I felt. "You followed me today? You were spying on me? It's none of your business!"

A look of pain shot through his face as if my words had stabbed him. Good. I wanted to hurt him as much as he was hurting me. So much for trust.

His hands unfolded and grabbed mine, gripping them tightly. I tried to pull them from his grasp, but he held on. Determined, I put my full strength into it and jerked them free, sliding my chair back as I did. Wincing at the sharp movement that pulled on his arm, his hands dropped back to his lap.

"Why?" I asked in a low hiss accompanied by my defiant glare.

"Please listen to me, Kathleen. I didn't follow you, and I wasn't spying on you. I didn't know you were going to McKay's house. I went there hoping to talk to the man. I got there just as you were arriving with that blond fellow. I didn't fancy going in then, so I waited."

I didn't say anything, just continued to stare at him. He took a deep breath and looked at me with such a look of pure hell on his face that I almost gave in right then. Only the sense of the violation of trust I felt kept me from going to him.

"Please believe me. I went to see McKay because I thought he might be able to help me. It had nothing to do with you."

"Help you? How could he help you?" I still couldn't believe it.

"I needed information that I thought McKay would know."

That wasn't much of an answer, certainly not one I would rebuild trust on. I cast a hard gaze at him. "If you expect me to believe you and trust you, you're going to have to level with me. For God's sake, tell me what's going on." I kept my voice low, but the anger and accusation remained palpable.

Owain closed his eyes for a moment then dropped his gaze. I felt as if he was shutting me out, making me nonexistent in his life, and I feared that would be his final decision. When he looked up again, I saw a look of commitment—his eyes appeared calmer. But I could see the muscles in his jaw flex with tension.

"All right. I do owe you more, but you must promise that what I tell you will go no further than you. It's important."

I hesitated. The last time I gave my word to him, I ended up holding back evidence from the police. "I promise," I stated, enunciating every syllable. "So long as it doesn't involve any legal complications for me. I won't lie to the authorities for you."

He seemed to think about that for a bit, then he nodded his agreement. When he started talking, his words came at a slower pace and with reluctance. "You must know that Sheila's death, and now Madlen's, haunt me—but I can't rest until some questions are answered. Part of the reason we fought was because she was involved with a group called the Preservers of the Light.

163

It's a religious organization, a pagan group. There are many others like it in the world, Wiccan groups, the Cornish revival societies, and others here in Wales. You get the idea. Some followers believe in the old gods. Others join for the ceremonies. Sheila was one of the former."

He paused to gaze at me a moment or two, perhaps to see how I reacted. I kept my face stony.

Taking a breath, he continued, "While I'm not the most religious man in the country, there were some things about the group that she'd gotten involved with that I couldn't accept. I was raised as a Christian, and you would have thought that an Irish girl would be as well rooted in it as I was, but her mother had lived in America long enough to expand her view. She found the old gods and the old religion far more appealing, maybe more romantic. We argued about it. I lost my temper and demanded that she give it up.

"Of course, that was a mistake, and she left. She came north and eventually met a fellow worshiper and became involved with a Light group in this area." He stopped again, his eyes peering at me.

I looked away from him this time, not wishing to reveal any of the thoughts in my mind as I tried to match this information with what I already knew.

"The group is headed by a druid called Gwyerion, who, I believe, is Aaron McKay. The man she'd met was called Tiernyon. This person was her guide, her teacher. I thought— I hoped, McKay could lead me to Tiernyon. I think he's the link I need."

At least, it made a little more sense now. I should have connected Toby's group with the "odd" religion Sheila Malone had been involved in. I still had questions. "How do you know that she met McKay and that this

Tiernyon was instructing her? Did you talk after you fought?"

He shook his head. "Sheila wrote a friend, another member of the Light group in Pembroke. I only found out recently from that friend."

"I see," I said, my voice soft but revealing nothing. More than he knew, I was beginning to piece it together. The friend, if my guess was right, was Awena. "So you had to find Tiernyon to ask him about Sheila. Why? Her death was an accident, wasn't it? Let her go."

His lower lip tightened. "Maybe it wasn't an accident. I can't let go until I know—until I'm certain. She won't rest. She'll haunt me until then. Can you understand that?"

I understood, and I didn't. I told him so. "What can you find out the police haven't already investigated? If it wasn't an accident, the police would have discovered it by now."

Why was I going along with this when I suspected he was involved? Did I need to believe he was innocent so much that I couldn't flat out ask him?

"Would they?" His voice sounded bitter. "Are all crimes in your country solved? Is Madlen's death an accident also? Is murder never ruled an accident?"

"Murder? *You're* calling it murder?" My voice reflected my disbelief. Could he really sit there and tell me he thought someone killed her when he was a suspect? "Your cousin as well?"

"It's a possibility. Oh, maybe not directly, but I believe Sheila was led to her death somehow. Why had she gone to the beach at that hour? In some ways, she was very Irish with the fear of the sea that flows in the blood of Connemara men; a respect for it that many don't understand these days. She wouldn't willingly go for a

165

swim in dark waters. And like Madlen, she was fully clothed."

"All right," I agreed. "Maybe you have a point. Now what?"

"Why did you go to see McKay?" he asked bluntly for the second time.

I met his eyes with annoyance in mine. "It's still none of your business, Mr. Thomas. But I'll tell you anyway. I'm doing research for a paper, you know that. The meeting with Aaron McKay was part of my research. That's all it was."

"And the man you were with?"

"That's definitely none of your business," I replied with the sting of acid in my tone.

His eyes searched mine for a moment, then he nodded his head slowly. "I see."

"I don't think you do." Even though I had no reason not to explain about Toby Morgan, I was still uncertain of Owain and unwilling to tell him about anything.

In the back of my mind, Toby's words about Sheila's lover taking her to the sea echoed like a never-ending chant along with that distant look on his face. Abruptly, I realized Owain was speaking again.

"—be that as it may, Kathleen, but I would like you to go away from here. Go do your research in Cardiff or Swansea for a while. If you need to find out about the Welsh, the research libraries are far better in those cities. The major population of Wales is in the south, and there are dozens of people you can talk to about customs, religion, and language. In fact, I'll give you letters of introduction to them.

"But I need you away from here—for now. I want you to be safe. Would you do that, please?"

I didn't answer him, my mind busily taking in what he was saying to me and raising more questions as I digested it. Safe from who or what? Why did he think I was in danger? What kind of threat?

Other questions presented themselves, but for now, only one burned in my thoughts. The one that was really the key to all of them.

"Where were you when Sheila died?" I blurted out, unable to contain it any longer. The accusation in my voice even startled me.

He looked stunned for several moments, as surprise and shock alternated on his face. Clearly, he didn't understand where the question had come from and why I was asking it. He sat back in the chair, his eyes meeting mine steadily for several long heartbeats before answering. "I was on a photo assignment in the Isles of Scilly, documenting island life on the various smaller islands in Britain for a magazine."

"Off the Cornish coast," I noted quietly. Not that far away. "Exactly where? Which island?"

"I don't know what you're driving at, but I wasn't on an island. I'd rented a boat, a small cabin cruiser. I was between islands, anchored for the night a good distance north of St. Martin's and the Eastern Isles. I needed to get away from people for a while, sort out my impressions of the islands, and look at the last of the photos." He paused, then added before I asked, "I was alone. I'm a good sailor. And I've been out alone several times, so it was nothing out of the ordinary for me. You can verify that if you need to."

As I gazed into the open frankness of his face, I yearned to believe him; accept that no deception hid behind those wide fern-green eyes. If he was telling me the truth, what had Toby witnessed? From the earnest look on his face, I found it difficult to believe Owain was deceiving me.

The expression on his face grew tender; his eyes seeming to blur at the edges with softness as he leaned towards me again. "I won't ask you what that was about. I have a pretty good idea anyway. Believe me, love. I was nowhere near Sheila when she died. I wish I had been. I might have been able to prevent it."

Slowly, my hand, on its own volition, for I'm certain I didn't instruct it, moved to touch his face. As my fingers lightly stroked his cheek, my stomach bubbled with excitement at the contact. Like a gossamer creature dancing next to a raging fire, I shimmered in fascination. Why did merely touching this man do this to me?

His lips parted into a gentle smile. "Now, would you do what I ask and please leave here?"

"I can't—," I started to reply, then his hand reached for mine, pulling it to his lips to gently kiss my fingers, then the back of it, and make my body tremble with his touch.

"Please. For my sake if not for your own," he repeated in an urgent whisper.

I shook my head in a stubborn refusal of his plea. "I'm not the one in trouble. You are. You're the one who's up to his neck in danger and worry. Quit trying to shoulder it all alone. Let me help you."

As he started to reply, the Stoners came into the lounge, announcing themselves as Louise's boisterous laugh followed a gruff clearing of the throat from Harry.

Owain immediately dropped his voice even lower, and I barely heard what he said. "There's nothing you can do except stay out of it. I won't have you in danger because of me."

"Then don't worry about me," I replied, keeping my voice down. "I can take care of myself. You've told me nothing to make me believe my life is in danger. I have a

few plans made that are in this area, so I'm not leaving."
I hoped he could detect the determination in my voice.

His frown told me he did, and he sighed deeply, the
sudden slump of his shoulders reminding me he was an
exhausted man. "At least, take care," he warned in that
same low voice.

"Mr. Thomas! I didn't expect to see you down
tonight," John Linton declared as he came across the
room towards us.

Owain took a deep breath, sat back, and replaced
the displeased look with one of pleasant companionship
that suggested he was merely chatting with me.

"I thought you were still upstairs resting," Linton
said, then added under his breath, "As you should be
right now." In the louder voice, he said, "I trust you're
feeling better then?"

Owain pulled his eyes away from me and spoke to
Linton. "I'm doing much better, thank you."

The proprietor gazed doubtfully at his exhausted-
looking face, but diplomatically inquired, "Will you have
dinner downstairs tonight?"

"Yes, certainly," Owain started, then hesitated,
unsure.

"Mr. Thomas and I will be dining together," I added
quickly.

Linton nodded his acknowledgment. "Of course."
Then with a smile, he moved on to talk to the other
guests.

I leaned forward to speak quietly to Owain again.
"After dinner, you're going to bed before you fall flat on
your face. You looked exhausted."

"I'm okay," he objected, although not too strongly.

With my face only a few short inches from his
mouth, I couldn't resist any longer. I pushed forward a

little until my lips met his in a kiss designed to stop any further statements of nonsense. Deepening as he responded, I nearly tumbled into his lap, but his good arm caught me and held me close. Breathless, I pulled away even though every fiber of my being cried for more. I straightened up and extended my hand to him.

We took my usual table in the dining room where it seemed a little more private, although we didn't continue the conversation from the lounge. In fact, Owain said little while we ate, but he seemed pleased with just my company. Content at being with him, I relished the sense of victory that I had somehow won something by asserting myself.

Following dinner, he offered no more objections to returning to his bed, and I resisted the urge to escort him there. With a slight smile, he slid his right hand behind my neck and planted a gentle kiss on my lips.

"I promise, I'll get some sleep," he said in that low, seductive purr. "But you must promise me that you'll be careful. Please."

I nodded, thinking he didn't look like he could do anything else, and I hugged him for a moment feeling the warmth of his body and fighting the urge to touch. "I'll be fine."

I waited for a few more moments, letting my eyes linger on him as he mounted the stairs, then I turned to go out for a special evening at the castle.

Chapter Seventeen

"...reliving the past fearfully..."

On designated evenings during the summer, local Welsh historical groups reenacted some of the battles that took place at the various castles throughout the country. On this night, Harlech Castle hosted a recreation of an attempt to take Edward's mighty fortress.

In anticipation of a large crowd, I hurried across the shortcut to the main road and made my way up the hill. Even though it was a lovely evening, clear and golden as it neared sunset, my mind churned neither on the beauty nor the reenactment I would be seeing, but on the man with whom I'd eaten dinner.

While I'd heard his story about his relationship with Sheila, I wondered how this tied in with his cousin. What had brought her to Harlech and what were the odds of her dying the same way his fiancée had? Why had he come here now and why keep the connection secret? Too many questions plagued me.

All of this left me feeling more confused than ever. My emotions interfered with my logic, banishing rational thought in favor of romantic reasoning. Despite my growing love for Owain, I couldn't get Toby's words out of my mind— "her lover had come for her." Could there be any other interpretation? Had there been any lover other than him?

What if he'd come for Sheila in his boat and convinced her to come with him again? Maybe they had fought, and she accidentally fell into the sea, then he panicked and left the area, telling the police he'd been in the Scilly Isles the whole time.

Annoyed with my thoughts, I shut it down. This was useless speculation. Playing what if didn't make anything real and I only came up with more unprovable theories.

I shoved these thoughts from my mind and tried to focus my full attention on the spectacle that was soon to unfold about me. I located a place to watch the activity that would afford a prime view of the drawbridge and the main gate of the castle. Splendidly attired in medieval armor and surcoats, many depicting the arms of people who actually fought in battle, the attacking combatants began to move into position.

On the battlements, the defenders stood ready to repel the attack. I knew from having read the history of Harlech that the castle had never been taken by battle but had fallen three times in its long history due to treachery and starvation.

The remarkable Welsh rebel Owain Glendower only took it when Henry IV had not been able to defend it properly, and the garrison had been reduced to twenty-one ill and starving men.

But breach those thick walls to gain entry? Not a chance. As the warriors now defending the castle demonstrated, a few men could hold this castle quite easily. As I watched the attack, I realized how sturdy the concentric designs of King Edward's castles were, and Harlech's own strategic location made it even more difficult to take.

Steel hitting steel rang out over the hills along with the shouts and cries of the men portraying their roles. Excited and enthralled children watched from benches set up for that purpose in a safe area for viewing. As exciting as it was, I realized it only provided a small sampling of what the real battle would have been. Thankfully, it also lacked the bloodshed.

Once the attackers were defeated, the small, but enthusiastic crowd began to disperse. From my vantage point, I studied the outline of the massive inner gate, which stood over eighty feet high and marveled at what the people of the twelfth century had created here. Awed by the knowledge, building skills, and engineering feats of the men of that era, I considered how many buildings modern men had erected that had lasted barely one century, let alone eight.

As the sun began to drop into the sea and the sky filled with red and orange hues, I strolled towards the shops near the castle. Most had closed for the night, but the pub remained open, and I stopped in for a pint of cider. About a dozen people, clustered in groups of three or four, sat at the tables while a couple of fellows hugged the bar. I took a seat a few down from them and ordered.

Although the pub had electricity, the lighting simulated torches and lanterns to continue the impression of the earlier centuries. Even though the walls were constructed with the same gray stone as the rest of town, the interior ones had been plastered and whitewashed to simulate the earlier era.

Many of the guests appeared to be tourists who'd come up for the show, but a few locals, including the two at the bar, lingered and chatted. I sipped my drink and people-watched, enjoying seeing the interaction that I sometimes felt was missing from modern life. I could speak. Here I was sitting off to the side by myself. Hypocrite, I chided in silence.

I stepped out into a dark world after the sun had set, and I'd spent more time in the pub than I thought I had.

Feeling the chill of the moist air, I turned back towards the sea and retraced my steps to the hotel.

Quite naturally, my mind returned to the problem of Sheila. Perhaps I'd made an erroneous assumption in concluding that the Irish girl Toby had known was Sheila. Could there have been two girls in the area at the same time that could fit the description? Possible, but not likely. Although Toby didn't actually say she'd died, I'd made that connection. Still, I was back to "what if" and I was gaining nothing from it.

I sighed and picked my way down the steep decline to the hotel. No sign of the moon tonight and the sky was like velvet sprinkled with rhinestones. A few lights glowed in the eyes of neat little houses that lined the street, but for the most part, only the smooth blackness filled my view. In the distance, I heard the hypnotic rhythm of the waves pounding against the shore as the clean, fresh sea air filled my lungs. It should have been peaceful and relaxing. Would have been if I could have switched my troubled thoughts off.

Just ahead, barely visible, the gate to the path that cut across the cliff face to the hotel stood open. Odd, I thought and stepped through, closing it behind me. From here, it was only a few minutes' walk to the warmth of the hotel. I hadn't realized how chilly I'd become, but now I shivered, finding my sweater inadequate and hurried along the path using my cell phone as a flashlight to illuminate the way.

The thick foliage of the trees and bracken at the side of the path muffled other sounds; even the ocean seemed distant. Heaviness hung in the air making it somehow harder to breathe and I felt like I fought my way through molasses. I glanced over my shoulder, aware of the inky blackness surrounding me, and I swallowed nervously. My stomach fluttered as a vision

174

of a horned monster popped into my brain. I stumbled, nearly falling to my knees. On the other side of the trees, I knew a fifty-foot or more drop waited if anyone was foolish enough to stray off this walk.

How easy it would be to fall from here on a night like this! How easy would it be to push someone, especially if you were a friend? As the hairs on the back of my neck rose like small antennae, I cursed myself for allowing my thoughts to wander again.

With an overwhelming sense of relief, I spotted the welcoming lights of the hotel lounge, lunged through the end gate, and hurried, almost breaking into a run, to the safety of the hotel.

Good lord, what had been in that cider? I wasn't the skittish type, but the combination of the brew, the excitement of the evening, and my own twisted thoughts had spooked me once I hit that dark path.

As usual, the television was on with three viewers perched on chairs before it, Harry Stoner and the two ladies who'd finally arrived yesterday. I hadn't met them, but they seemed ordinary enough, middle-aged companions sharing a trip up the Welsh coast.

I turned into the bar area where Louise Stoner, holding a tall, icy drink in her hand, occupied the barstool at the farthest end. I nodded an acknowledgment to her greeting, then ordered the Gaelic coffee as I slid onto the first seat. The last half hour had brought on a chill, not only from the cooling evening, and a warming drink seemed just the ticket.

John Linton brought it within a few minutes, and I hurried to wrap my fingers around the warmth of the hot coffee glass.

"Did you go up to the castle?" Louise inquired, lighting a cigarette.

I nodded and took a swallow of the coffee, relishing the whiskey-induced warmth that burned down my throat and into my stomach.

"I guess the play battle is a fair example of medieval warfare," Louise stated. "But I don't know much about that kind of thing. Harry and I went out last year for a look-see. It was good entertainment."

I got the distinct impression that Louise was making small talk when there was something else she'd rather talk about. Perhaps I could give her that opening.

"Yes, it really is a fair portrayal within limits. I didn't realize it was going on last year. Did the accident here affect the schedule any?"

"Oh, no," she responded quickly. "That was hushed up so fast hardly anybody knew about it."

"Hushed up? Why?"

As if that was a signal, she picked up her drink and shifted onto the stool next to me where she could lean closer while she talked. I glimpsed Linton's curious look, but he stepped farther away from the bar counter.

Louise spoke in a whisper, her face close to mine. "Can't say, really, why it was shut down so quickly. I suspect they didn't want to scare off any guests. Tourism is very important in this area, you know, and it did seem a bit peculiar."

Setting my own drink down, but keeping my hands wrapped around it, I prodded a little more. "In what way? She drowned, didn't she?"

Louise lowered her voice and leaned a little closer to me. "Well, that's what the official report was— accidental drowning. But the poor girl was badly bruised like there'd been a struggle, you know? I mean, there were marks on her arms and her face. I suppose she could have banged against the rocks or something. But, if you look at that beach out there, it's hard to imagine anyone bruising against it. To have drowned, she had to have gone swimming in it, and she definitely was not dressed for bathing."

"What do you mean?" Newspaper accounts I'd read said nothing about this, which made me wonder how Louise Stoner knew.

"Well, she had on a heavy gown or robe," Louise said dramatically, pausing for a moment to study my expression.

I'm afraid I didn't react as she'd expected as I simply stared at her trying to make the connection.

"Well, don't you see? A heavy gown would weigh her down terribly in the water. Nobody would be so stupid to wear one swimming."

"Oh... No, of course not." Now, I understood. Certainly not Sheila, not if she had a fear of water as Owain had said. She wouldn't have willingly gone into the sea, especially with the tides around here.

"How do you know all this?" I asked. "Did you actually see the body?"

She chuckled. "Oh, no, no, no... Not me. I talked to someone who knew someone who'd been on the beach when the girl washed up." Louise paused, taking another deep draw on the cigarette and washing it down with whatever she was drinking.

"This person said it was a red robe. It was decorated with a leaf design at the neckline and sleeves, not fancy, mind you, but sort of interwoven together. Of course, it had been torn in several places, you know. The whole thing was most peculiar, my dear. There were rumors about a boat offshore that night, but no one could find out anything about it."

"Yet the police ruled it an accident?"

Pursing her lips in a grim line, she nodded. "Reluctantly, I think. They questioned her fiancé, I heard, and thought he might be involved, but I gathered they couldn't prove anything."

"Her fiancé was from South Wales, wasn't he?" I inquired, fishing for more. How much did she know? Did she know that Owain was Sheila's fiancé?

"Yes, I believe so, but the police kept all that quiet. He was never officially charged. I gather he was a fairly well-known person."

Louise paused, swallowed another gulp of her drink before she set an elbow on the bar. "Truth told, I don't see how he could have been involved because I think that girl was simply one more of a string of strange happenings around here, and I believe they're connected. So, unless he comes to Harlech every summer, there's not much chance he's the one. Of course, I could be wrong." She said the last as if it was a doubtful prospect.

"What other strange events happened?" I asked, intrigued. I hadn't heard about any of this.

She studied me for a moment as if deciding if she should really tell me more, then went on. "Well, there were incidents with two other women, one each summer before last year. The first was a girl from France, a hiker, I believe. You know, college students come from all over to hike in the British Isles."

I nodded. I'd seen the students on the trains in their hiking shorts and shoes with their backpacks slung over one shoulder or deposited in fat lumps at their feet while they waited for the next stop. They all had a similar look, smiling, sun-tanned youth, and gaiety of spirit that students the world over displayed.

"Well, this girl was at a B&B up at Criccieth and decided to stay a few days after her friends left. One day,

178

she went out and never came back. She left her backpack at the house and never came back for it. Of course, the owner of the house reported it, and the constables investigated, but they never found anything. No trace. Eventually, they concluded she'd run off with a boyfriend. I gather her pals said she'd met a man and that was why she stayed behind. But, like the Irish girl last summer, no one seemed to know with whom she was involved."

Inexplicably, a chill touched my spine, its cold fingers working their way up to my neck. I took another sip of the coffee and asked Louise to continue.

"The one that happened two summers prior was not near as vague. In fact, it was horrible. A woman in her early thirties—German, I think, was found dead in a stone dance up in the hills here—just above the town. Near where you were caught in the storm, I believe."

The shock must have shown on my face because Louise stopped and peered anxiously at me. "Are you all right?"

"Yes, fine," I choked out. "A little surprised. Please do continue."

"I gather it was not a pretty sight. The woman was nude, stretched spread-eagled on the ground. Both her nipples had been sliced clean off, and her stomach was ripped open in a circle around her belly button. Her throat had been cut, but the authorities thought that was the last step. It was definitely a ritual killing."

"My God!" I breathed in shock. "Did the constables solve that murder?"

She shook her head. "'Fraid not. Of course, they questioned the people in the local pagan worship group, but they don't condone human, or even animal, sacrifice, so it wasn't a part of their rites. They don't even use that

179

stone monument. It was built about thirty years ago by a cult group from, coincidentally enough, Germany. None of that group are around here anymore."

As she paused, her mouth turned down in a sorrowful look. "Then there was that drowning a few days ago, another suspicious one, you know. And poor Mr. Thomas being shot this year. I suppose there's really nothing to connect them, but doesn't it seem peculiar? I mean, they all happened in the summer along this very stretch of coastline."

"It certainly is odd," I agreed. I found myself wondering if Owain had been in the area the previous three summers. For that matter, his home in Pembroke was only a few short hours away by car.

Louise raised an eyebrow as if it concluded her story, straightened up, pulled back from me, and swallowed another sip of her drink. She changed subjects, talking about Portmeirion now. I told her I had seen the unusual village a couple of days earlier.

"Isn't it a fascinating place? Such unique buildings! I believe they filmed a television show there, you know. Oh, what was it called?"

"The Prisoner," I supplied. "Yes, I know. It is quite the place." I drained the last of my coffee and added, "I'm afraid I've run out of steam, so if you'll excuse me, I'm off to bed."

As I got to my feet, she caught my hand in her left one and said, "Do take care, my dear. A single girl here could be in danger. I'd hate to see you end up like any of the others."

Surprised at the warning, I caught my breath before replying. "I'll be careful. Goodnight, Mrs. Stoner, and thanks for the information."

As I went up the stairs, I thought about the murders, for I now agreed that Sheila had been murdered. On the one hand, there was Owain, whom I couldn't believe would kill anyone, but what did I really know about him? In spite of what he said, he, too, had once been involved with a pagan worship group, as had Sheila. And, he was in a position to have studied other cult groups. In fact, did, as his photos of Brittany and Cornwall showed. But would he kill his cousin?

In his defense, he said he was here trying to locate Tiernyon, a name in a letter. Who was Tiernyon? A murderer? A witness? Or a non-existent person, a red herring dragged across my path to distract me?

When I was with the man, I loved him and trusted him, certainly felt no threat from him. Yet so much about him was uncertain, and the answers he offered did not suffice. I couldn't forget that someone had tried to kill him. The reason for that was one more unanswered question.

Although I checked the lock on the door of my room three times to verify it was secure, a reflection of the muddled state of my mind, I fell asleep with a bedside light burning.

Flames rose and danced in the circle, long tongues of them shooting towards the sky. In the center was the horned man, eyes blazing with yellow slits like an animal. His long fangs protruded from the corners of his mouth as he roared out something. Incomprehensible chanting and a ring of small goblin-like faces surrounded the demon and the flames. Dressed in blood-red garments, they danced counterclockwise around the circle. Behind the goblins, the stones of the dance shifted in the shadows of the flickering lights.

A man's hand gripped my arm, tugging at it, pulling me toward the fire. I resisted, putting my strength against his, screaming at the top of my lungs, but I was losing the battle. My heels dug into the grass, pulling up tuffs of it as he dragged me closer to the flames. I strained to see him, to see his face, but I only saw blackness beyond the powerful arm that held me. Nearly to the flames, I suddenly could see him. Mouth yawning wide, evil fangs dripping blood as he bent his face towards me, the horned god lunged for my throat. I shrieked in terror!

My eyes flew open to the semi-darkness of my room. I tried to shift my right arm and felt tightness around it. My heart raced in panic, then I saw the bedclothes tangled up around it, restricting my circulation. I let out an exasperated groan. Another damned dream!

But the light was off. I'd fallen asleep with it on. Listening for any noises in the room, I remained motionless on the bed while my heart pulsed more swiftly again.

It seemed quiet, no sounds of movement. After a few minutes, I reached carefully for the lamp, pressed the switch, and remained in darkness. I repeated the action twice before I exhaled a breath of relief. No one had invaded my room. The bulb had burned out.

Relieved, I untangled myself from the bed covers and padded across the room to the switch on the overhead light. I stopped at the washbasin and splashed cold water on my face. Filling a glass with water, I drank and stumbled back to bed. Owain was just down the hall,

I thought, remembering how it felt to have his arms around me. I wished I could go to him now and lie securely in the circle of them.

With a disappointed sigh, I dropped back against the pillows, closed my eyes, and prayed I wouldn't have another dream like that one.

Chapter Eighteen

"... and the seasons that will be..."

*W*hen one really cares about another person—friend, lover, mate—you seem to develop a second sense regarding that person. Somehow, you know when something is troubling him and can even anticipate his moves.

After that disturbing dream, I'd been unable to go back to sleep. I drowsed a little, woke fitfully, unable to get comfortable and reluctant to ease the leash on my psyche. Dreams can serve many purposes, I knew. They relieve anxieties, offered possible solutions to problems, and sometimes entertained. These dreams I'd been plagued with for the past few days did none of these functions. They frightened me, adding to the worries I already had.

My grandmother was true Irish, born in County Donegal, Ireland, and raised there until the potato famine forced the family to America in order to survive. Maire O'Connor never ceased to be the Gael even though she adopted the language and customs of her new country. I remembered, too vividly, the tales she told the children of the family about Irish fairies, the puca, the banshee, and the fierce race of our antecedents, who were the Celts.

Gran'ma Maire would wink at me, a twinkle in her periwinkle-blue eyes and say, "Kat'leen, a chara, 'tis special you are, my girl, for you have fairy blood in ya'. You're a fey child, just as your mother, meself, and me mother before me. One day, lass, 't'will serve ya' well."

Now, as I sat downstairs in the hotel lounge on a quiet morning and watched the glow of sunrise kiss the shadows of the earth to life, I remembered the old woman's words.

Fey—was it to be able to know the future or when something was about to happen? Were my terrifying dreams a warning then? If so, they were so cloaked I couldn't decipher them. But I did know one thing with certainty and that only required my waiting to confirm.

It wasn't a long wait, as I knew it wouldn't be. He came down quietly, careful not to disturb anyone. He wore a black mohair sweater over a dark shirt and black slacks. My heart quickened at the sight of him. I cleared my throat, speaking loud enough for him to hear, yet not allowing my voice to carry. "You, sir, are supposed to be resting in bed."

Startled, Owain turned towards me. Surprise flashed on his face, and for a moment—only a brief moment—the look of a small boy caught with his fingers in the jam jar. Then, his confidence asserted itself and he diverted into the lounge to face me.

"I've heard that rumor," he admitted, his voice low. "But I'm running out of time."

"Time to do what?"

He studied me for a few seconds. "Are you spying on me now, Kathleen?"

"Hardly that," I replied, trying to keep my voice steady. "I'm merely worried about a friend. What are you planning to do?"

Eyes locked on mine, he hesitated, scraped his teeth against his lower lip, then seemed to come to a decision. "Come with me, Kathleen."

"Where?"

"If you want to know what I'm about today, then come with me now. Otherwise, go back to bed and quit worrying about me." He waited, a slight smile touching his lips, not a kind smile, but one of satisfaction that he'd put the game back on my side of the board.

I took a deep breath. In the back of my mind, an inner voice warned me not to go. Caution, it advised. You don't really know this man.

But I met his eyes and somehow, I could see no danger in them. Not for me, although I knew they could show cold anger for others. Now there was confidence in them; he knew he'd won, either way.

"All right." I accepted his challenge. I was ready to go out, had dressed casually in slacks and a lightweight shirt. I picked up my handbag, rose, and joined him as he started towards the door.

Just as I knew he'd be down and going somewhere early this morning, I accepted that I would go with him. With a sense of déjà vu rippling in my mind, I followed him out the door and down the stone stairway to the parking lot.

Perhaps Gran'ma Maire was right that I had the fey gift. Or maybe being fey amounted to the ability to understand and anticipate what people would do. Be that as it may, one thing I knew with certainty was this stubborn fellow and I were destined to be together.

Without a word, he unlocked the passenger side of his metallic gray BMW, then held the door for me before going around and getting in. Well-tuned, the car purred to life instantly. He backed up sharply, swung the car around onto the highway, and pointed it north.

He picked up Highway 470 into the mountains of Snowdonia. Ever since that brief exchange of dialogue in the hotel, we'd said nothing, but now I cleared my throat and asked, "Where are we going?"

He glanced at me, a mere flick of his eyes that barely diverted his attention from the curves of the road. In that glance, I'd seen a hint of reserve or reluctance.

After a lengthy pause, he answered, "I have someone I have to see this morning. Since you're determined to get involved, I might as well have you along. At least, I'll know you're safe if you're with me."

I studied his profile, admiring the firm set of his jaw, the forceful-looking nose, and his deep-set eyes with long black eyelashes highlighted by thick dark eyebrows that gave such dramatic impact to his features. I wanted desperately to trust him.

"Why don't you just tell me the whole story? I keep getting bits and pieces, but they don't seem to fit."

His jaw tensed slightly, the muscle along it making a slight ripple, but he ignored my question, concentrating—or so it seemed—on his driving as he down-shifted the BMW to third before we started up a steeper incline. Around us, beautiful green valleys and long canyons of grass and forest stretched for miles. Here and there, the glint of water flashed through the trees.

I sat back, pouting, and making it clear I was displeased. What was the big secret today that he couldn't at least tell me where we were heading? I tried again. "Okay, you told me about Sheila. What about Madlen? Why was she here? Is it connected to Sheila's death?"

He spared a glance for me. "Later. Enjoy the drive for now."

As we climbed, we seemed to be getting into a pocket of fog. Starting out as an overcast morning, the day turned even darker. I shifted in my seat nervously, wondering where this trip was taking us.

"Are you hungry?" Owain asked after nearly a half-hour of silence.

"Tea would be nice. Answers would be better," I replied tersely after a moment or two to register what he'd said.

"There's a nice little restaurant in Blaenau Ffestiniog where we can get tea and scones. We'll be there in about ten minutes." He lips formed an amused arc. "You'll like the town, I think. It was a slate mining town, but the mines are closed now. That was a blow to the economy. And like a lot of people in North Wales, the locals are trying to keep their lives going. Visit the tourist information shop in town, or you can get—"

"Owain!" I interrupted. "I don't need a tour guide. I need to know what's going on. You told me I'm in danger and asked me to trust you, but you haven't given me one reason to do it."

He eased the car around another curve, slowed a little more than was necessary, then looked at me long enough to say, "I love you, Kathleen, and I want you safe. Isn't that reason enough?"

"Safe from what?" I repeated in exasperation. For the moment, I missed the first part of his statement. "We keep going round and round and getting nowhere."

"I'll tell you everything soon, I promise, but can't it wait until after breakfast?"

I frowned at him for a few moments, until his earlier words registered in my brain. "Wait. What did you say?"

"Can't it wait until after—"

"No! Before that. You said you loved me?"

He smirked, amusement obvious. "Does that surprise you?"

I stared hard at him, shook my head once, and looked away. I wasn't sure what to think now.

My local guide was right about one thing; Blaenau Ffestiniog did interest me very much. The fog on the town gave it a softened appearance, like a cloud city. It nestled in a valley surrounded by hills and mountains of lush green-shaded shrubs and trees. With the clouds hanging over the valley, the mountain peaks vanished into puffs of grayish-white. Like the slate from the mines that had given birth to the town, the walls were dark gray. We came in on a road that paralleled the railroad where he slowed to point out a particularly beautiful view of the railroad bridge curving into town with a slate mountain in the distance and row after row of the gray rock houses clustered together.

"That looks like an awfully narrow bridge," I commented as we passed by it.

"Narrow gauge railway," he supplied. "They used the small trains to haul the slate down to the sea. They still run, but now they haul tourists."

I grinned. "The locals adjusting and surviving?"

A calm, peaceful feeling enveloped me. Even if the town wasn't old, the sense of antiquity pervaded the area. Could it be the last stronghold of an Elven race? When I mentioned that to Owain, he laughed.

"I don't know about the elves, but this is one of the wilder areas of Wales and certainly, it was part of the unconquered realm of the early Celts. A lot of the customs and the language survived because the interior lands of Wales were difficult for the Romans and the English to reach, so they didn't bother. Without these strongholds, our language might have vanished."

With growing suspicion, I watched his face as he spoke. He parked the car, and on foot now, we strolled up the street to the restaurant. I thought I would gather details about Wales and the spirit of the Welsh from Toby, but I was finding more of that spirit and enthusiasm in Owain. Love and pride shone in his eyes now.

"Are you one of the Welsh nationalists?" I asked to confirm what I'd only now discovered.

"Guilty." A small, amused smile curved his lips, and his eyes crinkled at the edges.

"I should have deduced that sooner," I admitted with a shake of my head. If he'd fallen for me, the feeling was mutual.

He opened the door to a quaint little café and pushed me gently through, pointing to a table. After we'd ordered, he said, "Kathleen, I love my country. Our relationship with England is one of cooperation, but we are not English. I'm Welsh. First, last, and always, Welsh. English is like a secondary citizenship. Not all Welshmen feel this way, but I can't feel any other way about it.

"I was born around here, a little further south at Ffestiniog. It's not much different than here, and it wasn't easy growing up in this area, but there were lots of good times. I went fishing and riding, and I knew these hills pretty well. I love it here. I may live in South Wales, but my heart is still in the north."

"Then, do you advocate a separate nation for Wales?" I asked, surprised at this aspect of him.

He shook his head with a sad smile. "No. There's no way a free Wales could survive. How long could we last with tourism our primary income? Ireland's had a hard enough time of it, and the resources of Wales are even less. It's a fine dream, but not very realistic. But I do believe in the survival of our language, our customs, and our nationalism even if not as a separate nation."

Over our tea and scones, we talked more about the nationalists and the Plaid Cymru, who supported a free Wales. While he clearly sympathized with their point of view, he, like most of the Welsh who voted against separation over the years, was a realistic man, yet I could detect a longing in his voice for that once proud nation.

"Still, Wales has been under English rule for about four hundred and fifty years, and we experienced plenty of conflict before that. That's why the Norman and English kings built all these lovely castles the tourists now come to Wales to see." He leaned back in his chair and stretched his long legs out to one side. For the moment, he appeared to be feeling quite relaxed, more so than I'd seen him before.

"I wish I had this on tape," I groused, knowing that I'd never remember everything he said.

"Most of it is a matter of record," he said. "Nothing new and exciting in all my rambling. You'll hear it echoed by many of the people you talk to."

"Maybe. But you put it quite plainly. How about putting something else plainly?"

He didn't pretend to not know what I meant. "Let it wait a little longer, caru—love. I think some of it will be clear soon enough, then we'll talk."

Getting to his feet, he picked up the bill, dropped a pound coin tip on the table, and offered me his hand. It was a casual move, done naturally and without thought, yet in some ways, it demonstrated the possessive attitude he was beginning to develop towards me. Oddly, I didn't resent it and welcomed the connection.

We strolled back onto the street and turned towards the car lot. To the right, I noticed a turn off the main road. I poked his arm, "Where does that lead?"

"To the trains. BritRail comes in here from Llandudno Junction in the north, then you can take the Snowdonia Mountain Railway from here on down to the West Coast."

"That's the narrow-gauge train?"

"Yep. It's one of several that run in Wales. You can even take one up to the summit of Snowdon."

In delight, I grinned at him. "Really? Can we do that sometime? Together?"

He stopped mid-stride, turned to face me, and his fingers brushed lightly through my hair at my right temple. "Yes," he said softly. "There might be a together for us now."

For some reason, I felt a chill up my spine as he said this, and I recalled, somewhat reluctantly, my distrust of this man. It was alarming how easily he could disarm me when I was with him. He may have sensed this change in my thoughts because his hand dropped from my hair, and he turned back to the road.

"Let's get going. It's only another half hour from here," he said crisply as he picked up the pace to the car.

"Will you at least tell me where we're going?" I asked once we were on the road again.

"Betws-y-Coed," he replied.

"Where?" I repeated as another Welsh town name sounded like a jumble to me.

He laughed and said the name again slower, emphasizing the vowel sounds for me. "Betws-y-Coed. It's a little town a few miles inland from the northern coast. Mostly a tourist town these days, but it's charming and beautiful. You'll be able to see the mountains clearly from there."

"Bet-see-coid," I repeated, trying to get the sound down.

"Close enough," Owain conceded behind a suppressed grin.

"Don't be so damned smug about it," I muttered and slapped at his arm. "Now, why are we going there?"

"I told you. I have to meet someone at noon."

"And that's all you're going to tell me?"

"For now."

There was no point in pursuing it any further, so I leaned back and enjoyed the view. We came down out of the slate mountains into the verdant green of another valley.

I perceived a different ambiance in the North Wales countryside, hard to explain, but maybe best described as wildness. When compared to the neatly groomed fields of England and the almost stark look of the Scottish Highlands, Wales had an unkempt appearance. But the wildness wasn't forbidding as many wilderness areas are, more a look of a land that is loved by her inhabitants and left to wander as she will. In this, it bore a kinship with Ireland where the country also flourished in wild beauty.

Despite the surrounding splendor, my stomach fluttered with the uncertainty of this drive. What might lie ahead in Betws-y-Coed that was important enough to pull Owain away from his much-needed rest?

Chapter Nineteen

"...an excursion into the wild hills..."

*G*olden sunshine greeted us when we drove out of the fog into another valley. Not even one cloud interrupted the wash of light blue above the tree-clad mountains.

"It's a beautiful day," I stated, making a weather comment to break the silence we'd endured since leaving the slate-mining town.

"Here, it is. Closer to the coast there could be clouds and fog again. The weather is quite changeable; you never know what the Irish winds will blow in."

We came abruptly to Betws-y-Coed and, as advertised, it looked both charming and welcoming. Owain eased the car into a public lot near the town square, which was a large park. On the east side, I spotted the small train station that served the area. The Welsh Tourist Bureau occupied a building to the north of the square. The main street, which led up to the northern end alongside a picture-book babbling brook, branched off the west side.

Owain caught my elbow, urging me past the southern end of the square in the direction of the main street. We crossed the road and continued up a side road for a few hundred feet. Constructed mostly of stone, the houses off the main road looked like small but well-kept places where the locals lived undisturbed by the influx of "summer people" who descended on their village.

At a typical stone cottage with a gorgeous flowerbed adding a splash of color to the front, Owain paused to open the gray wooden gate set into the rock fence, then ushered me through it. While he knocked on the door, I studied the beautifully carved spoon that hung next to it.

An oversized Welsh love spoon. I'd seen them in a couple of gift shops, but the rougher finish of this one told me it was not one made for tourists. Within the lacing framework, the artist had carved a feather pen and an ink bottle on an old-fashioned school desktop. I knew enough about the custom of these spoons to know that usually the center design related in some way to the person who would receive it.

I was about to comment on this when the door opened, and a silver-haired older woman's face peered at us. Upon seeing Owain, the petite woman stepped forward, and her face crinkled with laugh lines as she grinned. She reached up to hug him, and he nearly lifted her off her feet with the exuberance of his greeting. She spoke to him in Welsh, her voice husky and robust with the sometimes-harsh tones of the language.

He replied briefly in the same tongue, then switched, for my benefit, to English. "This is Kathleen. She is a friend of mine from America. Kathleen, this is Aunt Min."

The elderly woman smiled, a charm to equal her nephew's flowed from her face. "Welcome to my home, Kathleen. Please come in."

Even as I mumbled a thank you and thought that I couldn't very well address her as Aunt Min, Owain said, "Her full name is Minerva, but everyone calls her Aunt Min. She used to be a schoolteacher."

"And Owain used to be one of my brattiest, although most clever, students," Aunt Min responded sharply. "Make yourselves comfortable, dears. I'll bring some tea."

Well, that explained the design on the love spoon. I took a seat on the delicately built Louis XIV-styled sofa while Owain settled himself in the sturdier-looking chair, but only briefly, for Aunt Min returned with a tray, and he was immediately on his feet to take it from her, setting it on the table. I noted that he moved his left arm with care, still mindful of his injury.

Watching him in this situation, I reflected once again how absurd it was to suspect him of murder, either premeditated or accidental. Aunt Min poured while he distributed the tea. As I accepted the delicate China cup from him, I noted the pattern looked like a Belleek design from Ireland. The good China: I felt honored.

Once we all had a cup, Aunt Min spoke up. "Well, Owain, how have you been? You're looking a bit worse for the wear."

He smiled, apparently accustomed to the lady's directness. "I'm fine. A little overworked and banged up, but fine. And you're looking remarkably fit."

"Oh, I keep busy since retirement," she agreed. "Doesn't do to sit about and stagnate, you know. I teach Sunday school classes, and I work with our art guild. There are still a few bright young minds around to shape and guide, my dear."

From there, the conversation went to some other recent changes in the area and back to the earlier times of Owain's school days. Casually, he mentioned that I was also a teacher and was researching a paper on Wales.

"That's wonderful!" Aunt Min exclaimed, clapping her hands once to punctuate her delight. "I'm so glad people are interested in our culture—and from America, at that."

I explained a little of what I was doing and added, "I would really love to talk to you more about this and the changes that have taken place in your lifetime. That is if you're willing?"

"Certainly. I believe there were bards in my bloodline because I do love to tell stories and relate histories. However, I suspect Owain didn't come here to listen to my tales. In spite of the casualness of your call, *hogyn*, I feel there's a distinct reason for this visit."

His lips tugged into a sly smile at whatever she'd said, and he set his cup down, folded his hands on his knee, and said, "Astute, as always, Aunt Min. I've come to ask you about pagan cults."

"Harmless groups," she said readily. "You know, we had a revival of interest in the old religion a couple of decades ago, more outsiders than locals, although there's always a few of our younger folk getting involved. There's a sort of romanticism in the Druids, even for us, but most people just play at it."

"Are there still some active?" he asked.

"I imagine so, but you know that already. I follow your work, you know. I saw your photo journey of the modern Druids. With all these old cromlechs and monuments cluttering the landscape, it's only logical that Wiccan and Druid groups would frolic in the countryside."

I almost laughed at the tone of scorn in Aunt Min's voice. She clearly dismissed the pagan-Druid groups as romantic children play-acting.

He was more serious as he asked, "Do you know of any who are into sacrifice?"

"Oh, my, no!" she responded immediately. "None are as barbaric as that! Most of them might use symbolic sacrifices, but the worst I've heard of is daisies and roses being tossed into a bonfire."

Owain laughed. "So, nothing more serious than that?"

"Well," she drew it out as she thought. "I do recall some incidents around Beddgelert several years ago. Animals were found, one a year for seven or eight years, that had been killed in what looked like a ritual method. They were always found the day after the summer solstice. The authorities thought it might be a local boy, a strange lad they had their eyes on, but they never could prove it. When the family moved away, the killing stopped."

"Do you remember the name?" To my ears, his voice carried an anxious tone.

"Oh, my, that was a long time ago," Aunt Min said as she gazed towards the window with a distant look in her eyes as if her bardic mind was leafing through the pages of the past. She shook her head, not finding the name she sought.

"That's all right," he interrupted. "And that's the only incident you know about?"

"In this area."

"What about Cardigan Bay?"

Unexpectedly, his not-so-casual question caused chill bumps to rise on my arms, the hairs prickling as if an ill wind had moved through this charming sunlit room.

Aunt Min gazed slyly at him, the look saying he already knew the answer, but she obliged anyway. "About six years ago, a sheep was found in a stone dance the day after the solstice. The hapless animal had been disemboweled, and the intestines scattered around the ground suggesting it was used for a druidic ritual. The same thing happened the following two years, and then it stopped."

"Do you suppose," he asked slowly, "that could be the same boy as in Beddgelert?"

Even as he asked the question, I recalled Louise Stoner's description of the German girl murdered in the stone dance above Harlech. A ritual killing.

"I guess it's possible, but that's reaching rather far," Aunt Min replied.

"Are you sure you can't remember that boy's name?" He pressed her a little. "It's very important, Aunt Min."

The elderly woman closed her eyes, picturing the past. "He was a towhead, slightly built. I recall seeing him a few times. His father owned a small piece of land outside the town. Winston! That was it—Sean Winston... No! Not Sean, Shane. Shane Winston."

"You're sure?"

"Yes, of course. Shane Winston. English father and a Welsh mother."

She watched his face, just as I did. While he looked thoughtful, he also seemed disappointed.

"That wasn't the name you were hoping for, was it?" she said.

Owain smiled, shaking his head gently. "No, but it's still a help. I do appreciate it, Aunt Min."

"Now, I don't suppose you're going to tell me why you're nosing about?"

The smile grew wider. "Not just yet. But I will when I get it all sorted out, I promise."

Aunt Min shook her head and addressed me. "I don't suppose this big blockhead has told you any more than he's telling me?"

I shook my head.

"I thought not. Well, whatever it is, Owain, try to stay out of trouble. But that's never been one of your strong points, has it?"

He managed to look hurt. "Now, Aunt Min—"

"Oh, don't pull that misunderstood innocent routine on me," she said with a dismissing hand gesture. "Just tell me the whole story when you can. And be careful."

"And you, young lady ...,," she leaned a bit forward as she spoke to me and her eyes twinkled, "... you take care of him and don't let him drag you into trouble."

"Aunt Min!" He muttered in disapproval as he sprang to his feet, then held out his hand to her. "We have to be going now. I have lots to do."

Caught off guard, I hastened to rise, the teacup clattering as I hurried to set it back on its saucer.

Aunt Min, too, rose from her chair. "It's been good to see you again and to meet you, Kathleen. You bring her back to see me, *hogyn*. You hear."

"I will," he promised and bent to kiss her cheek in goodbye.

Thanking her for the tea, I hugged the old woman with a feeling of genuine affection and promised I would be back to see her whether Owain brought me or not. After all, she had stories to tell.

As we walked back towards the town square, he dropped his right arm across my shoulders, a hint of discomfort showing as his eyes tightened a bit.

"How's the arm?" I asked.

In response, he pulled me a little closer, but he didn't say anything. A few lines creased his brow, as he seemed to be puzzling over what Aunt Min had said. She was right; he hadn't heard exactly what he wanted to hear. On the other hand, I hadn't heard anything to tie together the bits and pieces of the mystery surrounding the man next to me.

Back at the town square, we crossed Main Street to take us into the park. A harpist had set up in the shade of one of the numerous trees and was now playing a traditional air on a beautifully voiced Welsh lap harp. At his feet, he'd spread a tapestry cloth, and a few coins were scattered across it.

We stopped to listen for a few minutes. The melody sounded familiar, but I couldn't place it.

"*Llwyn Onn*." Owain identified the music for me. "'The Ash Grove.' It's an old tune. Luckily, much of our music has survived through the centuries. We have an annual bardic gathering, *Eisteddfod*, that helps."

The strains of the music moved me, the call of an ancient race of people played on an instrument that was as antique in design as the music. The Welsh harp was a symbol of Wales as much as the Irish harp represented that country. Owain's hand pressed on my shoulder, bidding me to move on.

Impulsively, I reached into my purse, withdrew a one-pound coin, and dropped it on the tapestry. The harper glanced up at me, a smile crossing his sun-tanned, roughly handsome face, then he bent his head again to the command of his harp.

Owain headed up the street, pulling me along with him, and crossed to walk alongside the road. He still looked troubled.

"A penny for your thoughts?" I asked.

He barely glanced at me. "They're pretty jumbled right now. Let's walk and maybe I can sort them out a bit."

More procrastination. He wasn't going to tell me anything.

Now that we were out in the sun again, the sweater I donned in the crisp morning grew too warm, so I slipped it off, placing it over my arm. I glanced at the various businesses across the street, then slipped Owain's arm off my shoulder.

"I'm going to get some food for lunch," I announced, and without waiting for his comment, dashed across the road and into a bakeshop.

Just walking in made me hungry, but I resisted the urge to buy one of everything and settled for half dozen meat and potato pasties, two apples, and two small bottles of orange juice.

I came out to find Owain waiting by the door. He'd slipped his sweater off now to reveal a short-sleeved gray shirt. A line of white gauze showed just under the cuff of the left sleeve.

Since I'd used my sweater to hold my purchases, I held it up to show him and said, "Let's find somewhere to sit and eat these."

"I know just the place." He caught my hand and, finding an opening in the traffic, led me across the street once again.

"Somewhere" turned out to be a rock in the middle of the brook. He guided me up the street and across the bridge over the water to the eastern side of town. There was a public park-like area scattered with boulders that provided a natural pathway into the brook. Quite a few people had already settled on these rocks, climbing on and off them while they cooled off in the water.

Children, in particular, found these great boulders as imaginative creations and walked the plank off their ship rocks or frolicked around their desert islands. Their laughter filled the air around the park.

However, Owain had a quieter place in mind as he continued up along the bank of the brook. Within a few minutes, we'd left the yells of the children and the crowds of people behind us. As we came around the curve, I caught my breath at the view of a serene pool with a large, flat-topped boulder just a giant step from the shore. Owain hopped across, then reach back to offer me his right hand.

After I emptied out the food, we used our sweaters as cushions and settled comfortably on the rock. Like Nature's gifts, tall trees lined the bank providing partial shade yet allowing dappled spots of sun to break through. The result provided just enough warmth while adding sparkling lights on the water.

Our pasties were still warm, and we ate them like a pair of starved rats as we realized just how hungry we'd gotten. At one point, Owain gently nudged my arm and pointed at the center of the pool where the silvery movement of a fish stirred the waters.

I breathed in the fresh, slightly moist air, and let it out slowly. An idyllic situation with the cold, sparkling water, and a slight breeze through the trees, I felt like we were the only two people in the universe; as if time had paused just for us and we could hold it here forever.

He leaned back, propping himself on his right elbow. In some ways, he seemed more at peace than I'd seen him before, yet his eyes still seem troubled as they flicked across the changing patterns of ripples in the pool. So much for time standing still.

Wrapping my arms around my knees, I introduced the subject yet again. "It's time you told me everything. I've gathered so many pieces to the puzzle that I can't make them fit, but I need to know. You can start with that conversation with Aunt Min."

His eyes met mine, and he studied me in that direct way he had, almost as if he could read my mind and my heart. With a shake of his head, he said, "That's probably a false trail. I had the names of the members of three pagan groups in this area, but Shane Winston isn't on the list. I hoped to make a connection there."

"Did you know about Winston already, before you talked to Aunt Min?"

"No, not at all. But, I did know about the sheep at that summer solstice. I vaguely recalled the story about some animal slayings several years back. I figured Minerva might know about it. She has the best memory of anyone I know. Anyway, I thought the animal rituals might be connected, and if I had a name I could associate with them, we'd have something to go on."

"We who?" I was more confused than ever.

"The Constable for Merionethshire, Tom Bowen, and myself—"

"Wait a minute," I interrupted. "You mean you're working with Bowen? I don't understand any of this. I think you'd better start at the beginning and tell me the whole story. Start with Sheila's death."

He slumped slightly, ordered his thoughts with a frown, and then began. "It starts before then. I believe the beginning was the sheep. I know you deduced from the conversation that the sheep were murdered in that stone ring above Harlech?"

I nodded. Yes, I figured out that much and I knew the German woman had been slain there. Even as I wondered if he knew about her, he went on.

"The sheep aren't the only victims. The following year, a French student disappeared. There was no trace of her, no clues as to what happened. The constables didn't see any connections to the sheep slayings other than she disappeared around June 21, summer solstice. Her family never heard anything about her after that.

"The next year, the summer before last, a German woman, Margretha Bokstein was visiting in Harlech. She met a man in a pagan cult and was attracted to him.

Apparently, being a romantic, she found him a most charming figure. Then she was found the morning after solstice in the same stone ring where the sheep had been sacrificed and in much the same way as the animal—a ritual murder, disemboweled and intestines spread across the ground."

I shuddered involuntarily. Even though I'd heard this from Louise, it was more horrifying listening to Owain's calm voice going over the details, giving more reality to the gruesome story that Louise had told.

He paused for a few moments. Now he stared at me and moved his hand to gently touch my hair and swallowed hard. "Last summer, the victim was Sheila. Although the method varied in that she drowned, there is more to it than that. From the bruises on her body, it looked like she had been pushed or pulled—possibly dragged—to her death. Bowen speculated she might have fallen from a high place, not along the shore at Harlech, and her body was carried to the sea and dumped from a boat."

His voice broke. He turned his head away from me so I wouldn't see the tears in his eyes. I waited in silence, knowing there was nothing I could do to ease his anguish although I rubbed my hand on his upper arm, offering comfort.

After a few moments, he spoke again, the strain evident in his voice. "She was wearing a scarlet robe with a mistletoe design interlaced around the neckline and hem. The mistletoe is a symbolic design for some Druid groups. There were traces of hemlock in her system. Not enough to kill her outright, but she was probably disoriented at that point. A symbol was cut into her right breast, a crude carving of a triskele. That's a round symbol with three-locking loops circling a central point. It was used as a decoration by the early Celtic tribes.

"Like the sacrifices the year before, this was obviously a ritual killing, but it didn't take the same aspects as the sheep and Margretha's death, so the authorities had nothing to link them together. Except for the date—the summer solstice."

"But surely they investigated?" I objected, horrified by this revelation.

He laughed bitterly. "Oh yes, they investigated. They talked to members of the various pagan groups. They found she was involved with McKay's group when she'd come north, but all of them swore she was alive and well after the ceremony." He stopped, took a deep breath, and met my eyes directly. "And they investigated me."

"Why?" I asked innocently. But I was now looking for the answers to the questions that had haunted me for the last two days.

As he shifted his position to sit up more, he looked pained by what he had to say. "I'm not untouched by these cults myself, Kathleen. A few years ago, I was an idealistic fool, a nationalist, and like many before me, I saw the pagans as part of my cultural heritage and got involved with one. It was a harmless show, and I quickly realized it was not really a representation of my culture. There's very little, if anything, in the modern services that were likely to have been part of the past. But for a short while, my name was part of a cult.

"So even though I haven't belonged for a long time, the fact that I did once, and that I studied and photographed pagan groups made me suspect. Then with Sheila being involved, it was easy to think that I had renewed my interest in it."

"But you hadn't?" I asked.

With a shake of his head, he continued, "Now, add to that a *witness*—"

He stressed the word indicating a distrust of the person as a reliable source, or at least, that's how I interpreted it.

"—who claims to have heard a motorboat on the night Sheila died. And where was I? On a bloody boat in the waters off St. Martin's and quite alone. I really was working on my assignment, adjusting photos, and planning my next shots. I was also taking some time for myself to get my thoughts together. Trying to work out my problems with Sheila so we could get back together. So, I spent three days on a boat with no witnesses."

When Owain looked at me again, his eyes grew wider and his brow furrowed as begged, "Please, believe me; I was nowhere near here when Sheila died. I had the devil of the time convincing the local constabulary I hadn't brought the boat north. I think the only reason they didn't arrest me was the lack of evidence. Still, the only person who didn't believe I killed her was Tom Bowen."

A lot had fallen into place now, past and present. Even the house in the South with its strange hill was most likely acquired during his interest in the pagan religion. "So how does that connect to Madlen?"

"At the time, I thought there was more involved in this than the killings. There's been some drug-running along the coast, and Porthmadog Bay is a likely spot to come ashore during the night for a drug exchange. Maddie worked for the organized crime unit in Cardiff, so I discussed it with her. We figured the murders might be a diversion for the drug running and the boat the witness heard could very well have been one leaving Porthmadog. So, she came here to investigate."

"This is really confusing. So, you suspect someone in one of the groups of being a murderer *and* a drug runner?",

He nodded. "I thought he would be connected with one of the pagan groups in this area. He has a sick mind, and he needs to be stopped before someone else is hurt or killed. Do you see now why I'm worried about you?"

"But I'm not involved with any pagan groups," I stated flatly. "Don't you see? Sheila was a member of the cult; so was the German lady. Quite probably, the French girl was as well. Maybe Madlen infiltrated the group and they learned about it, making her the next victim."

"You contacted McKay's group," he interrupted me to point out. "That's an involvement."

"You're reaching for it!" I snapped back. "Did it occur to you that your killer might be a loner? It may be a coincidence that Sheila was with McKay's group that night, then she met this other person, the murderer, later on."

Exasperated, he turned his head away from me, gnawing on his lower lip as he did so. He spoke tightly. "Yes. That did occur to me, but I can't find out anything! At least, not until now. This name is the first real lead I've gotten."

Suddenly, he turned to face me again, this time placing both hands on my shoulders. The look on his face said he would like to shake me until I came to my senses, but he just let his hands rest there. "I'm certain Tiernyon is the key. Either he is the killer, or he knows him and is part of it. Please, go away from here for a few days until this is over. Please."

I hugged him, pulling him closer. "My God, I love your concern about me! But don't worry. I'm perfectly safe. McKay's group is harmless. Besides, Toby is watching out for me."

"The blond fellow?"

"Uh-huh. He's a friend."

Owain's face looked solemn. "And you trust him?"

"Yes, of course," I replied quickly. "He's a kind, thoughtful person. He would never let anyone hurt me."

"Do you trust me?"

I hesitated. Lord knows why, but I did. Certainly, I trusted him, but there was still that doubt in my mind. The pause was long enough. He laughed sharply, dropped his hands from me, and sat back.

"And well you should not! Nor should you trust anyone you barely know. But, my love, you can trust me. I don't want anything to happen to you."

"You seem to be the only one in danger," I reminded him as I gently laid my hand on his arm just at the edge of the bandage. "How is your arm doing?"

"Sore, but I'm getting along well enough."

"Who shot you?"

He shook his head. "I honestly don't know. I think it might've been Tiernyon. I didn't see him, but I made some inquiries around town. I'd been at the stone ring a little earlier."

"What? I was there just before I found you."

From what he said, I must have missed him by perhaps no more than forty-five minutes, but he hadn't ventured off the path through the woods until he'd come to the hillside. He'd felt someone was following him, yet whenever he paused to look around, there was no one.

"You could have been killed," I said. "You still could be. Why don't you back off and let Constable Bowen handle this?"

"I'm safe enough," he answered stubbornly. "If he wanted me dead, I would be. I was an easy target on that hillside. No, it was just a warning. He didn't want me around. But it means I'm on the right track, and I have to make the connection before tomorrow night."

"Tomorrow night?"

"June 21st, summer solstice. Promise me you'll not do anything with anyone tomorrow night. You'll stay safely indoors." The urgency in his voice spoke to his fear of what might happen.

I almost told him McKay's group was having a solstice celebration this coming night, but I didn't. I figured if I told him, he would try to stop me from going. And I was determined to go. No harm could come to me with a group of people around and Toby watching out for me. I nodded and agreed I would stay at the hotel the following night.

He exhaled a shaky breath, the tension in him melting away as he cupped the back of my neck, drawing me toward him. His kiss found me, not in a rush, but with a reverence that made my pulse flutter—first, a soft brush against one eyelid, then the other, each touch a vow. His lips drifted to the bridge of my nose, following its path downward in tender, deliberate caresses until they finally met my mouth.

There, the softness vanished. His kiss deepened, hungry, raw, pulling an answering fire from me. He guided me backward until the cool stone cradled my head, then slid down beside me, gathering me into his arms. I curled into him instinctively, feeling the steady beat of his heart against my side.

Above us, the sun wheeled across the sky, casting shifting ribbons of light across the water — but the world beyond our small sanctuary faded. In that moment, the only journey we cared about was the one we made across each other's bodies, learning, lingering, daring more with every breathless second.

The world beyond the water waited, dangerous and unrelenting — but for now, we had carved out this one stolen moment, and neither of us dared to let go.

Chapter Twenty

"...tracking the legend through the highlands..."

*A*s Owain swung the BMW onto the side road, I jumped in surprise. I hadn't expected the sudden turn. He looked apologetic. "Sorry. That turn snuck up on me."

"I didn't even see it," I admitted. "Where are we heading?"

"Beddgelert. I just want to drive through and take a quick look around."

"Find Winston's old farm?"

He flashed a charming grin. "Clever girl."

We sped along a back road that barely allowed room for one car. I only hoped no traffic came at us from the other direction. At one point, we had a particularly clear view of the top of Snowdon and Owain pointed it out to me.

"The Welsh name is *Yr Wyddfa*. It means the barrow," he informed me.

"Well, that sounds prettier than Snowdon, but why call it a mound?" Gazing up at the heights of the mountain, at over 3560 feet, the tallest in southern Britain, I saw how it had acquired both names. Even now, a hint of snow glistened on the rounded top.

"It ties into the Arthurian legend. Mostly, the Welsh just call this whole area *Eryri*, our highlands."

Despite the narrow back road, we made good time to Beddgelert. As we came into the village, I caught my breath at the exquisite beauty of the town. Like Betws-y-Coed, it resembled a fairytale village adorned with a multitude of green-shaded trees and ferns. Picturesque stone arched bridges crossed the broad, shallow river that threaded through it. Astonished, I decided the whole of Wales must be an elaborately designed tourist park.

He stopped the car on the main street, turned off the ignition, but left the key. "I'll only be a couple of minutes. Wait here."

While he ran into the chemist's, I remained in the car and studied the shops along the streets. One of them bore a large sign with the word *Croeso* above an illustration of the Celtic cross in which a curved dog's body made a circle of the cross. *Croeso*, I knew, meant welcome, but I wondered about the cross design.

When he returned, nearly ten minutes later, I asked him about the sign. He glanced at it as he started the car, then laughed. "It's called Beddgelert's cross. That was the dog's name. There's an old legend about it. The dog saved a baby from a wolf, but when his master—legend claims Prince Llewellyn—came home, he saw blood everywhere and thought the dog had attacked the baby, so he killed the dog. Then he found the wolf's body and realized the dog killed the wolf and it was the wolf's blood, not the baby's that covered everything."

"Really?" I asked as he pointed the car out of town. I made a mental note to return and spend a lot more time in this quiet village.

He smiled. "I told you; it's a legend. But it adds a little glamour to the town, a bit of history, whether it's true or not. No one knows."

He shrugged. "The old Winston place is about five miles out. I don't imagine there's anything there, but I'd like to take a look."

I'd expected as much. He was determined to follow through on this scant lead. I asked, "Did anyone at the drugstore recall Shane Winston?"

"I talked to two people there who remembered the family, not the boy specifically except to say that he was an odd one."

As he had anticipated, there wasn't much to find at the farm. Deserted now, wild ferns and grasses had overtaken the land. He caught my hand as we walked out into the fields towards the old house. A line of trees that marked the slope of another hill bordered the few acres of open land where a half-dozen plump sheep grazed, paying no mind at all to us. We strolled a short way into the trees where he paused and gazed around the grove. He sighed in discouragement.

"There's really nothing here—" he started, then suddenly froze, his eyes narrowing and he let his breath out slowly.

"What is it?" I asked, alarmed by the look on his face.

He moved closer to one of the trees, reached to touch it. Coming up next to him, I saw the scarred carving in the trunk—rounded, with regular-shaped circles within the rondels linking around a central point. Methodically, he ran his fingers along the ridges of the carving.

Suddenly, I felt uneasy. "Owain? What is that?"

He stepped back, tore his eyes away from it. "It's a triskele—like the one carved on Sheila."

"Oh, my God!" I whispered, a prickle of alarm causing me to shudder. "You don't suppose?"

"It's a good possibility. Shane Winston just might be our man." He caught my arm again. "Come on. I want to see Tom Bowen now."

I turned with him, started to say, "it's about time," when Owain abruptly threw me to the ground at almost the same instant I heard a loud crack like the sound from a rifle being fired. Lying flat on the grass, the rich earthy smell of it practically shoved up my nose, I realized that he was sprawled half over me, protecting my body with his.

I drew my breath to speak, heard his insistent shushing hiss, and clamped my mouth shut. A few moments later, he raised his head up cautiously to look around. In the stillness of the woods, I heard the heaviness of his breathing, the fitful pounding of my own heart, and I was acutely aware of the lack of other sounds. Had it really been a rifle shot? Another warning?

Just as Owain started to lever himself off me, another crack echoed in the hills, more distant than before, and he burst into laughter and sat up. "Car backfiring!"

Relieved, I pulled myself into a sitting position and breathed deeply. Despite that knowledge, I was shaking, as was he and he winced, then rubbed at his sore arm.

"Are you all right?" I asked concerned that he'd hurt his arm again.

He nodded. "Just pulled it a bit. Let's go. I want to get out of here."

I understood that desire quite well. I didn't care much for the place either.

Within forty minutes, we'd come down Highway 496 and back to Porthmadog. From there it was a quick trip down the coast to Harlech.

Tom Bowen listened patiently as Owain related his story about Shane Winston and about the mark on the tree.

A few times, Bowen nodded his head, but he didn't speak until Owain had finished. "So, you think this Winston fellow is responsible for the murders, or at least Sheila's murder? And for the attempt on you as well?"

"Most likely," Owain replied. "It certainly seems to fit, don't you think?"

"Not a stray bullet from a hunter anymore, then?" Bowen commented dryly, refusing to agree with him.

My man was losing patience. "Are you going to help me or not, Tom?"

The Constable motioned for him to calm down. "I'll do what I can, but you know it's a long shot. I haven't heard of anyone by that name in this area. However, I'll put it out on the wire. Now, don't go charging off on your own again."

"And tomorrow night?" he asked caustically.

"We're all set. If anyone uses that dance tomorrow night, we'll catch them." Bowen thumped the top of his desk to emphasize his words.

"I'm going with you, Tom."

Bowen was quiet voiced but firm. "We've been through this already. It's police business. You stay out of it."

Owain's face clouded, his green eyes turning hard, and he muttered something in Welsh to which Bowen replied in that same language. Even though the Constable had spoken in his usual soft tones, the disapproval rang clear.

"Come on, Kathleen," Owain ordered as he whirled around and stormed out the door without waiting for me.

I cast a hasty glance at Bowen, who shrugged indifferently. "He'll get over it."

I ran to catch up with Owain.

He was already in the car; his head slumped against his arm on the steering wheel. He straightened up when I got in, but he didn't look at me. His face was pale with tension and anger. By the time we reached the hotel parking lot, Owain was biting his lip against the pain.

"What am I going to do with you?" I asked, concern showing itself as exasperation.

He glanced at me without replying.

Shaking my head, I added, in a gentler tone, "Come on. Let's get you upstairs."

Once I got him into bed, yet again, I examined his arm as I changed the bandage to make sure he hadn't pulled any stitches. Bruised and swollen, it looked painful but intact, so I carefully redressed it. I sat by him, massaging his neck and shoulder muscles while he swallowed a pain pill.

"You've really got to rest more," I said firmly. I rubbed my thumb against a hard knot in his shoulder muscle.

"I can't until this is settled," he objected. "There isn't much time now, and I've got to find Tiernyon or Winston or whatever his name is."

"Well, you can't do it if you fall flat on your face," I stated emphatically. "Besides, Bowen told you to stay out of it. Let him take care of it; it's his job."

"Kathleen! I thought you understood—"

"I do understand, but there's only so much you can do. Now, you rest, or I'll take you to the nearest hospital where you won't have a choice. What good are you going to be if you collapse?"

That got through a bit. He frowned, frustration evident on his face, but he agreed, more or less.

I closed the curtains, kissed him once more, and slipped out of the room to let him sleep. As I pulled the door shut behind me, I reflected that this was the third time in two days I'd tried to get him to stay in bed.

Owain Thomas was undeniably a stubborn man.

Chapter Twenty-One

"... dancing in the moon's light..."

*P*acing around the patio of the hotel, I waited for Toby to come for me. He'd said seven-thirty and been clear I should meet him there instead of inside. I hadn't asked why, but now I wondered if I'd heard him correctly.

In the meantime, I'd had too much time to think about the events of the day and of Owain's warning to me. While I had no hesitation at all about attending the ceremony, it nonetheless made me nervous knowing that he would not be pleased when he found out I'd gone anyway.

It did occur to me that attending the ceremony might provide the opportunity to observe the rest of the members of this particular pagan group. If Owain was correct in his theory that Tiernyon was associated with one, then perhaps I might notice someone who could be a likely suspect.

With such thoughts in mind, I greeted Toby enthusiastically as he came up the steps from the car park. "I thought you'd be here earlier. I've been worrying for the last twenty minutes that you'd forgotten."

Laughing, he caught my hands, then stepped back to look me over. "How could I forget ya, Kat'leen? Not ever. But the ceremony doesn't start until sunset, so we have plenty of time."

I noticed the way his eyes ran over my clothes. I had put on a plain light blue cotton dress, the simplest one I had with me, and I hoped it was appropriate for the ceremony. Now, seeing the almost frown on his face, I was worried it wouldn't do. "Is this all right?"

"For now," he said. "But let's get going."

As I picked up my handbag and sweater, I noticed Sarah Linton watching from the door to the patio. How long had she been there? It might have been my imagination, but I thought I saw a frown of disapproval on her face. I shrugged it off and took Toby's hand as he led the way.

He'd borrowed a car for the evening, an old blue Ford Escort, but it was clean and had been recently washed. With a flourish, he proudly held the door for me. As I climbed in, I reflected that being with him made me feel like a high school sophomore on her first date. He had that kind of charm about him.

Yet, for all this feeling of recaptured youth with Toby, I preferred the seriousness of Owain. The guilt I felt for a few moments as he pointed the car southward was not just that I was sneaking off to witness the pagan ritual, but that I was going with another man. Telling myself that Owain and I had no commitment didn't alleviate the guilt.

If I'd ever ordered up a perfect summer evening, this one was it. The pale orange ball of the sun hovered on the horizon of the sea seeming reluctant to leave the sky. Casting its rays of golden light across the surface of Cardigan Bay, they reflected mirror-like in the calm waters.

From the point just above the Dyffryn Cairns, the view was spectacular. I shivered in anticipation of the celebration to come. For all my Christian upbringing, thinking about the quaint pageantry of a Druidic ritual

220

excited me. That the ceremony might have had its roots in ancient sacrificial worship was inconsequential at this moment.

Gently, hesitant to break into my enjoyment of the evening, Toby touched my hand and urged me to continue up the hill with him. He carried a bundle under his arm; a bulky, paper-wrapped parcel that he'd said contained a surprise for me. He stubbornly wouldn't reveal its contents and told me I would have to wait until we were at the grove of trees where the Celtic man-stone stood.

With a lingering gaze at the glimmering water, I turned to follow him on up. We came to the copse of trees at the top of the hill. Behind us, I heard footfalls on the ground and glanced back to where a young girl and a man who looked to be in his early twenties followed, hurrying up the incline. They both wore white robes, tied at the waist with blue and gold braided cord belts. They smiled and waved at Toby before veering to the south to approach the man-stone more directly.

Toby guided me into the line of trees, then stopped, set the bundle on the ground, and opened it. White material showed through the opening. He picked up a corner, lifted the fabric up, then held it out to me. "I thought this would be more appropriate tonight. Then you won't feel out of place."

Once he lifted the garment, I saw a long white gauzy gown with fabric flowers around the neckline and the bells of the sleeves. "It's beautiful, Toby. Are you sure I should wear it?"

"Absolutely. Go ahead and put it on."

In delight, I reached for the gown, noticing another white fabric in the package, and asked, "Yours?"

"Yes, a Druid's robe. I'm still lower-ranked, but I am one of the officiating Druids." He lifted the garment and held it up to display before me. Much like mine, it was a simple design with a border of intricate interlace at the neckline worked in red and blue threads. In the center of the breast was a large round circle with three interlaced knots worked around a central hub. Again, the Celtic tradition of the power of three showed in the design.

Having displayed the robe for me, he again encouraged me to put the gown on. "You can change in that thicket of shrubs," he said and pointed the way to the curtain of tall bushes that were at the edge of the grove.

Within a few minutes, I'd stripped off the blue dress and donned the lovely gown. It fit loosely, the long sleeves draping freely. The low-cut neckline barely covered the tops of my shoulders. Toby had included a blue and gold interlaced macramé belt that wrapped around my waist, then tied with six long strands of cord to hang elegantly down the front. I felt like a medieval princess regally clad for the ball. Satisfied with the fit, I made a bundle of my blue dress and returned to where I'd left Toby.

He had changed as well and now looked official in his Druid's robe. The leather belt around his waist bore an intricate interlaced pattern tooled into it. Securing it, he used a silvery buckle, comprised of a knot of intertwining dragons trying to swallow each other's tails. It was very old looking, but when I commented on it, Toby said, "It's a reproduction of an ancient cloak clasp. The original would be very valuable, but this only cost a few quid."

He paused, studied me a few moments, then grinned his approval. "You look lovely, Kat'leen. There's only one more thing needed."

He bent again to the bag and pulled out a band of flowers—roses, daisies and Sweet William, mixed with green leaves. Stepping close to me, he placed it on my head. The mixed scent of the flowers teased my senses with a bouquet of early summer fragrances, pleasant and sweet.

"Now, you are perfect," he declared. "You have the beauty and bearing of the goddess Rhiannon."

With a bit of hesitation, I smiled shyly and dropped a small curtsy. "Thank you, my lord."

With a flourish, Toby looped his arm around mine to escort me to the gathering at the man-stone. As we walked ceremoniously up the path, he spoke quietly. "Now, most of the ceremony will be in Welsh so you won't understand the words, but I'll explain it afterward.

"There are five basic parts to the ceremony. First will be the gathering chant when all the celebrants come together in the grove. Second, there will be the opening prayer to the goddess followed by the young maidens' dance. Next will be the Invocation of Peace with the head Druid asking the powers to bring peace and harmony to the world, and the congregation will join in with a song."

He paused and stopped our progress as he faced me, his eyes intent. "Now, the fourth part is the naming rite at which new members are given their personal names. These are the power names and are always very secret, so you won't hear any of them spoken out. The head druid whispers the name only to the recipient. The last phase is a symbolic sacrifice into the fire and accompanying dance."

I nodded thinking it really didn't sound like much, and I had to remind myself that the rite was symbolic and as sacred to these people as Christian ritual was to me. When we stepped to the edge of the clearing, I saw the little grove had taken on different trappings for the evening.

The man-stone was draped in a white robe and crown with a berry leaf garland giving it a more human appearance, yet the carved face retained the cruel expression of an ancient warrior gazing in defiance over the clearing. Each of the surrounding border trees displayed banners with ancient symbols appliquéd on them. Wishing I could photograph them, I tried to memorize the images and guessed the symbols represented various deities of the religion.

In the center, the fire ring held a timber structure built up within the confines of the stones. At the top, a small wooden casket engulfed with flowers waited for the final part of the ceremony. Around the edge of the fire pit, about a dozen reed torches, unlit, leaned against the stones.

As I started to step into the clearing, Toby caught my arm. "Wait," he said softly. "It is not yet the moment."

Puzzled, my eyes darted toward him and noted the intent expression on his face. His lively blue eyes flicked around the edges of the clearing, then back to the man-stone. What was he waiting for? Though I wondered, I remained silent and waited for his approval to move.

As if a signal had been given, the chant began, a rhythmic stirring of unintelligible words that were repeated over and over. What started with perhaps only a dozen voices, Toby's included, began to grow as other voices joined in. Still, no one moved, no figures entered the clearing. As the chant grew louder, it filled the grove, echoing in the hills until it seemed as if hundreds of voices were repeating the words.

Then from the trees behind the man-stone, the High Druid stepped into the circle, positioning himself dramatically, just in front of the Neolithic rock. As I stared at the alien-looking figure, dressed in a green robe similar to Toby's, I found it difficult to believe he was the kind Scotsman I'd spoken to a couple of days earlier. The ornate headdress, a metallic-looking corona, he wore wholly covered his skull, pulling his eyes tightly and giving them a slanted look. Below his head, a vast starburst metal collar engulfed his neck and shoulders tying the solar image together. Below that, he wore a breastplate with intertwined golden dragons enameled on it.

McKay, or rather, Gwyerion in this guise, wore a broadsword at his hip and carried a gold scepter topped with a ruby-colored stone in his right hand. Raising the rod before him, he grasped the free end with his other hand and lifted it horizontally over his head. Taking a deep breath that lifted the breastplate and collar visibly, Gwyerion called out a word in Welsh. It was not one of the dozen or so, I recognized.

I felt Toby's hand on my arm, and I reluctantly tore my gaze from Gwyerion to glance at him.

"Wait," he mouthed then stepped into the circle at the same time as another druid, dressed in the same manner as Toby, entered from about half-way along the ring of trees on the opposite side. Still chanting, each took their places, one on either side of the High Druid and the triad was complete. Gwyerion lowered his scepter, a clear signal for the rest of the congregation to begin assembling.

Echoes of the Past

They came out of the trees, wraith-like, materializing where I had not seen any indication anyone was there. They came alone or in pairs, each taking his or her place around the clearing until it almost filled with worshipers except for the center around the fire ring. All wore gowns or loose tunics of white, yellow, or green. Once everyone came out, I stepped forward to stand at the back, still at the edge of the trees, where I could observe the ceremony without drawing attention.

At a unseen signal, the chanting stopped leaving a stillness in the grove that felt eerie. For a few moments, time seemed to suspend when I heard no sound at all— not a bird's voice or even a whisper of a breeze through the foliage. A shiver of anticipation raced through my spine, and I held my breath.

Floating through the silence, a woman's soft voice sang in a crystalline soprano, the Welsh words sounding mystical. One by one, more female voices joined in.

As the music grew and changed tempo, several young girls, possibly pre-teens, for they were smaller than the average fourteen-year-old was, stepped into the ring of space around the fire. They danced in a counterclockwise circle with joyful steps and graceful turns. As they whirled, their simple white gowns, unadorned except for sky blue cord ropes circling their waists, flowed out giving the illusion of blossoming flowers.

When the singers came to the chorus of the song, the familiarity of the tune clicked in my brain and, in the rhythm of the words, I recognized a song I'd sung as a girl but had not quite heard with this melody.

I knew it as "Simple Gifts," but I'd also heard it as "Lord of the Dance." My mind supplied the English words. I'd often heard a Christian version, but at this moment, the pagan words I'd learned from a friend held more meaning.

With the sun nearly gone from the sky and the twilight shadows already falling on the hills of North Wales, the ceremony and worship seemed as if they'd arrived through a time portal from the past. Along with the thought came a vision of the portal dolmens at the burial cairns below us. Curiously, I wondered if psychologically, they were indeed a portal to the age that created them. Would these people be out on this hillside celebrating on archaic religion if those relics of Neolithic times and a pagan ancestry were not in such evidence around them?

A few words came unbidden into my mind, but the rest were unremembered fragments as the voices continued to sing the verse in the hauntingly melodic Welsh language. The hairs on my neck prickled with a chill of the unknown as if something quite unearthly was happening here.

As the song ended, the dancing ceased, and each of the girls picked up a torch from the edge of the fire pit before approaching Gwyerion. With the dim light in the clearing, I couldn't see any details, but as each girl held the torch to the druid, it burst into flame with the spark appearing to come from his fingertips.

A trick, surely, perhaps a small lighter in his fingers? One by one, as the torches sparked to life, the girls retreated to the back and assembled at stations next to each of the banner-draped trees.

Once they were in position, Gwyerion began to speak again. This must be the prayer for peace, I thought, as I took the time to let my gaze wander across the faces of the gathered worshipers. Perhaps fifty or more of them, they ranged in age from small children of five or six to old people, gray-haired and bent. Rapture and enchantment played across some faces while others seemed bored or disinterested. Some, like me, might have found it curious and witnessed the ceremony with a touch of cynicism. They would probably be dropouts as Owain Thomas was, yet most were clearly devoted members of this group. They were ordinary faces; men, women, boys, girls, who, for the most part, bore the facial features and coloring of the local area.

I worked my way quietly around the edge of the circle to see as many people as possible, looking for a face that seemed sinister among this gathering of fifty-plus people. Surprisingly, I spotted two familiar faces, Margaret Hale and Freda Weintraub, the two ladies who were staying only a couple of nights at Harlech on their way to the north.

How odd they should join in the celebration. It crossed my mind that perhaps those two tied in with Tiernyon, then almost laughed out loud at my own suspicions. Like most of these people, they were merely innocent worshipers, two more people who paid homage to the old gods and were no more sinister than the young girls dancing around the fire. Realizing I'd let Owain's words influence my thinking, I set my amateur sleuthing aside.

While I studied the congregation, the ceremonies moved into yet another phase as seven of the gathering came forward to stand in a circle around the pyre. One by one, Gwyerion summoned them to him, and they came escorted by either Toby or the other druid. Each stood a few moments before Gwyerion, long enough for an exchange of words, which no one could hear, then returned to the circle.

The naming ceremony, a symbolic version of the ancient ritual, I surmised. As McKay had explained when

228

I'd spoken to him earlier, no one could really be sure of what took place in those earlier Celtic rites, and this was a modern guess at what might have occurred. The one thing that was certain was that it was a very private ceremony and only for those involved. In fact, I found this part a bit boring since it was an intimate occasion for those seven people and tended to ignore the rest of the gathering.

But if I found it dull, it was clear from the expressions on the faces of most of the watchers they did not. Eyes were intense, even misty, as they witness this individual moment for each of the initiates. Perhaps for some, it was the vivid memory of their own special moment or, for others, the anticipation of that time to come for them.

I felt apart from those around me, clearly an outsider in this world. It seemed theatrical, a moment in a bizarre play and very much an alien scene to my reality. A shiver of unease caused me to shake despite the warmth of my gown. I found myself considering both Toby and Owain in a different light.

Until this moment, I had an image of Toby as an innocent, yet he clearly had some experiences and diversions outside the norm. Nothing was wrong with that, I assured myself; however, I wondered what had occurred in his life that had led him to this worship.

Whatever had summoned Owain to—what had he said? A mistaken belief that it would recapture his Welsh roots? —he'd turned away from it. Yet Sheila had found something in it, just as these people did, something that Christianity, or any of the more conventional religions, did not seem to provide.

The last of the newly named members resumed their places in the semi-circle before Gwyerion raised his staff above his head and spoke with power, his voice filling the forest. The words seem terribly ancient, archaic even for Welsh.

"Oh, great God of my fathers, see these newly born before you and grant them your protection and power."

Startled to hear the words in English at my ear, I turned sharply to discover Toby standing next to me. I'd not noticed him move away from his place near Gwyerion. He wasn't looking at me, but he continued to translate the words.

"Let no others know the names of power and let no one invoke them without your divine protection. Your power protects; your power preserves."

The congregation picked up these last words and repeated them several times, the sound building in strength to ring like a choir on a hillside Cathedral. At last, Gwyerion lowered his scepter, and the chanting ceased abruptly, with only an echo of the voices reverberating through the hills for a few moments.

In the absence of sound, a strange serenity settled on the hillside giving a feeling of unity with the earth. In what seemed to be slow motion, Gwyerion reached for a torch from the maiden standing nearest to him.

Holding it aloft, the High Druid marched languidly around the circle, allowing the glow to reflect off the faces of the worshipers before he stopped in front of the wooden pyre within the fire pit. Again, he spoke the ritual words in Welsh following them with a dramatic flourish of his arm as he plunged the torch into the heart of the pyre.

Instantly, the wood flared up, dry branches within the timber cage catching swiftly and leaping upward to set the sturdier pieces aflame. Within a few minutes, it was a roaring bonfire. Moving in an east to west circle, the congregation approached the fire, tossing their offerings into the reddish-gold inferno. Without variation, the sacrifices consisted of plants, flowers, and nuts. Those wearing garlands of flowers tossed the whole strands into the flames.

Caught up in the pageantry with Toby still at my elbow, I followed behind the others and lifted the wreath from my hair. As I started to toss it into the fire, Toby's hand caught my arm, grasping it firmly just above the elbow. Uncertain of his action, I shifted my eyes to meet his, a moment of fear tweaking my stomach, but he only slid his hand down my arm to touch the garland.

He murmured something in Welsh, the only word of which I recognized as "Rhiannon." With a nod, he indicated I should now toss it.

A moment later, the vibrant flowers danced like small fairies in the flames for an instant before they plunged into the pyre's furiously burning core to be devoured. Startled by my perception, I shuddered.

Toby's hand shifted back up my arm as he guided me away from the central ring towards the trees surrounding the clearing. "You did well. The goddess accepted your offering."

I frowned, feeling the tightness in my face, as I heard his words.

The *goddess accepted* it? What did he mean?

Chapter Twenty-Two

"...learning the desires of the gods..."

To my astonishment, I discovered most of the gathering had dispersed, vanishing as quietly as they came and only a few people besides Toby, Gwyerion, and I remained. Toby pulled my hand to lead me away from the clearing, into the woods, and through the trees towards higher ground.

Still under the spell of the last ceremony, I spoke softly, afraid my voice might carry. "What was that last bit about? Why did you touch my garland also?"

"You're not a member of our group, so I wanted to add my power to the offering for the goddess to accept it." He spoke matter-of-factly as if he honestly believed it made a difference. If it hadn't been for the earnest look in his eyes, I might very well have laughed at such a preposterous statement. As it was, I smiled in amusement, but he took it as acceptance.

"The gods would welcome you anyway," he added. "You're really one of us, you know."

"What's the significance of the flowers and the fire?" I asked, ignoring his suggestion that I was a part of this group.

"At these rites, it's customary to make an offering to the gods—most especially at this time of year to Morrigan, the goddess of the Earth and fertility. The flowers are symbolic, a substitute for other living things. In ancient times, a sacrifice would have taken place, usually an animal—although sometimes humans were used, particularly when a God needed to be appeased or especially honored."

"That's barbaric!" I blurted out. "How could killing some poor animal, or worse yet, a person, have any effect on a god's ego?"

Toby's eyes narrowed. "But it does, my lovely one. I know it does. The gods give many blessings to those who worship and respect them."

His face moved closer to mine, his hand circling my neck to pull me into his kiss. Not a passionate kiss, his mouth brushed dryly against my lips.

"You are lovely, my dear Rhiannon," he whispered as he pulled back, still holding my hand.

"Why do you call me that? I'm hardly worthy of the name." Even if he was teasing, I found it disconcerting that he referred to me by a goddess's name.

He seemed quite caught up in the theatrics of the evening, but it made me nervous. This was not the same person I'd been out with before. I started to walk again, wanting to head back down to the town, and he fell in beside me, his hand firmly grasping mine.

To break the awkward silence and because his whole story nagged at me more than ever, I said, "Toby, do you remember when you were telling me about that girl you loved, the Irish one?"

He nodded.

"You said she left you to go to her lover. Did you actually see him?"

"Of course," he said without hesitation.

"Could you identify him? Did you see him clearly enough to recognize him?" I felt a touch of excitement as well as dread as I asked the question. What if it really had been Owain?

Toby looked at me, a peculiar look on his face, and his eyes seemed to search mine. "Oh, yes, Rhiannon. I know him. He came to get what was his. and I could not prevent it. It was ordained, you see. He came from the ocean for her, a god rising from the sea on magnificent foaming steeds."

"God?" I asked, choking on the word as the unsettling feeling of apprehension built in me. Was he still relating things to this imaginative ceremony? My mind refused to consider any other possibility at this point. "You mean her fiancé?"

Toby grinned, a reverent look shading his eyes. "Oh, no. Her lover, her lord, came for her—Lir, the God of the Sea to whom she was dedicated."

"You mean she was sacrificed?" I sputtered. My throat went dry as I began to absorb what he was saying.

With a gentle shake of his head, Toby touched my cheek and snaked his other arm around my waist. "She wasn't sacrificed. She was elevated to a higher level, taken by a god. And in gratitude, Lir gave me power and strength."

His arm tightened to hold me against him as he continued. "And you, my dear Rhiannon, loveliest of all goddesses, belong with the greatest God of all, with Llew as his partner."

My mouth completely dry now, I croaked out, "You want to offer me to a god, Tiernyon? It is Tiernyon, isn't it?"

The ugly grin spread across his face as his eyes narrowed. "It's one of my names. I suppose Owain Thomas told you that. But I am more than Tiernyon. Like Cernunnos, I am the Hunter. Because I serve the gods, they reward me."

"But— But haven't you already sacrificed that woman on the beach? Wasn't she killed the same way as

Shiela?" Even though it hadn't been the solstice, I'd thought Madlen had become the victim for the year.

Toby sounded amused and irritated at the same time as he replied, "The cop? No, of course not. She was not worthy. But she meant trouble and needed to be silenced. Just another drowning victim."

So, Madlen had discovered the truth, and he'd killed her. A dam of comprehension broke in me, flooding my thoughts with the proof before me.

Though it seemed impossible that sweet, simple Toby could be the monster we'd been hunting, his dangerous side had become terrifyingly real. His grip tightened on my arm as I struggled to pull away, and I screamed—raw and loud, desperate for someone, anyone, to hear. I prayed the whole cult wasn't as crazed as Toby Morgan.

At the sound of my scream, he lunged to muffle me. I twisted, ducking my head and jerking side to side, dodging his grasp. His fingers slipped at my waist, and I seized the moment—kicking hard. My foot struck his legs, landing solid hits, but he barely flinched.

Again, he reached for my mouth, and this time I bit him—hard. My teeth clamped down on his hand as I jabbed wildly with fists and elbows, hitting anything I could reach. His grunts of pain told me I'd found my mark.

My right elbow slammed into his gut. His grip slackened.

I shoved him with everything I had and sprinted uphill. Another scream ripped from my throat, but mostly I focused on running. On surviving.

Behind me, twigs snapped and earth thudded under pounding feet—he was chasing me. I veered into a thicket of trees, branches lashing at my arms. Risking a glance back, I spotted him—white robe catching moonlight, a glint of metal flashing in his hand.

His knife. The ritual blade.

Panic surged. I pushed harder, darting toward deeper cover. My lungs burned. My side ached. The initial burst of adrenaline had begun to fade, leaving me heavy-legged and breathless.

Then—my foot snagged on a root. I crashed to my knees with a cry, sharp pain radiating from where I struck a jagged stone. But the scrape didn't matter. I scrambled up, limping, hand braced against trunks as I staggered forward.

Too late.

With a crashing burst of motion, Toby caught up and hurled himself at me. I went down hard again, the impact jolting through me. I twisted onto my back and cocked my fist, ready to strike.

But he was faster.

Toby pinned me, one hand slamming over my mouth. I braced for madness in his eyes—some feral glint of the monster he'd become.

Instead, his face was eerily calm.

Tender, almost.

Like a hunter admiring a captured fox. That was the worst part. The boy who'd once taken me on a picnic in the hills now looked down at me like I was his prize.

And still, he wore the same gentle smile.

That quiet composure made the moment feel unreal—like a dream I couldn't wake from.

"It's all right, Rhiannon," he whispered, his voice soft, almost paternal. "There's nothing to fear. Tonight, you take your place by Llew's side. You'll be worshiped as a goddess. You'll enter the High Kingdom. It's your destiny. I knew it the moment I saw you. You understand that, don't you?"

I should have been terrified. I should have screamed again. But that surreal calm was disorienting, like I was watching it all from somewhere outside my body. I nodded, dazed and silent, like a stunned animal.

"Good girl," he said, soothingly. "Now, if you stay quiet, I'll take my hand away. No screaming. I'll be gentle. You won't feel a thing."

He spoke as if promising pleasure, not death. So calm. So reasonable.

Why hadn't I listened to Owain?

Don't trust anyone, he'd said.

And like a fool, I'd trusted Toby.

If no one had heard my screams, I'd never get to tell Owain he'd been right. Still playing along, I nodded again.

Toby slowly lifted his hand, hovering it just inches from my face, ready to clamp it back if I made a sound. My lips were cracked with dryness, my throat raw.

"So... you gain more power now, Tiernyon," I said at last, surprised at how steady my voice sounded. "The gods must be grateful."

His smug smile stretched wider. "Most assuredly. It's been far too long since they were shown proper respect. With every offering, my strength grows. I am the vessel of their will. And Llew—he required something special. Someone with spirit. With beauty. A true Rhiannon."

"Then you've made a mistake," I said, keeping my tone even. Maybe I could still stall him, use his beliefs against him. "I'm not her. I'm not special. Rhiannon was life itself, the essence of the Earth. No human could come close. To pretend otherwise is sacrilege. It will anger Llew."

His fingers stroked my hair, dirt-streaked strands tangled around his knuckles as he stared with sick reverence.

"That's true, to a point," he murmured. "But Rhiannon *will* possess you. She chose you. She speaks to me—I'm her Hunter. I serve her, and I bring her what she asks. You."

His hand tightened on the knife.

"The blade is sharp. You won't feel a thing. In moments, you'll be in the Otherworld."

Like hell.

I gathered my strength, ready to strike, to kick, to claw—anything.

Then, from the trees—

A shout.

My name.

A voice I knew. A voice that cut through the horror and the haze like a lifeline.

Help had come.

"Owain! Here—" I shouted, my voice ragged with panic.

Toby's hand lunged to silence me, but I jerked my head aside just in time. His palm caught only part of my mouth. I sank my teeth into the fleshy pad beneath his thumb—biting down with everything I had.

He howled and wrenched his hand free, glaring at me. The knife rose high in his other hand, catching the moonlight like an omen. My eyes locked on the blade, and a new terror surged through me. But Owain's voice—closer now—cut through the fear like lightning through fog.

"Kathleen!" he called again.

Fueled by the sound of him, I twisted and shoved, kicking wildly. I bucked Toby off-balance and scrambled to my feet. He was behind me—I could feel him there, a beast breathing down my spine. I didn't dare look back.

Then his fingers clamped around my ankle.

I kicked backward instinctively—wrong move. He seized my leg and yanked hard, dragging me toward him.

I twisted around just in time to see a shadow arc through the air—Owain.

He collided with Toby in a blur of motion, knocking him off me with brutal force.

I didn't wait to see more. Crawling like a wounded animal, I dragged myself to the nearest tree, arms clutching the rough trunk for support. My breath came in gasps. I was covered in grass stains and dirt, my white gown ripped in half a dozen places. I stared dumbly at the damage, disbelieving it all—until I heard the grunts and struggle behind me.

Owain and Toby were locked in a desperate fight, tangled on the forest floor. Owain wrestled for the knife, fingers locked around Toby's wrist. But Toby was stronger now, driven by something savage. He slammed his knee into Owain's stomach, knocking him backward against a tree trunk with a sickening thud.

I flinched at the impact. My own breath caught in sympathy—then horror—as I saw the glint of the raised blade.

"**No!**" I screamed as Toby plunged it down.

Owain twisted at the last moment, and I couldn't tell if the knife had hit or missed—but it was enough to snap me out of my frozen shock. He was losing. If I didn't act, he'd die.

Frantically, I scanned the forest floor for anything I could use. Twigs and brush were useless—but then I spotted it: a stone, the size of a football, half-buried in the earth.

I lunged for it, fingers clawing at the dirt, breaking nails in my desperation. It was heavier than it looked, but adrenaline gave me the strength I needed. Behind me, Owain cried out in pain again.

I rose, staggering toward them with the stone gripped tight in both hands.

The knife was gone, but Toby was still on top, slamming punches into Owain's side and gut. Owain jerked with each blow, trying to fight back, but Toby was relentless.

He turned to search for the knife again—his mistake.

I raised the stone and hurled both it and myself at him.

The rock grazed his head, and my body slammed into his side. He collapsed beneath me, dazed. I landed hard on top of him and, with a cry, began pounding my fists against him, no longer caring where I hit or how badly it hurt.

I drew back for another strike—when a voice cut through the madness.

"No! You don't need to do that, lassie."

McKay's hands caught my arm, then wrapped around me, lifting me off Toby's back. For one panicked heartbeat, I thought he might be another threat.

But the way Toby reacted erased all doubt.

Snarling, Toby shoved us both aside. I was so weak, it barely took effort to send me sprawling. McKay stumbled to one knee beside me.

Then came another shout—someone crashing through the brush.

Toby turned to flee, panic now overriding ritual.

But he didn't make it.

240

From the side, Owain launched himself like a panther, rising into a perfect arc before his arms clamped around Toby's legs. The two of them hit the ground hard—and this time, Toby didn't get back up.

Both men crashed to the forest floor with loud grunts and cries. Even as Toby twisted, trying to kick free, Constable Bowen burst onto the scene, a heavy club gripped in his hand.

Toby's eyes widened as he saw the constable charging. With one last desperate effort, he kicked savagely at Owain's injured shoulder.

Owain's sharp yelp made me flinch—but even in pain, he refused to release his grip.

Bowen reached them in two strides, straddled Toby's back, and raised the club high, ready to strike. Only then did Toby freeze, his body going rigid beneath the threat.

With rough efficiency, Bowen yanked Toby upright and snapped handcuffs around his wrists. He shoved him aside with a snarl of disgust, then turned worriedly to Owain.

"You all right?"

Owain managed to roll onto his back, nodding weakly. I stumbled to him on legs that barely held me and dropped down beside him.

"Toby is Tiernyon!" I blurted out, breathless and dazed.

A look of weary amazement crossed his face before he rasped out, "Figured that much. Told you not to trust him."

Rely on Owain to get an *I-told-you-so* in, even now.

Annoyance flared—then vanished in a rush of gratitude when he groaned trying to sit up. I slid an arm carefully around his shoulders and felt the damp stickiness soaking through his shirt.

"Oh, crap—you're bleeding again!"

He grimaced, leaning against me. "Think I pulled a stitch or two loose."

It was stupid, reckless even, but I couldn't help myself. I hugged him tightly—enough to make him wince—and planted a hard, grateful kiss on his mouth. His body tensed with pain, but he said nothing, just wrapped his good arm around me and squeezed my shoulder in return.

Hot tears spilled down my cheeks as I pressed my face against his shoulder, breathing him in, needing the solidity of him to anchor me.

At last, pulling back, I looked at him: dirt-streaked face, messy hair, torn clothes. God, I loved him.

"You're wonderful," I whispered hoarsely. "But you're a mess."

He barked a rough, broken laugh. "You're not exactly tidy yourself, my lady."

"Need a hand?" a voice asked behind us.

Startled, I turned and remembered McKay—still standing nearby, watching everything with a faint grin.

I smiled sheepishly and looked back to Owain. "You can help me get him to his feet," I said, offering my hand.

Between the two of us, we managed to lever Owain upright, though he protested every inch of the way that he was fine. McKay chuckled under his breath at my fussing as I checked Owain's shoulder in the faint moonlight.

"Well, you both seem to be managing," McKay said. "I'll go down and see what the constable's done with young Toby Morgan."

"Locked him away, I hope," I muttered as McKay vanished into the trees.

I turned back to Owain, studying his pale, pinched face in the silvered light—and for the first time, doubt gnawed at me. Would I really be able to manage him if he collapsed again? Was this nightmare *truly* over?

As if reading my mind, Owain brushed my hair gently back from my face, kissed my forehead, and murmured, "I'm all right, Kathleen. It's over now."

I nodded and pressed myself against his side, steadying both of us. His arm dropped heavily across my shoulders as we started down the hill together.

Over. Finally over.

The realization made me almost giddy, like I could laugh or cry—or both. In fact, I started to giggle, shaky and half-hysterical.

Then, all at once, my knees buckled. The world tilted sharply—

Owain's arm tightened around me just as everything went black.

The last thing I felt was the strength of his arms, and the last thing I heard was his whisper: "I've got you."

Chapter Twenty-Three

"... the joy of sweet rebirth..."

Constrained—I hadn't escaped at all.

He came toward me, a dark shape drifting across the circle like a shadow come alive. I struggled, arms bound, fighting the ropes that bit into my wrists. I squeezed my eyes shut, but when I opened them again—

Toby's face loomed, twisted and contorted like a beast from some ancient nightmare. His mouth opened in a gaping snarl, and long, curved fangs jutted down like wolfish canines. On his head—

Antlers.

Not worn. Grown.

Stag's antlers erupted from his skull, and his grip turned vice-like on my arms as I screamed—

"Kathleen! It's all right, my love. It's all right."

Not Toby's voice.

And the arms holding me were warm, strong, and familiar—not the ones from my dream.

I peeled open my eyes. Light green irises swam into view, gazing at me with fierce concern. Owain.

I was lying on the ground, cradled against him, his good arm propping me upright while his other hand stroked my hair. A sliver of moon now crept through the trees, giving the world a silver glow. It hadn't been long—but long enough for fear to root deep.

244

"Are you okay?" he asked, his voice low.

"I— I think so. I've never fainted before." My voice came out cracked and raw. "I had a nightmare. About Toby. It was— He— That wasn't real, right?"

Owain shook his head. "He's gone. Taken away. He won't hurt you again."

I reached for him, burying myself in the circle of his embrace. His hand threaded through my hair. His lips touched my forehead, my eyelids—soft, loving, calming. Then he kissed me deeply, and I clung to him, every nerve still raw, but grateful—so grateful—to be alive.

Only when I felt the sticky warmth beneath my palm did I remember his injury.

"You're bleeding again," I murmured, drawing back.

"It's nothing," he said, wincing slightly. "Just a stitch or two."

Stubborn fool. I hugged him gently, careful of the shoulder, and kissed him again—relief and love crashing into one another. His arm circled my back and I felt his breath catch.

"I thought I'd be too late," he whispered.

"You weren't. Just in time, love."

He held me close, eyes scanning the trees above the clearing. "We'd better go while we still can."

We rose slowly, awkward and unsteady like drunks after last call. My knee ached fiercely from where I'd hit it earlier, and I leaned against him more than I meant to. But Owain held firm, guiding me through the woods, past the clearing, past the silent stones.

I shivered as we neared the burial cairns. My skin prickled.

"It's only nerves," he murmured, pulling me closer. "There are no spirits there."

"Then why are you whispering?"

He gave a faint smile, squeezing my shoulder, but I didn't relax until the cromlechs were behind us and we reached the gate above the road.

By the time we made it to Owain's BMW, exhaustion had sunk its claws into me. My knee throbbed. Every limb ached. Owain leaned against the car, rummaging for his keys while I stared back at the hillside. It looked so peaceful now. Serene. No trace of fire. No hint of the nightmare we'd just escaped.

I could have died, I thought, cold realization hitting like a slap. I nearly did.

"Kathleen, can you drive?"

Something in his voice wasn't right.

I turned slowly. "Yes, I think so. Why? Is something—?"

I froze.

His face had gone pale. Ashen. His right hand held out the keys. His left arm hovered stiffly from his side. My mouth went dry.

"What's wrong?"

Before he could answer, another voice—sharp, female, clipped—spoke from the shadows.

"Just get in the car, Miss Donahue. And don't try anything clever, or your boyfriend may join his old fiancée."

Owain tilted his head ever so slightly. My eyes followed his cue—to the back seat.

I didn't see her face.

But I saw the barrel of a rifle resting on the top of the passenger seat. Pointed squarely at Owain's chest.

Heart hammering, I took the keys and walked slowly to the driver's side. When I got in, the rifle vanished back into the darkness, but it didn't go far.

"Now, you get in, Mr. Thomas," the woman ordered.

Owain obeyed, easing into the passenger seat with deliberate care.

"You will drive us back to Harlech," she said. "To the constable's office. Quickly. Safely. No detours. No signals. Or I blow a hole through your lover."

"Yes," I whispered, gripping the wheel. My hands shook. I looked at Owain, who sat perfectly still, eyes fixed straight ahead.

I started the car and turned onto the road heading north.

So much for adrenaline. They said fear could fuel you. Give you strength.

I felt none of it. Just a heavy, cold numbness. A creeping certainty that we weren't going to make it. That Owain and I would die, and not in any romantic, storybook way.

Just... dead.

Images flashed: my parents. Friends. Annie Meister, my sixth-grade teacher. People I'd never see again.

Owain broke the silence.

"It's all right, Kathleen," he said softly, the words low, calm—steadying.

I glanced at him—but before he could say more, the woman snapped, "No talking."

He obeyed, but gave me the briefest look. Then, subtly, he lifted his right hand and dipped his palm downward.

A signal?

I didn't know what it meant, but I needed to be ready. I rolled the window down a few inches. "I need air."

"You may. But don't be stupid," she warned.

The wind cooled my face. I took a deep breath. Owain had a plan. He had to.

The rest of the drive passed in tense silence. My mind ticked through every woman I'd met in the last few days—trying to place that voice.

Not Sarah. Not Mrs. James. Not the hotel guests. Margaret Hale? Freda Weintraub?

None felt right—but I knew that voice.

The constable's office came into view far sooner than I wanted. I pulled up slowly and killed the engine.

"It's possible Bowen took Morgan elsewhere," Owain said quietly. "To Aberystwyth, maybe."

"I told you to be quiet," the woman hissed. "He's here."

Her voice grew cold and sharp. "Miss Donahue, leave the keys in the ignition. Get out. Stand by the front of the car. Now."

I opened the door slowly, every movement deliberate. The rifle was still pointed at Owain.

I stepped out, walked around to the front of the car, and turned back.

If she was going to shoot me, I wanted to look her in the eye.

And that's when it happened.

Owain moved.

His body dropped forward. The seat slammed backward.

A gunshot split the air.

I think I screamed.

I dove for cover, flinging myself beneath the front of the car.

Fear driving me, I crept toward the back of the car, hoping to get far enough away to act—*to do something*. Above me, scuffling broke out. The car rocked with sudden force, then went eerily still.

I froze, breath caught, heart thundering.

"Are you all right, Kathleen? Where are you?"

Relief surged through me. "Here, Owain!" I called and scrambled toward the side where he now stood.

Rising to my knees, then to my feet, I finally saw him—leaning against the car, rifle in one hand, a police club in the other. The woman lay crumpled across the back seat, black cloak twisted around her limbs. The hood had slipped back to reveal a wave of ash-blonde hair and a pointed nose.

Of course.

Abigail Halsted—the cool, unflappable group historian. She'd driven me to Swansea, full of polite smiles and passive judgment. She must've resented having to babysit the "sacrifice" before tonight's ceremony.

I threw my arms around Owain in a fierce hug. "That was incredibly dangerous. She could have—"

My words cut off as he winced, knees buckling beneath him. I stumbled with him to the ground, trying to brace his weight.

"I'm sorry," I said. "I wasn't thinking. Are you all right?"

He gripped the door handle and hauled himself upright, with my help. "Just... a little dizzy," he managed, his voice thin. His arms trembled from the effort.

I helped ease him into the passenger seat. Under the car's interior light, he looked worse than I'd feared. His face was pale, gray even. Cuts and bruises marred his skin. Dirt and dried blood streaked his clothes. Leaves clung to him like battle scars.

Still, he gave me a lopsided smile. "We're quite the pair."

I chuckled, exhausted. "We look like we've been in a horror movie. But we'd better deal with the baggage in the backseat before she wakes up."

He passed me the rifle. I left him the club and hobbled to the constable's office.

Locked.

Of course.

Owain was probably right—Bowen had likely taken Toby elsewhere. Luckily, I found a public phone nearby and managed to call the authorities.

By the time I returned, I was limping badly, my knee throbbing and my muscles screaming with every step. I climbed back into the driver's seat and glanced at Abigail—still unconscious.

"Help's on the way."

While I was gone, Owain had used strips of his shirt to bind her wrists behind her back. Now he sat with the rifle propped casually but pointed directly at her.

"Are you hurt, Kathleen?" he asked, eyeing my awkward movement.

"Banged up. Like you." I forced a smile. "A hot bath, antiseptic, and twelve hours of sleep should fix most of it. You?"

"About the same." He sighed. "Could've been worse."

There was a beat of quiet. Then he asked, gently, "Why didn't you tell me you were going with Toby tonight?"

It wasn't accusatory. Just... weary.

I hesitated. "I was confused, Owain. I didn't know who I could trust. It never occurred to me Toby could be so twisted. Did you suspect him?"

A pause. "A little. I just didn't want you around any of those groups. Something felt... off."

I frowned. "Then how did you find us? You were sleeping when I left."

He shifted, wincing as he leaned sideways to better see me. "Turns out you have a nosy hotel proprietress.

250

She trusted me more than she trusted Toby. When I woke and found you gone, I asked around, then called Bowen. He was already in motion—there was intel about a drug drop scheduled for the solstice night. We figured if they moved the drugs early, they might move the ceremony too."

I studied his face, watching the way he still favored his injured side. "Bowen met you here? To catch drug runners?"

He nodded.

"Wait—are you saying this cult is connected to a drug ring?" My heart sank. "You didn't come just for me. You came to stop the drugs."

"Not just the drugs," he said. "It's all connected. Toby Morgan—Tiernyon—was the linchpin. And this one," he nodded toward Abigail, "is his accomplice. After tonight's ceremony, they planned to take a boat out, exchange cash for drugs from the continent—and likely dump your body in the sea."

I stared at him. "No way. Toby? He didn't seem like... like that."

"He didn't seem like a murderer either," Owain said quietly.

I had no answer for that.

Owain winced again as he shifted the rifle a little.

"How bad your arm?" I asked.

He sighed. "I'm afraid Dr. Evans is going to have to put a couple of stitches back in. Tomorrow."

"Ouch," I sympathized, then said, "So, you didn't come specifically to save me."

"The Hell I didn't! When I first found out you'd gone, I checked the stone ring above Harlech, thinking that was where Toby had taken you. I confess, I had a few choice words to say about you at that point, but I was

251

apprehensive when I didn't find you there. Then the Stoner woman remembered that one of the two women, who were there at the hotel, said something about a summer celebration at Dyffryn. That's when we connected with that clearing above the cairns. Even at that, we almost didn't make it in time."

So close, I thought. *Death had come so close.* I owed both Sarah Linton and Louise Stoner a debt for that. I never thought I'd be so grateful for gossipy women.

Owain closed his eyes again, his head dropping against the headrest. I started to ask him about Shane Winston and how he figured into this, but I changed my mind. We could talk about that later. Better now to let him rest.

I turned instead to watch the lump in the back seat and wait for help. Abigail still seemed to be out, but I didn't count on it and took the rifle from Owain, aiming it at her.

Luckily, a police car came soon. The constable who pulled in beside me was young and half-asleep. I told him what had happened and that Constable Bowen could fill him in on more. Although the lad was confused, he hauled Abigail out.

Very much awake now, she kicked at him and fought until I poked her in the back with the rifle and growled, "Don't tempt me, Abigail."

Glad I didn't have to follow up on those words, I handed the rifle over to the constable after he marched his prisoner into the office and secured her. Promising we'd come in for a statement the next day, I returned to the car.

A few minutes later, I pulled the car into the parking area below the hotel. As I switch the engine off, I stared at the climb up the hillside and wished for a nice easy walk to the door. It had seemed so charming when I first decided to stay here.

I nudged Owain's leg, shaking him awake. "We're at the hotel, but I don't know if we can make it up the hill."

"We can lean on each other," Owain said as he sat up and groaned. "I'd carry you, but I haven't the strength."

Chapter Twenty-Four

"...releasing the past and looking forward..."

*S*taggering up that hill took nearly as long as the drive from Dyffryn to Harlech. We stumbled, leaning heavily on each other, too exhausted to speak, driven only by the lure of hot showers and a warm bed.

Despite our best efforts to slip upstairs quietly, Sarah Linton heard us. She fluttered out like an anxious mother hen, tut-tutting under her breath. I suspected she'd been waiting up for us.

I sent her to fetch my bathrobe while I pointed Owain toward the nearest bath.

"Get undressed," I ordered as I turned on the water and adjusted the temperature. When I looked back, Owain was sagging against the door, having managed only two buttons on his shirt.

"You look exhausted," I said, crossing to him.

He didn't protest as I took over the task. Gently, I slid the shirt off his shoulders. He winced, and I bit my lip at the sight revealed underneath: bruises bloomed across his chest and ribs, and a shallow knife graze scored his right side. Worse, nearly every stitch along his wounded arm had torn loose.

I let out a slow, queasy breath.

A knock at the door interrupted me. I opened it just enough to find Sarah standing there, holding my robe out at arm's length. Her wide eyes took in the scene before I snatched the robe from her hand and shut the door firmly.

I finished undressing Owain, then stripped off my filthy gown. Wearing nothing but underwear, I led him into the shower.

Under the warm spray, I worked carefully, soaping his battered skin, washing away dirt, blood, and fear. He braced against the wall, gritting his teeth when my fingers skimmed his cuts, but never pushed me away.

Despite everything, despite the bruises and the blood, my heart hammered with the awareness of him. The strength in his back and shoulders, the lean grace of his body—even broken and hurting, he was still the most beautiful man I'd ever seen.

When I finished, I poured soap into my hands and began scrubbing myself down. To my surprise, Owain's hands brushed my shoulders, turning me gently so he could wash my back with the same tender care.

I closed my eyes, savoring the quiet intimacy of the moment—the slide of his fingers over my bruised skin, the simple touch of someone who cared.

His arms slipped around my waist, pulling me close. His mouth brushed the back of my neck, lingering along my shoulders, sending shivers racing down my spine.

"If I weren't so exhausted," he murmured against my skin, "I'd take full advantage of this."

I turned, tilting my face up to his. I ran my fingers along his jawline, sliding them into the damp hair at his nape.

"And if I wasn't so knackered, I'd let you," I whispered, smiling through my exhaustion.

His soft laugh rumbled against me, warm and real.

I brushed a kiss over his mouth—gentle this time— before leaning my forehead against his.

"Come on, love," I said, forcing myself to pull away. "Let's get you to bed before we both end up in a heap on this floor."

But, alas, it wasn't that easy.

*S*arah, bless her meddling heart, had called Dr. Evans after seeing the state of Owain's injuries. He arrived just after I finished wrapping Owain's arm in fresh bandages.

I shot Sarah a glare of pure irritation, but the doctor quickly shooed her out with a gruff hand wave.

Dr. Evans muttered under his breath in cross Welsh as he checked Owain over, his hands none too gentle. When I saw Owain flinch as the doctor prodded a deep bruise above his kidney, my annoyance faded. Maybe it was good Sarah had summoned him tonight after all.

Clearly displeased with his patient for gallivanting about the hills, Dr. Evans barked a fresh string of Welsh, most of which I didn't need a translation to understand.

Muttering about "two cracked ribs", he taped them carefully before restitching the wounds in Owain's arm.

When he finally finished with Owain, he turned his stern attention to me.

My knee was the worst of it—twisted and swollen from the fall. An elastic bandage took care of that, though he still took grim satisfaction in bandaging a few cuts and dousing both Owain and me in what must have been half a bottle of antiseptic. By the time he was done, we both smelled like a hospital ward.

"Both of you need rest," Dr. Evans announced roughly.

256

He handed Owain a pill and stood there, arms folded, until Owain swallowed it.

"That sedative will keep you quiet for a while," the doctor said grimly. "No getting out of bed for at least three days. Keep that arm still until it heals, do you understand?"

Owain nodded, though his mouth curved downward in a grumpy frown.

Then Dr. Evans turned his glower on me.

"And you—can you get yourself to bed, or do I need to give you something to help you sleep as well?"

I lifted my hands in a pacifying gesture. "No problem here. I'm ready for sleep. I just want a few minutes with him first."

The doctor grunted, nodded curtly, and finally left us in peace.

I sat stiffly on the edge of Owain's bed.

Soft, silver light streamed through the curtains as dawn brushed the eastern peaks of Snowdonia. It was going to be a beautiful day—
A day I wouldn't have seen if not for this man.

I ran my fingers tenderly through Owain's still-damp hair. He was nearly asleep already, but he managed to slide his hand on top of mine.

"Thank you," I whispered.

He cracked open an eye. "For what?"

"For being there when I needed you. For being so stubborn."

His lips curved into a faint, tired smile. "Well, the nightmare's over."

I leaned down, laid my head lightly on the pillow next to him, and kissed his cheek.

"I'm here for you now, love," I whispered. "I'll take care of you."

Grunting with the effort it cost him, Owain wrapped his good arm around my shoulders and pressed a feather-light kiss to my lips.

"We'll take care of each other," he murmured.

It sounded deliciously wonderful, I thought drowsily—taking care of each other.

I snuggled closer, basking in the warmth of his body, the steady beat of his heart, the safety of his arms. Owain's fingers sifted lazily through my hair, and I sighed in utter contentment.

Chapter Twenty-Five

... the dawn of a new day ...

*N*ot sure what penetrated my sleep— maybe the birds singing outside the window, maybe the sound of a train pulling into the station.

Whatever it was, I woke to find myself still nestled in Owain's arms, his right arm resting comfortably around my shoulders, the day much farther along than I'd expected.

I lifted myself up on one elbow and studied his sleeping face. Bruises marred his jawline and cheekbones, his lower lip was swollen, and yet— He'd done it for me.

Because of Owain, I was still alive.

Taking care not to disturb him, I leaned in and pressed a soft kiss to his mouth before easing out of bed. Quietly, I made my way back to my room and the cold emptiness of my own bed.

The next time I woke, the sun hung low in the western sky, already well on its way to the sea. Hunger— not pain—finally forced me up. Still aching from head to toe, I dressed carefully and hobbled downstairs, my knee protesting every step.

I paused at Owain's door on the way. He still slept soundly.

As much as I wanted to see him awake, to talk, I knew he needed the rest more.

Downstairs in the dining room, Sarah Linton spotted me immediately. She bustled over as a few guests lifted curious heads to stare.

"You look tired, Kathy," Sarah said, concern etching her face.

"I am," I agreed. "But I'm hungry too. Maybe some of your wonderful soup and brown bread?"

"Of course." She led me to a small table tucked behind a post, away from prying eyes. "More private, love."

"Thank you. And just water, please."

She nodded and hurried off. I sagged into my chair, grateful for the small kindness.

Sarah returned quickly with a steaming bowl of barley beef soup and a generous half loaf of bread. As she set it down, she leaned closer and whispered, "Constable Bowen's been by three times. He asked us to call as soon as you or Mr. Thomas woke. Shall I let him know?"

I sighed. "You'd better. Half the guests have seen me anyway."

She gave a little nod and hurried off. I turned to my soup, trying to focus on the simple pleasure of eating.

Bowen arrived just as I finished.

We retired to the lounge, Mrs. Linton thoughtfully closing the door behind us to keep interruptions at bay.

Bowen wasted no time.

"When do you think Mr. Thomas will wake?" he asked after I firmly refused to let him disturb Owain.

"If he's as tired as I am," I said, "not until tomorrow. But can't you tell me what happened with Toby Morgan?"

"We're holding him for now," Bowen said. "But I imagine he'll be transferred for medical evaluation."

"Medical evaluation?" I echoed, puzzled.

Bowen sipped from a glass of soda before answering. "He's a very sick man, Miss Donahue. There were drugs in his system—suggesting he's a user as well as a dealer. He had been institutionalized in Chester for a time before escaping and returning here, where he assumed the identity of Toby Morgan. Until Mr. Thomas made the connection, I didn't see it myself."

Something clicked. "Shane Winston," I murmured. "It was Toby who shot Owain that night, wasn't it?"

Bowen nodded grimly. "Yes. He claims he only meant to warn Mr. Thomas away. But once he decided you were to be his 'sacrifice,' he wasn't going to let anyone interfere."

"And Abigail?"

"His partner. In love with him, apparently." His voice softened slightly. "It's often the way, isn't it? A lonely, isolated girl led down the wrong path out of devotion."

I nodded slowly.

Maybe Abigail deserved some pity. Maybe.

I had followed the charming, seemingly shy man far enough myself to understand how easily one could be misled.

"What will happen to her?" I asked.

"She'll be charged, of course. Kidnapping. Assault. Possibly more, depending on what else turns up. She confessed enough to get herself into serious trouble."

"And Owain?" My voice trembled a little despite myself.

"Is he cleared?"

Bowen's gaze was steady. "Completely. Winston confessed to all the murders. Framing Mr. Thomas was a stroke of luck on Winston's part—but unplanned. For what it's worth," Bowen added, "I never truly believed

Mr. Thomas was guilty. His grief was too real. But with no leads..."

He shrugged. "All I could do was keep him away as best I could. Lucky for you," he said quietly, "I didn't succeed."

I smiled, a tired, grateful smile. "In more ways than one, Constable."

He rose, offering me a steadying hand as I climbed stiffly to my feet. "Thank you for speaking with me, Miss Donahue. If you'll ask Mr. Thomas to contact me when he's able?"

"I will."

Slowly, painfully, I climbed the stairs back to my room.

Nothing had changed here—same bedspread, same curtains, same peaceful view out toward the coast.

Only *I* had changed.

The line between sanity and insanity, between normal life and horror, could be razor-thin. I knew that now.

I drifted to the window, pulling back the curtain, staring into the growing dark.

Had there been signs? Warnings?

Maybe.

Maybe not.

Maybe Toby had simply lived in a different reality all along.

My gaze fell on the small diary I'd started keeping on this trip, resting untouched on the dresser.

I picked it up—but found I didn't want to open it. Not yet.

Instead, I curled up on the bed, tucking my knees close, and finally let the tears come.

Tears for Toby.

For Owain.

For myself.

For all the others lost along the way.

With my cheek pressed against the damp pillow, I let sleep take me again—ths time, deep and undisturbed.

$\mathcal{I}$ slept longer than I thought I would. It was well into the next day—around ten—when I woke again.

At first, I felt disoriented, wondering why I was still in bed so late.

Then memory flooded back—the horror at Dyffryn, the terror of being a victim—and Owain.

At the thought of him, a contented smile crossed my face.

There would be time now. Time to truly know each other. Time to let our newly found love grow.

Stretching like a satisfied cat, I flung myself from the   bed—
—and instantly regretted it.

A dozen muscles protested sharply, forcing me into a slower, hobbling advance toward the bathroom with my tan slacks and turquoise shirt in hand.

As I dressed, I made plans:

Check on Owain.

Maybe bring tea to his room.

He was bound to be hungry by now.

But when I stopped at his room, he was gone. The bed was rumpled and empty. The bathrooms vacant.

Concern quickly turned to frustration. Damn that man! Why couldn't he stay put?

I hurried downstairs as fast as my aching muscles allowed.

Sarah Linton sat at the desk, busily adding up someone's bill, but she smiled warmly when she saw me.

"Morning, Kathy. You're looking so much better. Nothing like a long sleep to help. I'll get you some tea—"

"Never mind that," I interrupted sharply. "Have you seen Mr. Thomas?"

She nodded. "He went out about an hour ago. Said he had something he had to do." She pursed her lips in a small pout. "He's a stubborn man, love."

"You can say that again," I muttered under my breath.

Outside, I scanned the brilliant blue bay. Something he had to do...

It didn't take long to guess where he'd gone.

Fifteen minutes later, after navigating the public path and dunes, I spotted him. A lone figure walking at the water's edge, slow and thoughtful.

I quickened my pace despite my protesting knee. When I finally caught up, I saw him standing still, staring out across the sea. The sling supported his injured arm, at   least. His hair ruffled gently in the breeze. In his good hand, he held something small and white.

A white rose.

I watched as he pressed the bloom tenderly to his lips, then tossed it into the foaming waves. He stood there, watching silently as the tide caught it and carried it away.

"Owain," I said softly.

He straightened his shoulders and turned, a faint smile tugging at the corner of his mouth.

"I figured you would come," he said.

I closed the distance between us, my heart aching at the sadness still shadowing his eyes. "Are you all right?"

He glanced down at the sand, then back at me. "Just laying ghosts to rest," he said simply.

He turned back to watch the rose drift away, smaller and smaller on the receding tide.

"A farewell to my Irish Rose," he said quietly.

Then he reached into the sling and drew out a second flower—a single red rosebud. He held it out to me.

"And a welcome to my American Rose."

Tears stung my eyes as I took the rose from him, breathing in the delicate fragrance.

I looked up at him—and in his eyes, I saw everything: tenderness, pain, resilience... and love.

I stepped into his embrace, sliding my arms around his neck, pulling him close.

His lips brushed my forehead, my cheeks, my mouth—gentle at first, then deepening as our desire stirred, real and vivid.

I threaded my fingers through his hair, savoring the closeness, the feel of him alive and real against me.

But I forced myself to pull back, my fingertips brushing lightly over the bruises on his face.

I summoned my best stern voice. "Now, Mr. Thomas, what do I have to do to keep you in bed?"

He thought for a long moment before his eyes twinkled with wicked amusement. "Well... there is one way..."

I feigned shock. "That's blackmail!"

"Uh-huh," he agreed smugly.

I laughed, heart swelling with love and relief.

"I love you, Owain," I whispered, pressing another kiss to his mouth.

Sliding my arm around his waist, I steered him back up the beach toward the charming little hotel perched on the cliff.

Toward the cozy room with its big, comfortable double bed.

And toward the life we would finally begin together.

The End

Author's Note: Thank you for reading my book. If you enjoyed it, please consider leaving a review or at least a rating. Your feedback is extremely important to me since it's a direct way of letting me know if you liked it and how much. It also helps my book to find more readers, so I would appreciate it.

Glossary of Welsh Words

I tried to limit my use of Welsh words in this novel, but most of the town names are in their Welsh form as you would see on the signs and train stations throughout Wales. It is a separate country from England, and the Welsh people are quite clear about the distinction. To help you with the pronunciation and meaning of the words I've used, here's a short glossary.

Aberystwyth (*aber-oust-with*) – A university town in mid-Wales – the prefix *aber* meaning at the mouth of and the *ystwyth* is the name of the river that empties into Cardigan Bay.

Beddgelert (BED-gel-ert) – A small village in Snowdonia.
Betws-y-Coed (betsy-si-coid) – A beautiful village in north Wales at the edge of Snowdonia.

Blaenau Ffestiniog (BLIGH-na Fes-TIN-iog) – A historic slate mining town in the mountains of north Wales.

Bwthyn Gwyntog (buth-in gwen-tog) – Windy Cottage, the name of Owain Thomas' home.

Caru (*kari*)- to love, or love – A term of endearment or affection.

Croeso (kro-SO) – Welcome.

Cromlech – (*krom-lek*) – A single chamber megalithic tomb.

Cymru (kim-ri) – Welsh word for Wales.

Dyffryn Ardudwy – (*dif-rin ar-did-we*) – A seaside village in North Wales and the location of the burial chamber of the same name.

Eisteddfod (*i-STED-fod*) – A gathering of bards, a festival of music and poetry.

Eryri (err-i-ri) – The high reaches of a mountain, the highlands, referenced to Snowdonia.

Gwyerion (*gwer-i-on*) – the druid name for McKay

Harlech (*har-lik*) – A coastal town and the location of Harlech Castle.

Hogyn (*ho-gin*) – A boy or a lad.

Llwyn Onn (*ssin-on*)– Original Welsh for the song *The Ash Grove*. Most English speakers pronounce the double l as "el" but in Welsh, it is aspirated when spoken and come out as a bit of a hiss.

Merionethshire (*mer-ion-eth-shir-a*) – A county in north Wales bordering on Cardigan Bay.

Plaid Cymru (plied kim-ri) – The Nationalist Party of Wales that was formed in 1925.

Porthmadog; also Porthmadoc (por-th-ma-dog) – A small coastal fishing town in North Wales and the train stop for Portmerion.

Portmerion (*port-mar-ion*) – A tourist village in North Wales designed by Sir Clough Williams-Ellis as a model village. The TV series *The Prisoner* was filmed here.

Pembroke (*pim-bruk*) – A city in south Wales on the coast where Pembroke Castle is located.

Tiernyon (*ter-ni-on*) – The secret Druid name for Toby.

Yr Wyddfa (*er-WETH-fa*) – The Welsh name for Snowdon. It means the barrow and comes from the myth that a giant buried there.

About the Author

Riona Kelly is the pen name Rene Averett used for romantic suspense novels. She also writes fantasy and science fiction under Lillian I. Wolfe and paranormal cozy mysteries, cookbooks, and children's books under her own name.

She hails from the southwestern United States where she was raised until 21, then she migrated to California. She lived there for several years before moving back east all the way to Las Vegas, Nevada and eventually moving north to the foothills of the Sierra Nevada Mountains.

She enjoys painting, drawing, music, and living an uncomplicated life while serving the needs of her feline companions. She's a fan of figure skating and has skated herself although not in a professional capacity. Writing is a passion so like it or not; there will be more books.

For more about Riona Kelly, visit her information site at Pynhavyn Press:

https://pynhavynpress.com/?page_id=271

or visit her website: https://rionakelly.online/

From the Author:

I hope you've enjoyed reading *Echoes of the Past*. It's a story that had its origin quite a few years ago following a trip to Wales. I fell in love with the country and the people; so naturally, I wanted to write a book about it. Although much of the story comes from the imagination, a good bit of it is rooted in the history and mystery of the land and the Welsh.

If you enjoyed the book, I hope you will consider leaving your honest review at the online store where you purchased it. Reviews are very important to both the writer and other readers. They are always appreciated, whether they are short or long.

This book is also available using Amazon AI Voices.. If you would like to sample it in advance, you can listen to a sample of the voice reading a few pages at this page:

https://www.amazon.com/dp/B07DXF38J9

My apologies to the wonderful people of Wales for all the Welsh words that are mispronounced in the audio book. I tried my best to teach the AI.

From Pynhavyn Press

By Riona Kelly – Romantic Suspense

California Dreaming
A Harvest of Secrets

A legacy shrouded in secrets.
A love rekindled in danger

American Rose Abroad Series
Signature of a Soul

No matter what the name on the canvas,
the painting itself is the signature of the
soul. A stolen painting. A whirlwind
romance. A dangerous secret.

From Pynhavyn Press

By Lillian I. Wolfe – SciFi & Fantasy

O'Ceagan Saga
Sci-Fi/Fantasy

Captain Grania O'Ceagan isn't just navigating the treacherous expanse of space aboard the space freighter *Mo Croidhe*, she's steering a course through the shadows of ancient myths. When two mysterious passengers—a banshee bound by fate and a duplicitous smuggler—board her ship, the journey to *Erinnua* becomes a quest that challenges the very fabric of reality.

As the *Mo Croidhe* cuts through the cosmos, Grania must unravel the enigmatic secrets of her passengers. With every light year traveled, the line between legend and fact blurs, unveiling hidden truths that
could spell their doom or salvation.

Join the crew of the *Mo Chroidhe* as each new novel is a new adventure across the Cosmos.

O'Ceagan's Legacy: Book 1
In Strange Waters – 1.5
Outer Rim: Book 2

From Pynhavyn Press

By Lillian I. Wolfe – SciFi & Fantasy

Funeral Singer Series

Paranormal/ Urban Fantasy

Music is Gillian Foster's passion, but her dreams of success are overshadowed by her struggles. When an accident grants her a paranormal talent, her life takes an unexpected turn. As a funeral singer, Gillian's consciousness is transported to an interim cemetery where she can communicate with the recently departed while singing. Bound to help these spirits complete their unfinished business, she faces more than just departed souls.

Dark entities haunt the transitional plane, posing a threat to both the souls in transit and the living. Identified as a danger, Gillian finds herself one soul against hundreds, desperately needing help.

Can she find others like her and rally enough support to stop the spread of evil threatening everyone she loves?

A Song for Marielle
A Song for Menafee
A Song of Betrayal
A Song of Forgiveness
A Song of Redemption

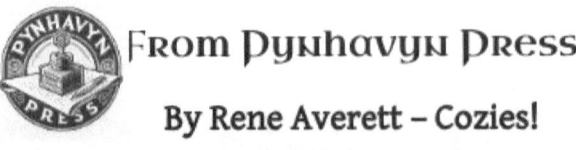